The Visco
with fury

'You'll forg...   ...ly,
'for not wi...   ...del
himself upo...

India bestowed her sweetest smile on him —
no mean achievement when she was boiling
with anger. 'I'd be similarly concerned if I
thought Richard was modelling himself on a
twelve-year-old,' she told him.

Lord Bardolph's anger was directed as much
against himself for having laid himself open to
such a remark as with India for having uttered
it. He delivered a pretension-squashing *coup*
de grâce. 'I find you impertinent, madam,'
he said.

Dear Reader

We welcome back Janet Edmonds with her Regency, A NABOB'S DAUGHTER, where India and Viscount Bardolph form an uneasy alliance. Julia Byrne is back with MY ENEMY, MY LOVE, a sizzling action-packed plot set in the Anarchy. Our American authors are Lindsay McKenna, well known to Silhouette readers, and Lucy Elliot, who offer an Apache heroine and the Civil War respectively. We hope these four stories will enthrall you — enjoy!

The Editor

Janet Edmonds was born in Portsmouth, but lived for years in the Cotswolds where she taught before deciding that writing was more fun. A breeder, exhibitor and judge of dogs, she now lives in an isolated house in the Fens run for the benefit of her dogs. She also has a son and a cat, and avoids any form of domestic activity if she can.

Recent titles by the same author:

THE DENMEAD INHERITANCE
FLIGHT FROM THE HAREM

A NABOB'S DAUGHTER

Janet Edmonds

MILLS & BOON

MILLS & BOON LIMITED
ETON HOUSE, 18–24 PARADISE ROAD
RICHMOND, SURREY, TW9 1SR

*First published in Great Britain 1993
by Mills & Boon Limited*

© Janet Edmonds 1993

*Australian copyright 1993
Philippine copyright 1993
This edition 1993*

ISBN 0 263 78240 9

*Set in 10½ on 12½ pt Linotron Times
04-9311-76598*

*Typeset in Great Britain by Centracet, Cambridge
Made and printed in Great Britain*

HISTORICAL NOTE

SMUGGLING has always been rife round our shores and East Anglia has never been an exception though I'm told that today drugs and illegal immigrants have replaced brandy, tea, lace and silk. Anything that carried heavy duty was smuggled and the smuggling of any commodity stopped as soon as the duty was discontinued — tea is perhaps the most notable case in point. Smuggling was a two-way traffic. For several centuries, in order to protect our weaving industry, it was illegal to export raw wool, so fleeces were smuggled out continuously until the Industrial Revolution lessened our dependence on one industry.

Almost everyone in rural areas, especially those near the coast, was involved to a greater or lesser extent. The customs service — interestingly, a much older institution than the police — was inadequately manned, heavily outnumbered, and widely hated even by law-abiding citizens. Its organisation was complex and hierarchical and those who worked for it did so at great personal risk.

The Fens have been systematically drained and extended since the seventeenth century, after previous sporadic attempts, and, ever since the Romans, earthworks have been used to keep back the sea. The coastline of the Wash is no longer what

5

it was during the Napoleonic Wars and Eaden's map of the area, surveyed in 1792, is the one I've used. Wisbech in those days was at the narrowest end of the wide estuary of the River Nene. Since the middle of the nineteenth century, the Nene has been deepened, straightened, narrowed and extended so that Wisbech is now over ten miles from the present estuary, though it remains a working port. Instead of a long and hazardous ford by Cross Keys House, there is now a Victorian swivel bridge across a much narrower stretch of water and Cross Keys House is now a hotel.

Impressment into both navy and army were lawful from the thirteenth century — 1206 in the case of the navy — and at least one of the events in this book is based on a true incident: a press-gang really was attacked by village women to the south of King's Lynn, in order to gain time for the men of the village to go into hiding, though this happened some years later than my book.

Janet Edmonds

CHAPTER ONE

'I SHOULD be very much obliged, madam, if you could keep this young blackguard on a tighter rein in future.' Lord Bardolph's voice froze the small parlour as dramatically as his tall figure dominated it.

India Leigh lifted her chin defiantly and drew herself up, irritated by the fact that even at her tallest she was at the disadvantage of having to look up into eyes which were as cold and unwelcoming as the waters of the Wash. 'Your language is extreme, my lord,' she said. 'My brother is only fourteen, after all, and he seems to have been aided and abetted in this little escapade by your own brother who is, I believe, the elder of the two.'

The Viscount had no choice but to concede the point. 'Bartram is sixteen, but I take leave to tell you he gave me no cause for concern until you and your brother came here.'

'Which does he lack — spirit or initiative?' India snapped. 'He must be remarkably easily led if he goes along with the hare-brained schemes of a fourteen-year-old.'

The fact that the same thought had often occurred to Lord Bardolph did not make it any easier to accept the comment when it came from an outsider whose origins, in so far as she was known to have

any, appeared to have been trade. He was unmoved
by her considerable beauty and by her undeniably
fine eyes, and if his opinion had been asked he
would have said that she dressed in a way most
inappropriate to such a remote spot. True, the green
velour of her dress would certainly keep at bay the
Fen winds, but the skilled cut by which its simple
lines were achieved, the quality of its braid and lace
trimmings, all pointed to a London dressmaker—
and an expensive one at that. None of this had
anything to do with the matter in hand, but all
conspired to fuel his annoyance.

'Bartram has not been allowed to run wild,' he
said repressively. 'I have endeavoured to inculate in
him a sense of duty, of what is fitting. Ultimately I
hope to see him embark on a career in the church
and such episodes as this are hardly helpful.'

'Goodness me!' India exclaimed. 'How very
pompous you are! I wonder if it has crossed your
mind to ask Bartram if he wants to go into the
church? From what I've seen of him—admittedly
not very much—I'd have said he was quite unsuited
but, naturally, I bow to your superior understanding
of him.'

The Viscount's mouth grew tight-lipped with fury.
'You're too generous, madam,' he said icily. 'You'll
forgive me, I'm sure, for not wishing to see my
brother model himself upon yours.'

India bestowed her sweetest smile on him—no
mean achievement when she was boiling with anger.
'I'd be similarly concerned if I thought Richard was

modelling himself on a twelve-year-old,' she told him.

Lord Bardolph's anger was directed as much against himself for having laid himself open to such a remark as with India for having uttered it. It wasn't often that someone succeeded in putting him at a disadvantage and he couldn't recall a woman ever having done so before. It wasn't an experience he was enjoying. He delivered a pretension-squashing *coup de grâce*.

'I find you impertinent, madam,' he said.

To his amazement, instead of flinching or shifting her gaze—which was the very least he had anticipated—India threw back her head and laughed. It was a full-throated laugh of genuine amusement which, had the circumstances been different, he might have found intriguingly attractive. As it was, it was so totally unexpected that it left him mystified. What woman with any pretensions to gentility could possibly find it amusing to be called impertinent?

India wiped her eye. 'Do forgive me, my lord,' she said. 'It really is too bad of me to laugh at you, especially when I suspect it isn't something you're used to. Pomposity really is counter-productive, you know. I'm surprised you haven't learned that.' Her tone became more confidential. 'I know one should never listen to gossip, but they say in the village that your bride elect left you quite literally at the altar. Now that isn't a humiliation I'd wish on anyone, but I feel bound to say that if you were half as pompous and downright rude to her as you have been to me, and so totally unable to see the lighter side of a situation, then, frankly, I'm not in the least surprised.'

No sooner were the words uttered than India knew she had gone too far by any standards. Had it been within her power to recall them, she would have done so. As it was, her colour rose in almost precise counterpoint to the paling of Lord Bardolph's. She opened her mouth to apologise but his retaliation was too swift.

He inclined his head in an ironic bow. 'You are no doubt aware of the speculation locally as to why a personable young woman such as yourself, the daughter, it's believed, of a nabob, should have returned unwed at the ripe age of twenty-three or four from the country after which she was named. . .a country where, one gathers, Englishwomen — especially single ones — are rather thin on the ground. Local speculators have obviously not been privy to the benefits of your shrewish tongue. I no longer find it remarkable that you returned an old maid, despite your fortune. Good morning, madam.'

India opened her mouth to protest that he was unfair and closed it again on the realisation that she was hardly in a position to complain. Before she could collect her thoughts sufficiently to enable her at least to try to smooth things down, he had gone, letting himself unceremoniously out of the house before the maid could be summoned.

India drew a deep breath and turned to the object of Lord Bardolph's visit. 'And what have you got to say for yourself, Richard?' she asked.

He was very nearly as tall as she was and it

wouldn't be long before she would be at as big a disadvantage in dealing with him as she had been with Bardolph, she thought.

Her brother merely grinned. 'My, that was a set-to, and no mistake,' he remarked. 'Do you know, you're trembling?'

She did, and was trying hard to control it. 'Don't change the subject. What's your version of this morning's events?'

'In general, I suppose Bardolph hasn't got it so very wrong, bearing in mind the source of his information,' Richard began.

'*Lord* Bardolph,' India corrected him. 'I don't think he'd welcome any familiarity from you, just now.'

Richard's grin broadened. 'I got the impression there wasn't going to be much opportunity for it from any member of this family,' he said.

Since there were only two members of it, this comment was more pointed than India liked to admit. 'Never mind that,' she said. 'What have you and the Honourable Bartram been up to?'

Richard's normally cheerful face clouded over. 'Will you listen to me? Really listen, I mean?'

'You know I will.'

'But you won't automatically believe Lord Bardolph just because he's an adult?'

'Not automatically or for that reason but it's only fair to say that, whatever difference of opinion we might have had, he didn't strike me as untruthful,' India warned him.

'I don't suppose he is,' Richard agreed, 'but the thing is, he took Mr Huggate's word for everything,'

'Then you'd better tell me your version of events,' his sister suggested. She pointed to a chair. 'Sit down and start at the beginning. I'll try not to interrupt.'

'Bart doesn't want to be a churchman, you know. He's got his heart set on being a sailor. Bardolph's got a yacht and sailing on it is the thing Bart most likes doing, only his brother's too busy most of the time to take him out. Bardolph says he wouldn't really like being a sailor at all because life in the navy isn't remotely like sailing on a private yacht.'

India felt that Lord Bardolph might have a valid argument there but she wasn't very clear what connection this had with the morning's brouhaha. 'This morning's events, Richard, if you don't mind. Get to the point.'

'I am. The thing is, wanting to be a sailor so badly means that Bart's made himself very knowledgeable about ships and the sea and all that and, barring going for a sail, there's nothing he enjoys quite so much as going out on to the salt-marshes and just watching.' He paused. 'As a matter of fact, Bardolph — *Lord* Bardolph, I mean — ought to thank me for trying to change Bart's ideas: I told him he wouldn't enjoy the sea so much if he had to come all the way from India on it. I told him it was a bit different from sailing up and down the coast on a diet of quail's eggs and champagne.'

'Quail's eggs and champagne?' India echoed, bemused. 'Am I supposed to believe those are the staple foods on board Lord Bardolph's boat?'

'I don't suppose they're the *staples*, exactly,' Richard admitted. 'I mean, you'd need to eat an awful lot of quail's eggs to fill you up, wouldn't you? It's just that they seem to be part of the attraction for Bart.'

'I doubt if much of either is served in the navy,' India remarked. 'I don't wish to be unkind, Richard, but Bartram does seem to be lacking in common sense.'

'Oh, he's quite stupid about a lot of things,' Richard agreed cheerfully, 'but he really does know a lot about ships and related things. He knows all the birds we see and a lot about their behaviour and all that. That's why I enjoy his company so much. After all, if I'm going to be a farmer, I need to know about these things, and if I decided to farm in this area, which Bart says is quite unlike any other—and I'm inclined to believe him—then the more I can learn from someone who really knows, the better.'

Since Richard's ambition was as big a bone of contention between them as Bartram's evidently was in his family, India, who had no stomach for another argument just yet, tried to turn the conversation away from the detour it appeared to have taken. 'This is all very fascinating, but I'm no nearer understanding what happened today.'

Richard shook his head. 'You're no nearer *know-ing*,' he told her, 'but you're much nearer *understanding*.'

India sighed. Sometimes she wished Richard were not quite so bright. She also wished he had waited another six or seven years before developing their late father's precision of argument. It might be very mind-forming and educational but in a fourteen-year-old boy it smacked of unwelcome precocity. 'It's *knowledge* I'm after,' she pointed out. 'You can *explain* after.'

'I shan't need to,' Richard chuckled. 'That's why we go to the marshes, and we go there often. From time to time there's a ship hove to some way off-shore, usually at low water just before the tide turns. Bart says it's a very dangerous thing to do because of the mud and sand shoals and that the master must be very skilled indeed. They weigh anchor as the tide rises and head off towards King's Lynn. We know that because we thought they were probably waiting for high-water so that they could get up the Nene to Wisbech, but they didn't. Bart thinks they must go on to King's Lynn, or maybe back to Holland.'

'Why Holland?' India asked.

'He says he can tell by the rigging she's a Dutchman—a ketch, he says. He explained it all to me, but I'm not really interested in all that business about gaffs and jibs and what-have-yous, so I only half listened and I certainly can't explain it to you. Does it matter?' He looked at her anxiously.

'Not in the least,' India assured him. 'In fact, it's probably quite a blessing because I wouldn't understand, either, and then you'd get annoyed. Go on.'

'As a matter of fact, I've only seen her once—the time we raced along the estuary to see where she went—but Bart's seen her several times, always previously at night.'

India frowned. 'Does that mean he has a bedroom overlooking the Wash?'

Richard grinned cheekily. 'No. He knows when the tide and the moon are going to be right and just slips out of the house. He says people come ashore. Smugglers, he says.'

India thought of the flat expanse of the salt-marsh backed by the embankment that stopped the sea encroaching on to the equally flat drained siltfields behind. 'I see. And where do they hide whatever it is they smuggle? In caves?'

'Don't be silly, India. How could they? Bart says, given the ketch's origins, the most likely contraband is Hollands. Gin, you know.'

'Yes, I do know what Hollands is,' she said. 'What does Bartram think they do with it?'

'They haven't really got much choice, have they? They must have an accomplice ashore who has somewhere where they can hide the goods until they can be moved.'

Light began to dawn. 'Do I infer that this is where this Mr Huggate enters the story?' India asked with misgivings.

'That's right. Got it in one. Bart says the place of possible concealment nearest to the spot where they land is Huggate's big barn. The one he built about ten years ago when he started to keep sheep. He said it was to store the fleeces and I dare say it was except that it seems a bit stupid to store a valuable crop so far from the house and the dogs. Anyway, Bart says the ketch was there last night. Now we'd previously agreed that next time it was there we'd go out first thing and root around that barn and see what we could find out. Before old Huggate's had time to shift it, you understand.'

'*Mr* Huggate,' India corrected automatically. 'Didn't it occur to you that this might be just a smidgeon dangerous?'

'Why? He wouldn't dare do anything in broad daylight, would he?' Richard said with the blithe confidence of extreme youth. 'We weren't going to be *obviously* searching for anything. We made it look as if we were just playing games around there.'

'What sort of games?'

'Hide-and-go-seek, that sort of thing; it justified one of us poking and prying into all sorts of nooks and crannies.'

'Including, presumably, Mr Huggate's barn.'

'Exactly. Well,' he amended, 'it would have done, only the barn was well and truly padlocked and there wasn't a chink anywhere.'

'Which is precisely what you'd expect if it was being used to store fleeces,' India pointed out.

'Or contraband.'

'You don't think this idea of contraband gin is a consequence of two boys having over-active imaginations and not enough to occupy their time?' India suggested.

'Then think of an alternative explanation,' Richard demanded, ignoring the insult.

'Maybe the Dutchman is buying the fleeces.'

'Then why not transport them to Wisbech — or Lynn — and ship them out from there? It would be a lot safer. Or it would be if it were legal.'

'Perhaps they go direct to Holland or somewhere else.'

'Perhaps they do but it's as much against the law to export English wool as it is to import Hollands gin without paying duty. Either way it's smuggling.' A thought struck him. 'Maybe we haven't considered the half of it. Maybe he's smuggling Hollands in and paying for it by smuggling wool out. Now there's a thought to ponder!'

India judged this to be an idea that was better not pursued. 'I take it Mr Huggate caught you?'

'We told him we were just playing games but I don't think he believed us. He said we were a bit old to be playing hide-and-go-seek.'

'I'd have to agree with him on that,' India commented.

'He marched us off to Bardolph—*Lord* Bardolph—and told him he'd caught us in his outhouses—which wasn't strictly true since you can hardly call a barn two hundred yards from all the other buildings an outhouse, can you? He told his lordship we'd been using Bart's spyglass to set straw on fire, which is absolutely untrue. Even if we'd wanted to, the sun isn't strong enough and we're not so stupid that we don't know *that*. Anyway, Lord Bardolph believed him and said he'd make good any damage if Mr Huggate would let him know what it amounted to, and Mr Huggate said fortunately he'd found us in time and it hadn't come to that but he'd be obliged if his lordship would make sure it never happened again and his land was now out of bounds to both of us and would his lordship please speak to you about me and make sure I was punished as well. Which he did,' Richard concluded.

'It seems to me I've maligned Bartram by saying he lacked spirit and initiative,' India said ruefully.

Richard shifted uneasily. 'Not entirely. I mean, he's the one that guessed what was going on but it was my idea to see what we could find out.'

'I see. Well, at least you've owned up to that. Tell me something which puzzles me: if Bartram really believed smuggling was going on, why on earth didn't he say something to his brother? Lord Bardolph is the biggest landowner in the area and a magistrate, He would be able to authorise "rooting around", as you put it, by the proper authorities and all this unpleasantness would have been avoided.'

'The thing is, Lord Bardolph isn't what you'd call a sympathetic brother. He's a half-brother, really: Bart's mother was the late Lord Bardolph's second wife and she died when he was born. There's sixteen years between them so they haven't much in common. Lord Bardolph is very good at administering set-downs, Bart says — and after listening to him just now, I can quite believe it. Bart says any suggestion of his gets a set-down and leaves him feeling about five years old and five inches high. He says his brother would just have laughed at him.'

India privately thought Bartram was probably right but judged it unwise to say so. 'All the same, that's whom he should have mentioned it to. Even if Bardolph didn't march straight over there, he might well have had the place watched, just to see whether there was any substance to Bartram's story.'

'He might, I suppose,' Richard said grudgingly. 'On the other hand, think how gratifying it would have been to be able to go to him with some *real* proof. That would have made Lord Bardolph think twice before being quite so dismissive of his brother's ideas in future.'

India supposed it would and had to concede that the boys' scheme, seen from the perspective of fourteen and sixteen, had a logic of its own. She sighed. 'I'm not saying I disbelieve you when you tell me Mr Huggate was lying, but I do think you've both been letting your imaginations run away with you and I think the Viscount has a case. I don't want you to have anything to do with Bartram for the time being and you can stay indoors for the next week. I'll see to it that you have some studying to do.'

He looked at her in horror. 'You mean I can't go out at all?'

India relented. 'You'll accompany me to church, of course, and I think I could allow you to come shopping with me. That ought to give you a bit of fresh air and exercise.'

'Thank you *very* much,' Richard snorted. 'I think I'd rather write essays.'

'That can be arranged. Now go up to your room and leave me in peace for a while. You've interfered with my day quite enough already.'

Richard took the hint with alacrity but paused by the door. 'How long is "for the time being"?' he asked.

It took a moment or two before India realised

what he meant. 'Till you can see Bartram again? I don't know. Till I say so, I suppose.'

'An indefinite sentence, in other words.'

'Something of the sort — and it serves you right.'

When Richard had left the room, India sank on to the sofa with a sigh of relief. Bardolph and her brother had between them given her more than enough to think about and now she needed time to work out the ramifications and decide how best to deal with it.

Since their parents had died within days of each other in an outbreak of cholera in Bangalore, India had found herself her brother's legal guardian with all the responsibilities that that entailed, chief among which was that of deciding their immediate future. Bardolph's gibe struck a raw nerve, not because she had any particular urge to acquire a husband just for the sake of it, as so many women seemed to do, but because a husband would have been a very useful asset in the present circumstances, due to the fact that the responsibility for those decisions would have been his. India was by nature far from indecisive and, had there been only her future to consider, things would have been much easier. Richard's future was another matter altogether.

She wondered whether, with hindsight, she had been foolish to reject all the suitors who had offered for her hand in India. Every summer her mother had taken her on the interminably long journey north to the mountains, to cities like Peshawar and Rawalpindi where it was reasonable to assume she might well find a husband among the government officers or the garrison. Her parents had had every reason to feel optimistic about her chances: India was not only extremely beautiful but was blessed with an exceedingly wealthy father — not quite what one might call a gentleman, perhaps, but rich enough for that to be overlooked by younger sons and ambitious civil servants. It had been known that a small fortune would be settled on her upon her marriage and a larger one on the death of her father. No, there had been no shortage of suitors.

Unfortunately all of them had fallen short of India's expectations in one way or another. There were those whose way of life suggested that it would take them very little time to get through her fortune and, since her parents' assessment of their qualities coincided with that of their daughter, they could only congratulate themselves on having raised a daughter with such discriminating good sense. They were less pleased when she rejected a suitor because he was too worthy or too serious, too domineering or too humourless.

'But that's just what one *needs* in a husband,' Mrs Leigh had protested on learning of the rejection of one eminently suitable young man. 'Your husband will have absolute control over you and your fortune. Worthiness and solidity are very necessary virtues in a husband.'

'But if I have to live with them for the rest of my life, unrelieved by any mitigating humour, I shall go quietly mad.'

Mrs Leigh could see her daughter's point though she had no intention of saying so. 'Nonsense,' she said. 'You refine too much upon humour. You can have too much of a good thing, you know.'

'Indeed you can. That's why I'm anxious to avoid too much worthiness or solidity. Papa strikes the right sort of balance so, Mama, if you can find me a young man with Papa's business acumen and his sense of humour, I'll do all I can to live up to your expectations.'

But it seemed that no such man existed or, if he did, he didn't live in India.

This wasn't as dispiriting as it might have been. Neither India nor her brother had ever been to England but both their parents had been born there. It stood to reason that there might well be a man — possibly even men — in England with characteristics closer to those she sought in a husband. Her mother smiled and shook her head when India suggested as much.

'Men are men, my dear,' she said. 'You'll find the full range in India. I'm afraid the idea that they're different in England is a case of the grass looking greener in the next field.'

Their parents' death changed all that. It was unthinkable that a young, unmarried woman should live alone in Bangalore with only the protection of a fourteen-year-old boy and some native servants. She must marry or return to England. This was the advice she received from all sides and India knew it to be sound even though she found it incongruously amusing that her counsellors invariably used the word 'return' despite the fact that she had never set foot in England in her life.

She gave marriage more serious consideration than ever before but could detect no improvement in the candidates for her hand and, in any case, felt that a lifelong commitment was not best entered into at short notice and when she was grieving deeply for her beloved parents. She and Richard would 'return' to England.

Another factor influenced her decision but it wasn't one she was prepared to mention to anyone else. Richard was young but he was also intelligent, ingenious and resourceful far beyond his years. He had a natural ability for getting into mischief and for leading others into it, too. India knew her parents had been keen to send him to England where they had felt that a few years at Oxford or Cambridge would not only complete his education in the way from which he was most likely to benefit, but also give him enough intellectual occupation to keep him out of the mischief his parents were sure was inspired as much by boredom as by naughtiness. Their satisfaction with this scheme was tempered with concern that at either place he might well gravitate towards the least desirable elements of university society without the mitigating influence of his family to redirect his activities into more desirable paths.

Both problems would be solved by going to England: she might find a compatible husband and Richard could go on to university while still remaining within reach of his sister's influence.

They had initially rented a house in the capital, a city which exceeded their highest expectations and reduced India to a wide-eyed schoolgirl up from the country. The shops, the warehouses, the mantua-makers and the milliners, to say nothing of the theatres, were a delight and India had been seriously considering acquiring an appropriate chaperon who could introduce her to respectable society, when she began to realise that Richard had become a cause for concern.

It had seemed quite reasonable for a spirited boy to resent being tied firmly to his sister's apron-strings and India had no initial qualms about letting him explore London on his own, just so long as he was home by the time she asked and told her where he was going. He was unfailingly obedient on the first score but she wasn't so sure about the last. That was to say that, while he might very well have visited the places he said he was visiting on any given day, she suspected that he added one or two less salubrious destinations to his itinerary. His conversation became interlarded with cant expressions at the meaning of some of which India could only guess. He became more careless of his appearance and, although India could refuse to let him leave the house until she was satisfied, she noticed that on his return he was a great deal more dishevelled than half a day's exploration of a great city warranted. When he told her that the allowance she made him was not nearly enough for 'a man about town', as he described himself, she became seriously concerned, knowing it to be on the generous side.

The lawyer who handled the family's affairs endorsed this view and tentatively suggested that Miss Leigh might be well advised to consider removing to a quieter town where there would be fewer distractions. He also suggested that she demand to know exactly what, where and with whom Richard spent his days, but this was not a piece of advice India was prepared to follow, knowing it would only be resented and, if Richard guessed she would disapprove, result in his lying to her. Far better quietly to find somewhere else to live and present him with a *fait accompli*.

Deciding where to go had been a problem because she had the whole of England, Scotland and Wales to choose from. The choice was really too great for comfort and she finally limited it to the areas of, but not too close to, both of the great university cities. After a lifetime spent in the Deccan, India thought it would make a pleasant change to live near the sea, a decision which further restricted her choice to the area north and east of Cambridge. She knew nothing of the Fens nor of the nature of the German Sea and barely noticed the quickly disguised surprise of the London agent she engaged to find a suitable house for them.

The house was entirely suitable and the location exactly what she had asked for but she was totally unprepared for the reality. She was quite unprepared for the high earthen embankment that kept the sea from flooding in across the fields created over the last hundred years by draining the marshes and consequently lower than the besieging sea itself, an embankment that effectively cut off any view of the sea unless one stood on top of it. She was quite unprepared for the merciless wind that howled interminably across the flat, open landscape. She was equally unprepared for the deeply suspicious reserve of the inhabitants of an isolated village, a reserve that was almost secrecy and contrasted starkly with the openness, the noise, the colour and the gossip of an Indian village.

The climate had a lot to do with that, of course: the wind, the cold and the rain were effective deterrents to the street life that was so much a feature of India. It was hardly surprising that people scurried home to shut out the weather behind stout doors and closed windows. It was primarily Richard who broke down the barriers of acceptance. He went everywhere, poking his nose into this and that, learning to catch moles and trap eels, wildfowling from a flatbottomed punt at dawn, and even struggling to master the stilts with which Fenmen traditionally crossed flooded stretches of land. And because the brother was invariably cheerful, no matter how wet and muddy he might be, the villagers gradually began to accept his sister too, especially as they began to realise that her fine London clothes and her undoubted wealth did not lead her to put on airs or 'fancy herself' as they had feared.

Even so, the social life of the little village was strictly limited. There was the vicar, the doctor and their families. There was a handful of farmers who kept themselves to themselves, a philosophy adhered to more stringently by Mr Huggate than by any of the others, and there was Edward Chelworth, Viscount Bardolph of Old Fen Hall.

Unfortunately the conventions of society held

good even in this remote spot and it was therefore only possible for India to receive and be received by the married ladies of the parish. The vicar and his wife took pity on her and decided that, for social reasons and despite his youth, Richard could be invited, too. It was clearly impossible, however, for the Viscount to pay a morning call on Miss Leigh or vice versa, a situation which, the vicar confided to his wife, was plainly ridiculous since it kept apart the two parishioners most eligible to be introduced to each other. He took very little comfort from the fact that both parties seemed entirely happy with the situation.

They met in church, of course. Or, to be more precise, they encountered one another entering and leaving. A courteous inclination of the head acknowledged the other's presence, together with a murmured, 'Good morning.'

On the basis of this level of acquaintance, India formed the impression that Lord Bardolph was cold, arrogant and decidedly high in the instep. For his part, the Viscount took one look at Miss Leigh's extravagantly modish apparel and dismissed her as a shallow, hen-witted butterfly — though admittedly a beautiful one — whose wealth had given her vulgar pretensions to gentility. On the rare occasions when he thought about her at all, it was with amazement that she had chosen to live in the Fens when London was so obviously very much more the sort of milieu in which she saw herself. It was most unlikely that she would stay here very long.

India was unsure whether to be relieved or

worried that Richard had made himself so very much at home here. He loved the Fens. Where his sister saw space, he saw skyscapes like none he had seen before. The lingering, spectacular sunsets and the glorious dawns more than compensated for the winds which drove the rain relentlessly before them. The people made him welcome, cautiously at first and then with amused willingness to let him into the secrets of surviving in this strange land. It was a land that spoke to his condition and he marvelled now at the degree of resentment he had felt when he first learned they were leaving London and coming here. He had always known that his parents intended him to complete his education at one or other of the great universities and he was neither surprised nor dismayed that India intended their wishes to be carried out. It was something to which he looked forward and the only regret he had on that score was that the present political situation ruled out any chance of undertaking The Grand Tour. What he had learned already from the Fens was what he intended to do with the rest of his life once his education was complete. He would be a farmer. Preferably a sheep farmer.

He had thought India would be pleased that he had settled on his future and was taken aback by her reaction, which was at first laughingly dismissive and then, when she realised this was no passing fancy, dismayed. Business was what they had been brought up in and one of the professions was what their parents had assumed Richard's education would lead to. Farming was what peasants did, though India

had to admit that that wasn't a word that fitted their
farming neighbours, least of all Viscount Bardolph.
What neither of them knew was that both their
parents had come from farming stock, so that a love
of the land was as firmly bred into Richard's bones —
if not into his sister's — as the sea was in those from
maritime families. It remained a source of friction
between them, so Richard let the matter drop. If
that led his sister to believe he had given up the
idea, it was too bad because, India notwithstanding,
he had every intention of pursuing that livelihood
and if India witheld the wherewithal once he had
finished his formal education, then so be it; there
would only be a few years before he had control
over his own fortune and then he could farm to his
heart's content. And he had every intention of doing
so.

Lord Bardolph returned to Old Fen Hall in a
humour that was far from sweet. He had been
bettered in a disagreement and had not enjoyed the
experience. It was particularly galling to know that
he had largely himself to blame and to recognise
that, although he had fired a telling parting shot, the
nature of it meant that he had lowered himself to
India Leigh's level, and there was little gratification
from that. Had she been a woman one could admire,
he might have applauded her quick thinking, but
there was very little to admire in Miss Leigh. There
was her beauty, of course, and he had already
remarked upon her eyes, which were large and dark,
well-spaced and set very slightly at an angle, giving

her an expression reminiscent of a deer. She had a
neat figure, too, and there was always her fortune.
Lord Bardolph had no interest in the latter and had
long ago learned to be wary of beautiful women
whose main purpose in life seemed to be the desire
to trap a title. To be fair, that didn't seem to be
India Leigh's ambition — or, if it were, she was going
a very strange way about achieving it — but there was
no denying she had struck a nerve.

Laura Newton had been beautiful and she had
used all her wiles to entrap the young Viscount into
a proposal of marriage. He had been quite besotted
with her fragile, pink-and-white beauty with its
fluttering eyelashes and breathless little voice that
made her seem infinitely vulnerable and very much
his junior instead of two years his senior. He hadn't
realised until after the proposal was uttered that
underneath that delicately palpitating exterior lay a
will of forged steel with a relentless determination to
have its own way. He hadn't realised until it was too
late that the smiles and the tinkling laughter were
social attributes, not indications of any real humour
and that, except where her own best interests were
involved, her mind was completely unformed.

He had been able to overlook most of the warning
signs until the day when she'd made it perfectly clear
that she had absolutely no intention whatsoever of
spending any part of their married life in the
country, much less in his beloved Fens. She hadn't
visited them but knew them to be remote and, it was
said, desolate, empty and, worst of all, unfashionable. From then on his infatuation had faded and

died but the realisation had come too late. He had proposed, he had been accepted — with considerable alacrity — and the betrothal had been announced. It was impossible for a gentleman to withdraw. The old adage about making your bed and lying on it was unpleasantly apposite.

The Viscount had stuck to his proposal. He had also stood unexpectedly firm over the choice of church for the ceremony. They would marry in the village church which served Old Fen Hall, the groomsman moving out of his own home and into the Hall so that the bride elect could be suitably accommodated until after the wedding.

Lord Bardolph had left London three weeks before the wedding to make sure everything at the Hall was as it should be; he had still harboured hopes that perhaps Laura might change her mind if she could be presented with perfection. He had been surprised but not disconcerted to receive a note from her to say that she was going to be delayed and wouldn't, in fact, arrive until the day before the wedding, and when the groomsman had arrived in the evening saying she still hadn't come Bardolph had experienced the first faint flutterings of hope. The most likely explanation, of course, was the mists or the state of the roads, and it was quite possible the ceremony might have to be postponed. Nevertheless, in the absence of any message to the contrary, the Viscount and the vicar had agreed they must carry on as if all were in order.

The messenger had arrived when everyone was at the church and Bardolph often wondered whether his timing had been at Laura's instigation. The message was brief and to the point: Miss Newton was crying off. She no longer had any wish to become Viscountess Bardolph.

The congregation had gasped with speculative dismay and genuine sympathy for the jilted bridegoom. Bardolph's feelings were mixed. It was not a pleasant experience to be an object of pity and probably—later—of ridicule. On the other hand he had had a lucky escape and resolved that he would take very good care never again to let infatuation warp his judgement.

The note had contained no explanation for the bride's action and Bardolph, knowing by now just how important his title had been to his intended, had asked the friend who had unnecessarily relinquished his home to go to London and find out. The Viscount drew immense satisfaction from the outcome. Miss Newton had made good use of his three weeks' absence from the capital to flutter her eyelashes at the Marquis of Quorndon, who had maliciously enjoyed playing her at her own game until she genuinely believed that it was only a matter of days before he, too, would propose—if only Bardolph were out of the way. Since a marquisate and later, when Quordon's father died, a duchy, far outranked anything she could hope for from Bardolph, she had decided the gamble was worth the toss. Some years later a well-bred but minor clergyman had rescued her from the shelf and he was now being pushed very effectively towards a bishospric with, Bardolph suspected, his wife's blue eyes fixed firmly on one or other of the archepiscopacies.

Bardolph grinned as he thought of it. It had been a lucky escape, all right, and well worth the nudges and whispers of the next few months, even years. No one knew his true feelings for the very simple fact that, if he had tried to explain them, people would only have thought he was putting a brave face on it. It was therefore no wonder that India Leigh had heard the popular version, and he certainly wasn't about to disillusion her. Her wealth had come from trade and her wardrobe was ostentatious in that it was costlier than either her status or her surroundings warranted, and it was therefore vulgar. That disposed of Miss Leigh, and if the thought occured to him, however fleetingly, that such a conclusion endorsed her assessment of him as pompous, he was angry enough to be able to dismiss it out of hand.

He wished he could dismiss her brother equally easily. He recognised in Richard Leigh much that he would have liked to see in Bartram. Until today, he hadn't deplored Richard's origins half as much as those of his sister. While he would have preferred Bartram to choose a friend of his own age, it was difficult to see how he could do so when village boys of sixteen had a living to earn and there was none of his own class. Richard Leigh was intelligent, with an enquiring mind and a maturity of judgement that belied his years. He was a born leader in a way that Bartram would never be. One of Bardolph's reasons for so strongly opposing his brother's ambitions to

join the navy was not the rigours of the life, useful
an excuse as that was, but his sad acknowledgement
of the fact that, while he could buy Bartram in, it
would be much more difficult to buy his promotion
once the boy had demonstrated his unsuitability for
any rank higher than lieutenant. Richard, on the
other hand, would do exceptionally well in the
services. It was ironic that his interests lay entirely
in the land.

He had no hesitation in assuming that the events
of the morning had been at young Leigh's instigation, especially since Bartram had once artlessly let
slip India's reason for coming here, and he could
hardly blame Huggate for being annoyed. Nathaniel
Huggate was not a man to whom one warmed. He
was a prosperous farmer who made very little noise
about his success and had the reclusive nature not
uncommon in Fenmen, but none of that made him a
liar and, in the absence of any rebuttal by the boys
or any attempt to justify their actions, he had no
option but to accept Huggate's word.

Richard Leigh had been dealt with, though
Bardolph had little faith in the ability of a butterfly
like India Leigh to exert any lasting influence on a
boy of Richard's strong-mindedness. Bartram, however, was under his control and that was a very
different matter.

He had told Bartram to go to the nursery and stay
there until he got back. It looked as if he had done
so. Bardolph handed his cloak, his hat and his gloves
to the manservant who came forward for them and
was about to ask him to tell Bartram to attend his

brother in the library when it occurred to him that it wasn't always a good idea to make too much use of the heavy hand. Instead, he went upstairs and opened the nursery door.

Bartram was sitting on the window-seat, looking down into the yew-framed garden below, but he turned a discontented face towards the door when he heard it open.

'Oh, it's you,' he said. 'You've been long enough.'

Bardolph held his temper in check and sat down in the old rocking-chair. Nurse used to tell him bed-time stories in this chair and its associations were of comfort and relaxation. He needed both just now. He forced himself to be pleasantly reasonable. 'I could hardly march young Leigh home and drop him on the doorstep without some sort of explanation, could I? Miss Leigh had to know what's been going on.'

'I'll bet *she* stood up for her brother,' Bartram said bitterly.

'I had the impression she was extremely angry about the whole business,' Bardolph said with perfect truth.

'Did she believe you as easily as you believed old Huggate?'

'She didn't accuse me of lying; she didn't even suggest I might be mistaken. I think I can assume she believed me.'

'And Richard? What did he have to say?'

'Nothing. He had the grace to look suitably crest-fallen. I don't think he's a boy who sulks.'

'Unlike me, you mean.'

'Your words, not mine.'

'Didn't she ask him for an explanation?'

'Not while I was there—any more than I'd have asked you for one if the positions had been reversed. I don't doubt they were demanded as soon as I'd left the house, however.'

Bartram snorted. 'I'd be very surprised if they were. Richard says he can do want he wants, that his sister doesn't interfere.'

Bardolph might have implied as much to India's face but, even if he believed it—and he wasn't at all sure he did—it wasn't a point he was prepared to concede to his brother. 'That wasn't the impression I got, but what Miss Leigh does or doesn't do is none of my concern. You are. I've listened to Huggate. Now I'll listen to you. What's your version?'

'My "version", if I chose to give one, would be the truth but you're not going to believe me, so I might as well save my breath.'

Bardolph sighed. 'Come on, Bart—you know me better than that.'

Bartram hesitated. If ever there was a time to tell Edward of his suspicions and the way they led up to this morning's escapade, it was now. Two considerations stopped him. He didn't doubt that sooner or later Edward would compare notes with India Leigh and if Richard had told a different story he'd be in even deeper trouble for lying than he already was for what, with any luck, would be interpreted as thoughtless mischief. The second cause of his hesitation was his deep-seated fear of ridicule. Everyone knew smuggling went on along the East Anglian coast and everyone knew that everyone else — well, everyone except Bardolph — took advantage of it to a greater or lesser degree even if they didn't actively participate. The cellars at Old Fen Hall were probably the only ones in the county where there wasn't a drop of liquor which had escaped paying duty. But to accuse a man like Nathaniel Huggate of wholesale smuggling would incur anger, which Bartram could cope with, and ridicule, which he couldn't. He and Richard might have convinced themselves it was true; convincing Edward was a different matter. At the very least, his story must tally with Richard's. The best thing would be to say nothing until they'd had a chance to talk about it.

'Do I? You never take anything I say seriously. You treat me like a child. Why should this be any different?'

'When you talk like a petulant, spoiled brat, it's hardly surprising if you're treated like one. Why don't you grow up? Or at the very least be your age? For God's sake, Bart, Richard Leigh is more of an adult than you are, for all he's two years younger.'

If Bardolph intended that remark to act as a spur, he misjudged it. Bartram sniffed and tossed his head in what was suspiciously like a flounce. 'Oh, yes, you'd much rather *he* was your brother, wouldn't you? His sister's sending him to Cambridge but I've noticed that although you went there, and so did Papa and Grandpapa, you've never mentioned sending me. I suppose you think it would be a waste of money.'

Bardolph frowned, unable to see any connection

with the complaint at hand and his brother's future. 'Then I'm sorry, Bart. I had no idea you harboured ambitions of a deeper education. If Cambridge is what you want, rest assured you shall have it. I thought your sole goal was the navy. You know my views on that. Believe me, I'd infinitely prefer to see you at university.'

Since Bartram hadn't the slightest interest in extending his education any further than was absolutely necessary and had only mentioned it at all out of pique, this immediate acceptance by his brother of a hitherto unknown ambition was decidedly unnerving. If he wasn't careful, he'd end up doing even more Latin and Greek than his tutors had already foisted on him.

'Yes, well, I might surprise you yet,' he said, retreating into childish dark innuendo.

'You already have,' Bardolph told him. 'However, perhaps we may discuss that another time. I'd like to return to the matter in hand. Since neither you nor young Leigh has been prepared to give me an alternative explanation for this morning's little fracas, I have no option but to accept Huggate's evaluation. You're gated for the next week — and I do mean gated: confined to the house. I'd like to say you can ride in the park, but quite frankly I don't trust you not to stray. Furthermore, you'll have nothing to do with Richard Leigh for the time being,' he concluded, unconsciously echoing India.

'And how long is that going to be?' Bartram asked. 'He's the only person round here that I've got anything in common with.'

'Until I say so. It will depend largely on your behaviour and your attitude.'

'In other words, you're forbidding it altogther.'

'That isn't what I meant and it isn't what I intend. Richard Leigh is probably the most suitable friend you're likely to find round here.' Bardolph paused. 'This is one of the problems of living here and it's one that would be solved by Cambridge. If that's really what you want, Bart, you've only to let me know.'

But Bartram wasn't going to let himself be trapped into something which held no appeal at all. He ignored the plea. 'If I'm confined to barracks, I might as well go somewhere more congenial than this,' he said, conveniently forgetting that the old nursery remained one of his favourite haunts. 'I'm going to my own room,' and, when there was no objection from his brother, he departed, taking very good care to slam the door behind him.

Lord Bardolph leaned back in the rocking-chair and absent-mindedly set it in motion with one small push of his booted foot. He did not enjoy taking the place of a father to his sulky, resentful brother. He knew he came down far too heavily on the boy; he lacked that lighter touch that their father had had, a touch which encouraged an affectionate respect. As Bartram got older, he had tried to become less didactic with him, but it was difficult to sustain when Bartram himself seemed unable to recognise any change. Perhaps the answer was to encourage him to join the navy in the hope either that fraternal encouragement would make him change his mind out of sheer perverseness, or that a year or two in his chosen profession would bring a request to be bought out. The trouble with that scheme was that, in a time of prolonged war, there was an uncomfortable probability that Bartram wouldn't live long enough to make the request, and Bardolph didn't think he could face the feeling of guilt that would ensue.

He had no real objection to the friendship with Richard Leigh and if it resulted in some of the younger boy's initiative rubbing off on the older one it would be a very good thing. It was a pity Richard was in the care of so pert a female. Had there been a father to consult, Bardolph would have suggested they put their heads together and agree on a term to the boys' separation. It would at least preclude their playing one guardian off against the other, as Bartram had tried to do. Bardolph had little to say in favour of Miss Leigh but she hadn't struck him as being a woman who would let her brother do as he pleased. He would be quite interested to know exactly what sort of punishment she had decided to mete out, because he had no doubt at all that as the door had closed behind him Richard had reaped the benefit of that highly accomplished tongue.

It was a problem to which he gave a great deal of thought.

CHAPTER TWO

INDIA read the note again.

Lord Bardolph hopes that Miss Leigh will consent to receive him on Tuesday morning, or at an alternative day and time that better suits her convenience, to discuss aspects of their brothers' friendship.

It was short and to the point and if he intended them to reach some sort of agreement on how best to deal with the boys it was a very good idea. If it meant she was going to be subjected to another tirade about her brother, it wasn't. India had no desire whatsoever to meet Lord Bardolph again, much less exchange words with him. Still, the wording was carefully chosen, the request entirely reasonable, and it would be both churlish and unreasonable to refuse him. It was an interview which would be easier if Richard weren't around, so India told her brother, with perfect truth, that his behaviour in the last few days had been impeccable and she was therefore prepared to relent a little and allow him to go fishing, provided he kept his word not to see Bartram Chelworth.

Richard couldn't believe his luck and India knew that, when he was fortified with a flagon of ale, a loaf of bread and a hunk of cheese, she wouldn't see him between an early breakfast and dinner.

Lord Bardolph was obviously making every effort to be civil, and India had no intention of being outdone when it came to civility. He declined an offer of refreshment, however. 'You're very kind, Miss Leigh, but since my visit will inevitably have set tongues wagging perhaps it would be in both our interests to make it as brief as possible.'

'Would you feel happier if I asked the maid to attend us?' India asked demurely.

He looked at her suspiciously, unsure whether he was right to detect sarcasm. He decided not. 'I don't think we need go to quite those lengths. I'll put my cards on the table, Miss Leigh. I don't know what you may have learned from your brother, but mine has given me no explanation at all for this business with Huggate and, although I know you hold Bartram in low esteem, I assure you he isn't usually as irresponsible as Huggate's story seems to suggest.'

Thus courteously reminded of her own discourtesy, India coloured and drew a deep breath. 'Lord Bardolph, I'm very conscious that on your last visit here my concern got the better of me and I made statements that went beyond the bounds of politeness. Will you accept my apology?'

Apology notwithstanding, it was gratifying to see him so completely taken aback. He smiled, and India observed that his normally saturnine features were changed utterly by the genuine warmth in his normally cold grey eyes.

'I think we both said things in the heat of the

moment that we may later have regretted,' he said. 'I know I did. Shall we try to put that unfortunate exchange behind us?'

'Nothing would give me greater pleasure,' India agreed warmly. 'Richard told me quite a lot. I think he was telling me the truth—apart from anything else, he is usually truthful—but they do seem to have been. . .well, misguided.'

'Would you be betraying a confidence to tell me what he said?'

India considered. There were some aspects of Richard's revelations which she would prefer not to divulge, if only because Bartram's somewhat partial interpretation of his brother's attitude was probably unjust and its retailing was not calculated to enhance the possibly fragile accord they had just established.

'The general gist of it seems to have been that they've got it into their heads that Mr Huggate—who, I must say, has always struck me as an eminently respectable man—is not just involved in smuggling but is in some way a mastermind behind it.'

'On what do they base this assumption?'

India shook her head. 'Largely because he has a very large barn some way from the main buildings, and on the observation of ships occasionally at anchor in the Wash.'

'What nonsense! Everyone locally knows exactly what that barn is for. He stores fleeces until he has enough to send to the clothiers.'

'That, in the boys' opinion, is all bluff,' India told him. 'In fact, while Richard was telling me all this, it occurred to him that Mr Huggate was involved in a two-way trade: contraband in and fleeces out. I'm afraid he does have a very vivid imagination,' she added apologetically.

'It's a characteristic of youth, I believe.' He smiled at a suddenly recollected memory. 'I remember when I was about twelve being firmly convinced that Jem Patrick, who was sexton at the time, dug corpses up again when the mourners had gone home, and served them to his family.'

India stared at him, fascinated. 'What on earth gave you that idea?'

'Evidence every bit as convincing as any the boys have got hold of, I assure you. For one thing, he looked like a hobgoblin and his wife like a witch and she did all her cooking the old way, in a huge iron pot hanging over the fire—you could see it through the open door of the cottage when you rode by. What else would you need such a big pot for? The fact that they had eight children and Jem was known to be one of the most successful poachers in the Fens didn't seem to me to have any relevance at all.'

'Did you tell anyone about it?'

'I kept it to myself until one summer when there hadn't been any deaths for several weeks and it occurred to me that the family must be getting pretty hungry and maybe, in the circumstances, Jem might supplement the pot with the odd naughty boy, so I decided I was only doing my duty by warning the younger children in the village to stay at home and be extra good. Their parents soon found out why the poor mites were terrified to set foot out of doors and, just like Huggate, they descended on the Hall to complain to my father.'

'What did he do?'

'He was appalled, of course. That was the only time in my life he ever gave me a thrashing—and that was the easy part of the punishment. I had to go to Jem Patrick and his wife and apologise. That taught me a lesson I've never forgotten. What made it all the harder was that the Patricks were so forgiving about it. In a way, I'd have felt better if he'd given me a thrashing, too. I can laugh about it now—mainly because those two poor souls are dead themselves so I no longer feel embarrassed every time I see them—but it wasn't funny at the time.'

India chuckled. 'I can imagine—and I must say it's a great comfort to know that you weren't *always* a pillar of rectitude. That makes you *much* more human.'

He stiffened. 'Is that how you see me? As an inhuman pillar?'

'Oh, dear, why don't I learn to think before I speak?' India lamented. 'Just when we seem to be getting on so much better, too. Mind you,' she added, consideringly, 'I suppose a pillar must by definition be inhuman. Still, it wasn't civil and I'm determined to be civil; I'm sorry.'

Disconcerted that, while India should apologise for her rudeness, she felt no need to modify her judgement of him, Bardolph suggested they return to the matter in hand. 'If Bartram really believed that story, why on earth didn't he come to me with it? He must have known I'm the person best situated both to look into the allegation and to do something about it if it proved true.'

'You didn't go to your father with a far more bizarre story,' India pointed out gently.

'True, and I suppose the reason was that I knew he wouldn't believe it.' He paused and looked at her. 'Is that why Bartram didn't come to me?'

'You'll have to ask him that, my lord. I've not spoken to him and it would hardly be right for me to repeat anything I might have heard at second hand.'

'Which means Richard has told you the reasons and I'm not far off the mark,' he said shrewdly. 'Dare I ask if you're punishing your brother?'

'Yes, of course. As much for giving Mr Huggate cause for concern as anything else.'

'Good. I think we ought to see whether we can co-ordinate the punishments we've meted out so that they're being treated more or less equally. I've gated Bartram for a week and told him he can't see Richard for the time being. When I was pressed to define that limitation, I told him it meant till I said he could. He wasn't very pleased. What's so funny?'

India had thrown back her head and was laughing that full-throated laugh that had so annoyed him before. He found it rather less annoying on this occasion, for some reason.

'We seem to have had identical conversations,' she told him. 'Mind you, I did concede that Richard could accompany me to church and to do the shopping.' She chuckled. 'He didn't think that was much of a mitigation to what he described as an indefinite sentence.'

Bardolph smiled ruefully. 'At least we're in perfect accord on one thing,' he said. 'Will you tell him the purpose of my visit?'

'He won't need to know anything about it. I told him that, since he'd been on such exceptionally good behaviour, I was going to relent for just one day and let him go fishing. He won't be back until dinnertime.'

'Didn't he think that rather odd?'

'I shouldn't think so. He'll just attribute it to my being in a singularly good mood today. I thought it quite likely I might not wish to discuss your visit with him.'

'Especially since he was present during my last one.'

'Precisely.'

'For how long do you suggest we sustain the ban on their meeting?' Bardolph asked.

'It must be long enough to be a punishment but not so long that they take to meeting clandestinely. I don't think we should do anything to encourage deceit, do you?'

'What would you say to a week confined to the house followed by a fortnight honour bound not to meet?'

'That sounds reasonable,' India said thoughtfully. 'Do we tell them we've set a limit?'

Bardolph considered the matter. 'I think not. A fortnight isn't really very long. If they don't know, it will seem much more severe than it's going to be.'

'Mmm. Are you sure that's wise?'

'It's only two weeks, for goodness' sake.'

'I suppose so,' India said doubtfully. 'They can't get up to much in that time, can they? Not on their own.'

Neither India nor Bardolph saw the surreptitious passing of a note between their brothers on the way out of church that Sunday. By that time, both boys had been told that their confinement to the house would end on Tuesday but that the ban on their meeting would continue 'indefinitely'. Richard had accepted this decision with resignation, but Bartram had grumbled for the rest of the day about its being unfair and he betted no such harsh fate had been allotted to Richard. Since Bardolph had no intention of telling his brother of his visit, he bore the grumbles with a better grace than Bartram had expected, thus depriving the younger of the self-righteous sense of grievance in which an outburst of anger would have allowed him to indulge.

It really was too bad. There was no justice in the world. Edward was out to thwart him at every turn and if Bartram weren't very careful he'd find himself packed off to Cambridge without a by-your-leave. It was no good talking to Edward, who was past being able to see reason. He would just have to take matters into his own hands. *That* would make Edward sorry.

Richard wasn't happy about the ban and objected to it as much on principle as because it bothered him unduly. He had plenty of other things to do even if they weren't as much fun on his own. Common sense told him that 'indefinitely' probably meant three or four weeks — less if he played his cards right. Common sense also told him that the better the grace with which he accepted it, the sooner it was likely to come to an end. He wasn't at all pleased to receive a note asking — no, demanding — that he and Bartram should meet on the outmarshes behind the sea-bank on the first day of their freedom.

His initial reaction was to reject the idea but when he re-read the message there was something about the wording which made him feel uncomfortable, especially since he wouldn't be able to let Bartram know he wasn't coming. It was brief yet managed to be both hysterical and despairing and hinted at some awful fate Bardolph had lined up for his brother. Richard couldn't see what that might be other than his well-established refusal to let Bartram go to sea, though perhaps the Viscount had come up with an alternative career for his brother. It was typical of Bartram to read too much into something his brother had said, just as — admittedly aided and abetted by Richard — he had read too much into Mr Huggate's activities. As Richard was now shamefacedly prepared to admit, they had let their imaginations run away with them.

The obvious thing to do — and certainly the most sensible — would be to take the note to India and ask for special dispensation, just this once, to let him meet his friend. He rejected it only because he wouldn't be a bit surprised if India, presumably still seething under Bardolph's insults, didn't go straight over to the Hall and demand that this time it should be the Viscount who kept a tighter rein on his brother. In that eventuality, Richard had no doubt that once India had left Bartram would get one of the sarcastic tongue-lashings he so dreaded. No, he couldn't tell India any more than he could leave his friend on the outmarshes feeling he had been deserted. It went against the grain to be deceitful and if India found out. . .well, he'd just have to cross that bridge when he came to it.

At least he wasn't obliged to lie. When India saw him going out her only words were a reminder to be back for dinner. No 'Where are you going?' or 'You won't see Bartram, will you?' He was perfectly willing to agree to be back for dinner. He had no intention of being anything else.

Bartram was already there and, judging by his manner, had been for some time. 'I began to think you weren't going to be able to give your sister the slip,' he said.

'Didn't have to,' Richard replied. 'I'm not gated any more. Just a week of that. I can go where I like, provided I don't see you.'

'Same here,' Bartram said, surprised. 'Do you think they've put their heads together?'

'Shouldn't think so,' Richard said positively. 'You weren't there when Bardolph took me home. Believe me, they didn't part good friends. I should think they'd both find it difficult to be barely polite to one another if they met in the street. What's this all about? I don't mind telling you, I was in two minds whether to come. I don't like deceiving India, not when I've given her my word. I grumble about her but she's not a bad sort. Even let me go fishing once when I was gated because I'd been taking it well. This had better be worth while because if she finds out she's going to be *really* angry.'

'Bardolph's sending me to Cambridge,' Bartram said dramatically.

Richard considered the matter. 'It's not exactly the Grand Tour — it's not exactly London, if it comes to that, but I should think there's plenty to do there. How long for?'

'You don't understand. It's to study.'

'What's wrong with that? He's not the sort to starve you of funds and from what I've heard there's plenty going on if you've the ready. Not that I've mentioned that to India, you understand,' he added hastily, 'and I'd be obliged if you wouldn't, either.'

'Don't you understand? It's his scheme to stop me going into the navy.'

'Maybe he just feels you should have a good education first,' Richard suggested.

'What use is Latin and Greek on the high seas?' Bartram asked. 'None, that's what. No, he's going to push me into the church.'

'Has he said so?' Richard asked, surprised. He wasn't at all sure what qualities were needed in a churchman but he somehow didn't think Bartram had them, and he didn't altogether share Bartram's opinion of his brother.

'No, of course not. He's not that stupid. He must know I wouldn't go along with it.'

'Then what makes you think that's his intention?'

'I can't think of any other reason for sending me

to Cambridge,' Bartram said. 'Besides, I've got a sort of hunch about it.'

'Look, I don't want to upset you, Bart, but haven't you noticed that these hunches of yours aren't exactly reliable?'

'You didn't see him. He sat in that rocking-chair cool as a cucumber and he wasn't the least bit concerned about what *I* wanted. Still, I've had plenty of time to think about it now, and I've decided what we're going to do.'

'"We"?' Richard echoed. 'What has all this got to do with me? Where do I come into it?'

'You're my friend, aren't you? I'm the first to admit that I've got the imagination but you've got the common sense—quite a lot of it, considering your age—so we make a good combination, so naturally we do things together.'

'What things?' Richard asked suspiciously. He liked this conversation less and less the further it progressed.

'Has your sister told you how long this ban on seeing each other is going to last?'

'No. She said it would be till she saw fit.'

'Exactly! Edward said much the same. He said it would be when he judged I'd had long enough to learn some sense. You know what it means, don't you?'

'That if we play our cards right and don't get up to any mischief in the meantime they'll lift it,' Richard reasoned.

'Don't you believe it. This ban will last until after Edward's packed me off to Cambridge. I expect he's already writing to his old college to ask them to take me.'

'Would that really be so bad? I mean, the trouble with this place is that there's absolutely no one to do things with — there's you and there's me. Apart from us everyone is either working or too old to be interested in fun. At least at Cambridge you'll make lots of friends in the same situation as yourself. I'm the one that'll be worst off, stuck here with nothing to do.'

'Which is why I've come up with this scheme,' Bartram told him, thinking that if ever there was a hot iron to be struck this was it. 'We run away. In the night,' he added.

Richard looked at him pityingly. 'I didn't imagine you meant in broad daylight,' he said scathingly. 'And what then? I've always thought running away sounded very uncomfortable: no proper food,' he explained with some feeling.

'We take food with us — there's bound to be plenty in your larder and mine — and we take lots of money. Well, as much as we can scrape together. I thought we could run away to sea. That way the navy'd feed us *and* pay us.'

'Oh, no, we don't — at least, I don't. I've had enough of the sea to last me a lifetime, thank you very much, and I can't imagine a rating in the navy — which is what we'd be — lives anything like as well as passengers who've paid for their cabins. And that isn't all that well, I can tell you. No, Bart. I am definitely *not* running away to sea.'

'I suppose it doesn't have to be the sea — not for

you, at any rate. What about the army? That would be exciting. You could be a drummer-boy, right at the forefront of what's going on.'

Richard gave the proposal due consideration. There was no denying its attractions were greater than those of the navy. There were one or two snags involved, though. 'The ones at the forefront get killed,' he said. 'Or else they lose bits, which is probably worse. I don't think the army's going to be much of an improvement on the navy, to tell you the truth.'

'And I thought you were adventurous!' Bartram said cuttingly. 'You just want a nice, easy life tied to your sister's apron-strings. At least I'm prepared to get up and *do* something about my situation.'

'That's not fair,' Richard retorted, stung. 'It's just that I don't want to join the army or the navy. I want to be a farmer and once I come into my own money that's what I'm going to do. In the meantime, I just have to pick up what I can about it, but I can't see that running away to sea is going to be any help at all.'

'Don't understand the attraction of farming, myself,' Bartram commented. 'I've lived in the country all my life and all I can see you get from it is tired and dirty and endless conversations about the price of grain or the prevalence of foot-rot. Still, if that's what you want, why not come with me and when we're far enough away you can get some work on the land — which you must admit will be first-class experience for you — and I'll enlist. What do you think?'

As an idea, it was a distinct improvement on its predecessors and a far more attractive prospect than sitting out the next seven years until he was controller of his own life. Seven years, even broken up by the diversions of Cambridge for some of them, was a very long time and Bartram was right: it was time which could be usefully spent gaining practical experience.

'They'd come after us as soon as they read our notes,' he said.

'Who said anything about leaving notes? We just disappear.'

'If we do that, they'll worry,' Richard objected.

'Edward won't. He'll be annoyed, because I'll have got the better of him, but deep down he'll just be relieved.'

'India will. She'll worry herself sick.'

'She'll soon get over it. She's not one of these silly, vapourish females and if she hasn't got to worry any more about keeping you out of trouble — which you told me you thought was why she'd come here in the first place — she'll be able to go back to London and find herself a rich husband or a title, or even both. At least she won't have to die an old maid, which is what'll happen if she has to stay here, because there are *no* eligible men at all.'

'Except your brother,' Richard said doubtfully.

'Edward? Don't be funny; he *hates* women. Besides, he's very high in the instep. I don't want to be rude about your sister, Richard, but let's face it, although she's an heiress and not the least frumpish, she just isn't the class that men like Edward marry.'

'And after the set-to they had the other week, I don't think she'd have him if he asked. Besides, she's not after a title. Never has been.' All the same, Richard knew that India had given up much that she enjoyed to get him away from the influence of bad company, which she had eventually admitted had been her purpose in coming to the Fens in the first place. He also knew that her chances of getting married diminished rapidly with every passing year. She was twenty-three already, an age which many regarded as beyond further hope. Perhaps by running away with Bartram he would indirectly be doing her a service. He still didn't like the idea of not telling her. Bartram might think what he chose, but Richard knew India would be both worried and upset. 'I don't mind coming,' he conceded at last, 'but we've got to let them know what we're doing.'

Bartram sighed with exasperation. He could think of no better guarantee of being ignominiously dragged home than letting Edward know his plans. Edward would simply alert every harbour-master and every enlistment officer on the east coast— probably even further afield than that— and ask them to have him delivered back to Old Fen Hall if he turned up and, since the reward would be generous, they would. If, on the other hand, there were no notes, it would be some time before he realised Bartram had run away and wasn't just off fishing. Then Edward would have to out-think him and decide not only where he was going but also which route he had taken. By the time he had worked it out and made a few false casts, Bartram would be on the high seas, out of his reach. It didn't occur to Bartram that his brother might be more than capable of out-thinking him.

'I'll tell you what we'll do,' he said. 'We'll compromise. We'll wait till we're well away from here and then you can write your sister a note assuring her that you're all right, and I'll post it when I've signed on. That way she won't know where *you* are, and I'll be at sea before she can let anything slip that might get back to Edward.'

'You would post it? You wouldn't forget?'

'Trust me. I'm your friend. In any case, why should I forget?'

Three nights later Bartram waited until the only sounds were the creaks and sighs of a sleeping house and crept downstairs and out through the kitchen and the dairy. There was no sound from the dogs who knew him well and the thick straw of their bedding deadened the restlessness of horses unaccustomed to be disturbed at this hour. It took precious time to muffle the hoofs of two horses before fetching their tack and saddling them up but they were essential minutes: it was one of Edward's obsessions that the stable yard was kept free of mud and straw, which meant that the sound of iron on granite cobbles would carry with absolute clarity to the coachman in his house adjacent to the yard, even if it didn't wake Edward himself.

He led the horses across the yard and round the bend of the drive to a spot where he could mount without fear of being spotted and then rode off at a fast trot to the place outside the village where he had agreed to meet Richard.

'You took your time,' Richard grumbled. 'I've been here hours.'

'I bet you haven't. I bet it just feels like hours,' Bartram said shrewdly. 'I had to wait till everyone was asleep and it took longer than I expected to muffle their hoofs. It was quite tricky trying to do it in the dark.' He was removing the cloths from the hoofs as he spoke. 'Did you get the food?' he asked as he straightened up.

Richard held up two sacks. 'Plenty. Cook will be furious when she finds out. There's bread and cheese, of course, the remains of today's mutton pie, a veal pie we're supposed to be having tomorrow— or today—and the remains of a roast chicken.'

'That ought to see us through a day or two. What about money?'

'The rest of my allowance and all of India's housekeeping money—about three guineas in all. I didn't like taking that. It felt like stealing.'

'Rubbish. You'd have eaten the food bought with it, wouldn't you? Well, then, you've just taken money to feed yourself when the victuals we've got run out. She'll be able to economise once you're gone, so she'll gain in the long run.'

It was a specious argument at best and did little to ease Richard's conscience. 'What about you?' he asked. 'Did you get any?'

Bartram smirked. 'A bit more than you,' he said. 'Edward had the rents in last week and they were still in his desk. The lock was quite easy to break. I didn't take it *all*, of course,' he said magnanimously. 'I haven't counted it, either, but there must be about fifty guineas in my pocket.'

Richard whistled through his teeth. 'Bardolph'll kill you if he gets hold of you,' he said.

'He's not going to get hold of me, is he? In any case, I doubt if he'll notice it's missing. What's fifty guineas to him? I've known him put more than that on a horse at the races and not bat an eyelid when it lost.'

Richard, accustomed to the society of wealthy merchants in Bangalore, any one of whom could have accounted for every last penny in their coffers, doubted whether Bardolph was any different but judged it wiser not to say so. He mounted his horse instead. 'Where are we going?' he asked.

'We'll make for Cross Keys House and the Wash Way,' Bartram said. 'I want to get to King's Lynn as quickly as I can and I'm sure you'll be able to find work the other side of the Nene. Or you can go further afield if you prefer. I've got to enlist before Edward catches up with me.'

'I don't much fancy crossing the river at night,' Richard objected. The Nene was fordable only at low water by the mile-and-a-quarter-long strip known as the Wash Way. On either side were treacherous stretches of mud and sand and when the tide swept in upriver it did so with deceptive speed and dangerous currents.

'Don't worry. I was born here. I know it well,' Bartram said with a confidence his friend couldn't entirely share.

'I don't think it's wise, anyway,' Richard said. 'By the time we get there, there may be one or two people about. They'll be able to tell Bardolph they saw us.'

That put a different complexion on it altogther and Bartram decided that hoodwinking his brother had better take priority over enlistment for the time being. 'We'll go along the Nene embankment to Wisbech and cross the river by the bridge there. We won't be so noticeable among the crowds. Then we'll go across to Downham Market to cross the Ouse and after that we can head north to King's Lynn. Or I can, if you've found yourself some work by then,' he amended.

'That sounds better,' Richard said. He rather thought he might part company soon after Downham Market and head across to Norwich where he must surely find some sort of work to tide him over until the next hiring fair. It would be very much easier to remain undiscovered in such a big city, too. One way and another, apart from the continuing feeling of unease about the way he had treated India, things looked as if they were turning out rather well.

CHAPTER THREE

LORD BARDOLPH'S valet tapped on his employer's door and, when there was no reply, turned the handle and went in, coughing discreetly. It took quite a prolonged bout of coughing to wake the Viscount, who was a heavy sleeper, but eventually he stirred.

The room with its heavy curtains was still dark. Lord Bardolph frowned. Sleep was still dulling his mind but something wasn't quite right. He was usually awoken by Folksworth's pulling back the curtains to let the morning light stream in.

'Draw the curtains, man,' he said. 'I can barely see you.'

There was an infinitesimal hesitation before the valet did as he was told and the thin, pre-dawn grey struggled manfully over the windowsill, lightening the room without illuminating it. Bardolph groaned. 'Good God, Folksworth, what time is it?'

The valet coughed again, apologetically this time. 'A little after a quarter-past five, my lord.'

'Quarter-past *what*? No—don't repeat it.' Lord Bardolph sat up and looked steadily at his valet. 'You know me too well to risk waking me up unnecessarily. Something's happened. Out with it.'

'I think perhaps you'd better speak to Gidding, my lord. He's waiting outside.'

'Gidding? The groom?'

Folksworth gave a small, deferential bow. 'We only employ one of that name, I believe, my lord.'

'Yes, of course we do. I'm still only half awake. Send him in.'

Bob Gidding was acutely embarrassed at being ushered into Lord Bardolph's bedroom and would infinitely have preferred the valet to convey the news but Mr Folksworth had seemed to think it would be all right. . . He pulled his forelock. 'Good morning, my lord,' he began.

'Good morning, Gidding, though I've a strong suspicion this visit means it isn't. What's the matter?'

'It's the horses, my lord. Well, two of them. Fanfare and Clarion, my lord.'

'What's wrong with them?'

'I don't rightly know as anything is,' Gidding replied, punctiliously truthful. 'The thing is, there's no way of knowing, seeing as how they're not there.'

'Not in their boxes, you mean?'

'That's right, my lord.'

'Have you checked the paddocks? They haven't been turned out?'

'First thing I thought of, my lord, just in case they'd been needed in the night — though why they'd be put back in a paddock to catch their deaths instead of in their boxes is beyond me. No sign of them. Their tack's gone, too.'

Lord Bardolph's eyes narrowed. 'When you say "their tack", do you mean quite specifically their tack or just the tack for two horses?'

'No, my lord. I mean their tack.'

'Right. Get back to the stables and have a look round to see if you can find anything to indicate which way they've gone,' Bardolph instructed, throwing back the bedclothes and swinging his legs on to the floor. 'Folksworth, my riding clothes.'

He was washed, shaved and dressed in record time even if, Folksworth thought regretfully, it showed. His visit to the stables only confirmed what the groom had already told him and a close examination of the scythed grass bordering the drive revealed nothing. Whoever had taken them had used the right tack and the dogs hadn't barked. The implication was clear: it hadn't been strangers.

'Have all the grooms turned up this morning?'

'Yes, my lord, I checked. Mr Folksworth and the housekeeper are checking the indoor staff. It did cross my mind, my lord — if you'll forgive the impertinence — that, seeing as how Fanfare is Mr Bartram's mount, maybe he's taken them.'

'The same thought had occurred to me but you know as well as I do my brother isn't noted for getting up early.'

'Except when he's fishing.'

'True, but he doesn't take a horse with him, much less two. I'll go and check. If he's not there at least we'll know who to look for.'

Despite the fact that he could think of nothing with sufficient lure to get his brother out of bed in the middle of the night, Bardolph wasn't entirely surprised to find Bartram's room empty and his bed unslept in. The counterpane had been removed and the blankets turned back by the maid the previous evening and an indentation suggested that it had been lain on but not in.

Bardolph called his valet. 'Folksworth, would you be so kind as to find out for me what my brother has taken in the way of clothes and ask Cook to check the larder? I shall be in the library if I'm needed.'

Lord Bardolph's desk was in the library. It was a large and very beautiful escritoire with drawers and pigeon-holes above the cherry-wood writing surface. Two doors closed over these so that a clean line with intricate marquetry was what met the eye when the desk wasn't in use. As he crossed to the chair at which he conducted much of the estate's business, Bardolph noticed that the lock had been forced and the doors stood slightly ajar. He frowned and then remembered the rents that he had locked away until he next rode in to Wisbech to deposit it in Jonathan Peckover's bank.

He opened the drawer in which three bags of coins had been placed and was initially surprised to find them all there, but when he took them out one of them weighed very much lighter than he thought it should. He opened it. It was the bag containing guineas and a quick count proved it to be forty-eight guineas short.

Bardolph frowned. A common thief would have taken all the money, not a relatively small part. A common thief would not have taken one horse, let alone two, because of the danger of the dogs waking up the household or, even if they could be quietened, the sound of hoofs waking the coachman. What was more, it was highly unlikely to be sheer coincidence that the money, the horses and his brother were all missing from their beds at the same time. The missing money suggested that this was no schoolboy prank, no midnight steeplechase and he had a sinking feeling that the only possible explanation was that Bartram had run away.

There remained the puzzle of two horses, unless Bartram had taken enough clothes with him to need a baggage horse. It seemed unlikely and then he recalled that Clarion's riding tack had gone and a saddle was not much use for transporting baggage. It followed therefore that there were two horses because there were two riders.

Richard Leigh?

The Leighs maintained no stable. When Richard wanted to ride, he hired a hack from a small local livery stable and they certainly wouldn't hire a hack to a fourteen-year-old in the middle of the night. Bartram would have faced no such problem.

Richard Leigh.

If that young scoundrel had persuaded Bartram to put up the horses and the cash, what was he providing? It would be interesting to find out. It would be even more interesting to discover what their game was and where they were headed but, since there was still an outside chance that Richard Leigh had nothing to do with all this, the first imperative must be to find out whether he was still soundly asleep in his bed or whether he, too, was missing. It was a pity the recently improved relations with Miss Leigh would have to be jeopardised but that couldn't be helped. He would ride over there straight away.

But first he had to try to discover which way Bartram and two horses — and probably a second rider — had gone. While someone saddled his horse, he told Gidding to organise everyone who could ride into teams which would quarter the Fens in the hope of finding someone who had seen them. Every farm was to be visited, every drove explored and the people at every settlement questioned. Since Bartram's ambition was to go to sea, and since his achievement of it would place him beyond his brother's reach for some years to come, the searcher's first priority must be the Wash Way. It was the shortest route to King's Lynn and, although the present state of the tide made it uncrossable and delay therefore inevitable, there was a very good chance the boys would have been spotted. Both Bartram and the horses would have been recognised in that area, an additional advantage which wouldn't necessarily hold true if they had gone elsewhere.

India's maid was as diffident about waking up her mistress as ever Lord Bardolph's valet had been a short while previously, though her method was more direct. She shook her.

India stirred and sat up. 'Eliza? Whatever's the matter? What time is it?'

'Seven o'clock, Miss Leigh, and I'm sorry, I really am, but there's a gentleman in the parlour to see you.'

'At seven in the morning? Don't be ridiculous. And if there is, tell him to go away and come back at a more civilised hour.'

'From the look on his face, he'd refuse point-blank,' Eliza told her. 'In fact, I wouldn't be a bit surprised if he came straight up and hauled you out of bed himself. It's Lord Bardolph,' she added as if this explained everything.

India frowned. 'Lord Bardolph? What on earth can he want at this unearthly hour?'

'I'm sure I couldn't say, Miss Leigh. He didn't look about to tell the likes of me. "Just fetch her", he says when I asks what it was about. Shall I tell him to come back later?'

India resisted the temptation to say yes. She couldn't delude herself that Bardolph was in the habit of paying morning-calls at this hour so whatever had brought him here must be important. 'Tell his lordship I'll be with him as soon as I'm half presentable.'

While Eliza conveyed this message to its destination, India hastily put on a peignoir of sapphire-blue edged with swansdown and held together under the bosom with a jewelled clasp. She freshened her face in cold water and hastily re-braided her dark hair in one plait which hung over her shoulder. It would do, in so far as such intimate attire could be held to 'do' when entertaining an uninvited man. Only the obvious urgency indicated by the hour could possibly excuse her not dressing properly and taking her time over it. If he didn't approve, that was just too bad—he should at least have sent a warning message.

Despite the fact that he was in no mood to approve of anything connected with the Leighs until and unless Richard proved to be sound sleep in his bed, Lord Bardolph was distinctly appreciative of the picture India presented when she came into the room. A woman who could look so good so early and at such short notice was nothing if not resourceful, though, in India's case, he had to admit she started with the very best in raw materials.

He bowed. 'I apologise for the hour, Miss Leigh.'

'And so you should. I fully intended to have you sent packing but my maid seemed to think it was important.'

'Your maid was right. I certainly don't customarily make morning-calls at this hour, and not on single ladies. At least, not on those with pretensions to gentility.'

'In precisely the same way that I don't customarily receive men in my dressing-gown. Gentlemen, of course, don't make it necessary.'

Bardolph felt his lips twitch. '*Touché*, Miss Leigh. And now may we consider the pleasantries completed? The purpose of my visit really is rather urgent. Tell me, do you happen to know where your brother is at this moment?'

'I've always heard that some members of the aristocracy are noted for their eccentricity,' India told him, 'but I didn't guess it might extend to checking up at unseemly hours on where lesser mortals might be. It isn't any of your business, my lord, but since it isn't of the slightest importance, either, I take leave to tell you that Richard is still sound asleep.'

'In his bed?'

India appeared to consider the question. 'In India he sometimes slept on the veranda but it's very warm in India, you understand, and the wind doesn't blow you off your feet. Besides, we don't have a veranda here. Don't be silly—of course in his bed.'

Lord Bardolph held his temper in check with an effort. 'I wonder if you'd do me the very great favour of checking?'

India looked at him in silence for a few moments and then went over to the door. 'Eliza!' she called when she'd opened it. 'Would you go and wake Richard up and tell him to come down here immediately, please?' She turned back to her visitor. 'Will that satisfy you, sir?'

'Admirably. Believe me, Miss Leigh, I hope he materialises.'

It was Eliza who materialised. 'I'm sorry, madam, but he's not there.'

'Not there? He must be. Snuggled under the bedclothes, perhaps.'

The maid shook her head. 'The bed hasn't been slept in and Cook says can she have a word?'

'Tell her not now. It will have to wait until I've worked this out. If he's not in bed, where is he?'

'With respect, madam, I think you should see Cook,' Eliza suggested.

'You think she can throw some light on this? Very well, ask her to come along.'

Cook had come with the Leighs from London, largely because she knew a good position when she saw it. She was very Welsh, very red in the face and very angry. 'There's a load of snide, underhand and deceitful wretches these Fenmen are,' she began. 'I can cope with the wind, I can even cope with their heathenish language most of the time but I can't and I won't cope with thievery and that's the truth, madam.'

'What thievery?' India asked.

Cook held out one massive hand and counted off her losses on her fingers. 'There's yesterday's mutton pie gone, what's left of it, and today's veal pie as well. There's no sign of the cold chicken and the bread-crock's empty. And that's not the end of it for there's no sign of that lovely cheese we'd only just cut into. There's gone they all are, madam. Quite gone and what I'm going to feed us all on today is more than I know.'

'I'm sure you'll succeed in conjuring something up,' India told her, 'and as soon as I'm presentable we'll see about replacing what we can.'

'What are you going to do about the thief? That's what I want to know,' Cook declared.

'I'm sure Lord Bardolph will be able to tell us,' India told her. 'His lordship's a magistrate. Who better?'

'Rest assured he'll be hanged, drawn and quartered,' the Viscount interjected.

Cook nodded. 'I suppose that'll have to do but it doesn't go far enough, if you ask me.' She turned back as she reached the door. 'That wasn't quite all, come to think of it. There's two empty flour sacks gone missing. I keeps them, you see. They comes in useful for all sorts of things, but two of them's not there now.'

'I dare say the thief used them to transport the victuals,' Lord Bardolph suggested affably.

'I dare say your lorship's right,' the cook agreed and left the room to conjure up a breakfast of pancakes, ham, scrambled eggs and kidneys, which was the most she felt able to concoct after so great a shock.

'I shouldn't think you could go much further than hanging, quartering and drawing,' India remarked as the door closed behind Mrs Newport's broad beam.

'Believe me, I'm considering it,' Lord Bardolph said grimly. 'Two of my horses and forty-eight guineas have also been taken.'

'There can't be a connection,' India protested. 'The items missing are so disparate, Unless. . .' her voice tailed away and she looked at him in alarm as the implications of this news coupled with the very fact of his being here dawned on her.

'Quite,' he said sardonically. 'Miss Leigh, would you be kind enough to check whether you have any money missing?'

'But I keep very little in the house — just enough for our day-to-day needs. Nothing like forty-eight guineas.'

'Nevertheless, I'd appreciate it if you'd check.'

'I shall have to leave you for a moment.'

'I dare say I shall survive.'

When she returned, she was both chastened and angry. 'I owe you an apology, my lord,' she said. 'All my housekeeping money is gone. I can't tell you exactly how much it was because it was all in small change but it doesn't compare with your loss. I'd estimate it to have been very slightly in excess of three pounds. It begins to look as if the boys have gone together, your brother providing the mounts and the money, mine providing sustenance and such money as he could find. Richard will have had some of his allowance left but that won't amount to more than a few shillings. Why on earth have they run away?'

'That's a question they can answer when we've caught them. For the moment I'm more concerned to know where they're heading.'

'You don't think perhaps that the "why" might give some clue to the "where"?' India asked.

'It might, I suppose. Do you know of any reason your brother might have had?'

'No, none,' India said, shaking her head. 'One is tempted to think the recent bother with Mr Huggate may lie behind it but I don't think Richard was at all resentful of his punishment. He took it remarkably well considering he had no idea how long it was going to last.'

'That's more than I can say for Bartram.' He hesitated. 'I don't wish to be unkind, Miss Leigh, but do you think Richard's clever enough to pretend to accept his punishment while actually planning to do something about it himself?'

India considered it. 'I think he's clever enough,' she admitted. 'I don't think he's sufficiently devious, though. Apart from anything else, I don't think he'd want to cause me the anxiety he knows I'd suffer.'

'Yet he seems to have done precisely that,' Lord Bardolph said gently.

'He does, doesn't he?' There was a wistful note in India's voice which made her seem suddenly very vulnerable and the Viscount was conscious of a desire to protect her from any further anxiety—a desire which, since he held her responsible for her brother's behaviour, was quite irrational in the present circumstances. Then she visibly brightened as a thought struck her. 'You don't think they've taken it upon themselves to prove that their suspicions of Mr Huggate are correct? That they intend to keep watch until they're in a position to produce irrefutable evidence of his involvement?'

'That's logical enough and I certainly wouldn't put it past them—goodness knows, they're silly enough.' Then he shook his head. 'It's an attractive idea but it won't fadge: there's an outside possibility they might be able to conceal themselves for what might amount to several weeks, but they'd never be able to hide two horses. Besides, they wouldn't need horses—they'd only be a few miles from home.'

'Their goal might be London,' India offered reluctantly. 'Richard was very put out when he learned we were leaving. Would that appeal to Bartram?'

'It might well, though he's never expressed any interest. If he were on his own, I'd say he's run away to sea. His great ambition is to join the navy—a career for which I consider him totally unsuited.'

'Have you told him so?'

'Frequently,' he replied, surprised.

India nodded. 'Yes, you would. So that's very

likely what Bartram would do if he were on his own, but he's not, and no one will ever persuade Richard to run away to sea. I've no reason to believe he ever harboured any dreams in that direction but, if he had, the voyage from India will have killed them. He hated it. He said he intended never again to set foot on a ship no matter what. His ambition is to be a farmer.'

'I've never heard of anyone running away to work on a farm,' Bardolph commented.

In spite of her anxiety, India chuckled. 'Neither have I,' she admitted, 'but they must have had some destination in mind.'

'It begins to look as if the steps I took before coming here are our only hope,' the Viscount told her. 'I've taken every available man off his work and they're quartering the whole locality in the hope of picking up the boys' trail. Someone must have seen them, and if two boys on horseback don't attract attention *per se* the quality of their horseflesh will.'

'They must be aware of that,' India said doubtfully. 'They may very well sell them and buy more mundane mounts.'

'If they do,' Bardolph said grimly, 'I'll make them wish they'd never been born.'

'And Cook will help you,' India said, trying to lighten his anger.

He laughed in spite of himself. 'She'd probably do an even better job than I. In the meantime, I'll let you know as soon as I've any news.'

India reached out without thinking and laid her hand on his arm. 'You will let me know immediately,

won't you?' she pleaded, looking up into his grey
eyes. 'I mean, you won't leave telling me until
you've sorted everything out?'

Bardolph laid his hand on hers. 'Immediately, I
promise. As soon as I have any news at all, I'll ride
over and let you know.' He smiled reassuringly.
'Don't worry, Miss Leigh. Both boys are more than
capable of looking after themselves for a few days.
It's only a matter of finding out their direction,
following them and bringing them back. If it's any
comfort to you, I promise any punishment meted
out to Richard will be at your hands, not mine.'

India smiled ruefully. 'Thank you, my lord,
though I feel bound to confess that Richard might
take rather more notice of you. You're quite formidable when you're angry, you know.'

'Am I? I'd never have guessed you found me so.'

India dropped her gaze and her long dark lashes
fluttered over her eyes. 'I'm a very good actress, you
see,' she said.

'Ah, is that what it is? I'm afraid I attributed it to
your having the hide of one of your Indian ele-
phants. I'm delighted to learn I was wrong.'

It was jokingly, almost flirtatiously said and India
was unsure how to respond so she hid her confusion
by changing the subject.

'We're wasting precious time, my lord. I'll look
forward to hearing news.'

He bowed. 'And I shall look forward to delivering
it, Miss Leigh.'

Lord Bardolph returned to the Hall in a far better
humour than might have been expected. Nothing

had transpired to change his opinion that, whatever the boys were up to, Richard Leigh lay behind it, but he no longer judged that young man's sister to be in any way blameworthy. On the contrary, her reactions had been everything he could have hoped for, if not what he had dared to expect. He was beginning to wonder whether he might not have misjudged the lady altogether.

Bartram and Richard reached Wisbech in very good time and, more importantly from their point of view, without having been observed, so far as they could tell. Plenty of people saw them in Wisbech but none seemed to take undue notice of them. It was market day and buyers and sellers, regular tradesmen and itinerant peddlars, were congregating on the market-place, while the quay was crowded with fishing-boats and cargo-ships. Bartram looked at them wistfully as they rode over the bridge upstream of the main basin.

'We could always sign on on one of these,' he told his companion.

'I'm not signing on anything,' Richard told him. 'Besides, this isn't the place. It's far too close to home. Someone would be bound to recognise you and it wouldn't take Bardolph long to get here — I dare say he could make it before the next high tide. In any case, I thought you wanted the navy? No chance of that here.'

Both arguments were irrefutable but Bartram was deep in thought all the way to Downham Market. Here they agreed they were far enough away and had a big enough start to risk stopping for a rest and some luncheon. Each boy was so sunk in his own thoughts that he scarcely noticed the other was, too. Bartram was the first to break the silence.

'I've been thinking,' he said, 'and I've come up with a scheme that will suit both of us better than our original plan. It was seeing all those ships in Wisbech that gave me the idea. I know you don't want to go to sea, but why don't we sign on together to work our passage over to the Continent, then I can join a *foreign* navy and you can farm there? There are some very good farms in the Low Countries, I've heard, to say nothing of Belgium and France.'

'You don't think it might be a bit dangerous farming in country that's at war with my own?' Richard suggested.

'Well, not France, perhaps or Belgium, but there's always Denmark and any number of German countries — Hanover, Saxony, places like that.'

'Don't you ever read any newspapers?' Richard looked at his companion in amazement. 'Almost everywhere is under French rule. Denmark isn't and neither is Prussia, and I don't fancy either of them. I'm not going to Norway or Sweden, either. As for you joining a foreign navy, you must be quite demented. *What* foreign navy? Most of them will clap you in irons as soon as they see you.'

'Yes, well, it was just an idea,' Bartram said sulkily.

'And just about the worst one you've ever had,' Richard told him with the bluntness of a true friend.

'I've been thinking, too. It seems to me that this is a good place for us to separate and go our own ways. You can head back northwards to Lynn and enlist, while I go west and south into Bedfordshire and Hertfordshire where I'm not going to have any difficulty finding a good farm. What do you say?'

Bartram said nothing for some time. Richard's suggestion came as a very nasty shock. At the back of his mind he had never really believed that the younger boy would want to separate when it came down to it. He had been quietly confident that he would be able to persuade Richard that the sea was really quite good fun. He might himself have to relinquish his naval ambitions in order to persuade Richard to sign on for a spell on a coastal trader — something that didn't make the sort of voyage that had given Richard so pronounced a dislike of sea-travel. Why, such ships were rarely out of sight of land and it stood to reason that, while the sea could undoubtedly be, well, a little choppy round the coast, it couldn't compare with what one might expect to meet in the middle of the Atlantic. So pleased was Bartram with this plan that he had convinced himself that he had only to put it to Richard for his friend to accept it but his rejection of Bartram's modified version was so adamant that Bartram hesitated to put its predecessor in case that, too, was rejected with the minimum of thought. And now here was Richard wanting to split up already, fired by a thoroughly selfish wish to pursue his own ambition no matter how inconvenient it was to his companion.

'I think it's much too soon,' he said at last. 'Let's both carry on to King's Lynn. It'll be much easier there to cover our tracks, and if you do decide to stick to this bizarre idea of farming you can head towards Norwich. Better agricultural land round there.'

'Is there? Maybe I should strike out for there from here. Get there all the quicker.'

This was not at all what Bartram had in mind. 'Well, you won't,' he said spitefully, 'because you'll have to walk. I couldn't let you go on unsupervised with one of my brother's horses. He'd kill me.'

'Only if he caught you, and I thought the whole point of this was to get away from him,' Richard said, startled by this sudden change in his friend.

'Figure of speech,' Bartram said lamely. 'The thing is, these aren't the sort of bloodstock you're used to riding. Much better stick with me for a bit longer till you've really got the hang of them. Actually, once we get to Lynn and I've signed on, I shan't need either of them, so you might as well have them both then. You can always keep one and sell the other. That would compensate for the small amount of money you brought with you.'

Richard hesitated. The prospect of walking any great distance, especially in riding boots, was not an appealing one. On the other hand, there was much to be said for continuing to Lynn if at the end of it he came away with both animals. He wasn't at all sure that Bartram could be entirely trusted to keep his word since he was already taking for granted certain alterations to the original agreed plan. However, if Richard did stay with him to Lynn, Bartram could hardly then turn round and refuse to let him keep Clarion, even if by that time he'd decided not to include Fanfare. It didn't, after all, make very much difference where they split up but it made a considerable one if obstinacy lost Richard a mount.

'All right,' he said. 'I'll come with you to Lynn.'

When Lord Bardolph called at Abbot's Lodge towards evening that day, India jumped up to greet him, oblivious to decorum.

'You've some news?' she asked. 'You've heard something? Do tell me, my lord. Don't keep me in suspense. You've no idea how worried I've been.'

Lord Bardolph took her outstretched hands and guided her towards the sofa. 'I've come here for no other purpose than to tell you what I've discovered. Now be a good girl; sit down, take three deep breaths and when you're a little calmer I'll tell you.'

India found it surprisingly reassuring to be spoken to as if she were once more a child, and did as she was told. 'Now, my lord,' she said, 'I think I'm calm enough. What have you discovered?'

'Fortunately for us, country people, no matter how reticent they may be, are both extremely observant and quite remarkably inquisitive. I'll wager anything you like that Richard will believe them to have been totally unobserved and Bartram — who's lived here long enough to know better — is probably of the same opinion. In fact they were seen approaching the Wash Way but changed their minds and rode along the embankment to Wisbech.'

'The person who saw them was quite sure it was them?' India asked anxiously.

'I gather the light was too poor to identify the riders, but he was quite sure about the horses. A fisherman landing his catch at the Nene Quay in Wisbech recognised Bartram, who was riding over the bridge into the town. No one seems to have taken any particular notice of two horsemen in the town itself, but since it was market day that's hardly surprising. They were next spotted at Outwell. At least, the horses were and note was taken because the riders seemed rather young to have been entrusted with such prime horseflesh.' He frowned. 'I hope they give those animals a good, long rest. To get as far as they have, I'd hazard a guess based on the distance they've travelled in the first day that there haven't been too many rests so far and I doubt if they've dismounted and led the horses much today, either. It looks as if Downham Market is their immediate destination so I've sent someone there to find out which route they've taken. I'm still putting my money on King's Lynn, in which case I shall be there before them tomorrow, but I shan't know for sure until someone gets a message back to me, and I don't expect that until the early hours. It's a full moon and I've arranged changes of horses so that there's no unnecessary delay. At all events, I shall leave the Hall as near as possible at first light. My guess is they'll sleep very soundly tonight and wake up feeling sufficiently safe from pursuit to be in no particular hurry.'

'I do hope they choose a clean inn for the night,' India commented.

'Whatever happened to your romantic soul, your sense of adventure?' Bardolph asked. 'Where would be the fun in running away and sleeping in an *inn*? No, they'll be wrapped in a blanket under the stars. Much more the thing, I assure you. Besides, an innkeeper would remember them.'

'Then I hope it doesn't rain,' India insisted.

'I, on the other hand, hope it does. Serve them right.'

India laughed reluctantly but it seemed to Bardolph she was preoccupied.

'Is something still bothering you?' he asked gently.

'I was just thinking—do you have such a thing as a side-saddle in the stables?'

'Several. Why?'

'I think I ought to come with you.'

If she had intended to startle the Viscount, she couldn't have succeeded more gratifyingly. 'Come with me? I've never heard such nonsense in my life. Totally unfitting,' he declared.

'I can ride, you know,' India said indignantly. 'Quite well, as a matter of fact. The only reason I don't do so here is that the livery stable doesn't have a horse that will carry a lady's saddle. I've ridden quite long distances in India so you needn't be afraid I shan't keep up.'

'That isn't the point,' Bardolph said. 'I'm going on my own so there'll be no chaperon and, in any case, I'm likely to be away over at least one night. Your reputation would be ruined.'

'Now who's talking nonsense?' India retorted. 'I'm an old maid—hadn't you heard? Quite on the shelf, I believe. Old maids don't have reputations to lose.'

'If there's any truth in that outrageous statement at all—which I beg leave to doubt—you're not nearly an old enough old maid for it to apply to you.'

India, momentarily diverted, looked at him speculatively. 'I *think* you've almost been betrayed into a compliment,' she said. 'You really must be careful, my lord. When you're alone in a room with a woman, such remarks could be used to compromise you. I understand you're generally considered a *very* good catch,' she added ingenuously.

'A good catch I may be, but no one who knows me would take me for a big enough flat to lay myself open to being compromised by a nabob's daughter. Which, madam, is precisely why you will not accompany me, no matter how outstanding a horsewoman you may be. In fact, now I come to think about it, although we still have some side-saddles in the tackroom, we no longer have any horses trained to carry them.'

'That would appear to clinch the argument, wouldn't it?' India said with deceptive meekness.

Bardolph looked at her and frowned. It was certainly an irrefutable argument, though he doubted whether she believed it, but his admittedly brief acquaintance with her had not accustomed him to such tame acquiescence on her part. 'One would have thought so,' he agreed.

'Then nothing remains but for me to thank you for keeping me informed and to wish you good luck for tomorrow,' she said.

He bowed. 'I hope that next time I call it will be as the bearer of good news.'

'To say nothing of a brother,' India pointed out.

'That too, of course. Goodnight, Miss Leigh. I hope your mind is sufficiently at ease for you to be able to sleep well.'

'I'm quite sure I can depend on you, my lord. Goodnight.'

Lord Bardolph paused briefly before swinging himself into his saddle. He had an uncomfortable feeling that, although everything indicated that he had won the argument, there was nevertheless something behind it. India Leigh had capitulated far too easily. It was hard to see what else she could have done in the circumstances and she certainly didn't lack enough intelligence to recognise that fact. All the same, he couldn't help feeling slightly uneasy.

When the door had closed behind him, India sat in silence for several minutes before going over to the looking-glass that hung over the fire-place. It was a large, ornately framed glass and if one stood far enough back one could almost see oneself from top to toe. She was only very slightly taller than Richard; an inch, no more.

She went over to the little writing-desk, dipped pen into ink and wrote. Then she called Eliza.

'Get the gardener's boy to take this round to the livery stable,' she said.

CHAPTER FOUR

A NIGHT under the stars might be romantic and adventurous and what one did when one ran away but it was also exceedingly uncomfortable and, in Richard's opinion, just plain stupid when one was barely a mile from Downham Market and had a total of over fifty guineas. He thought the risk of a landlord's remembering them was a small chance to take when set against the advantages of a hot meal, a comfortable bed and a proper breakfast. Bartram disagreed.

It was Bartram's concern for the horses that had kept them from pushing on any further yesterday. He said they had pushed them as far and as fast as they had dared in order to put as much distance as possible between them and their relatives — by which Richard suspected he meant Lord Bardolph, since India could pose no threat in that respect. They would lay up somewhere snug for the rest of the afternoon and the night, and go on their way in the morning, but this time they'd put the horses' well-being first.

While no one could possibly criticise a desire to look after the horses, Richard found it distinctly odd that Bartram's primary motive still seemed to be to avoid aggravating his brother's ire. Bardolph would undoubtedly be furious if his horses were ruined but, since Bartram would be on the high seas and Richard the other side of Norwich, it was hard to see how the Viscount was going to find either of them even if his horses did somehow get back into his possession.

Richard sat up and rubbed the stiffer parts of his anatomy before clambering over the bank in the lee of which they had spent the night, and slaking his thirst in the drain on the other side. These wide, canal-like water-courses had been built over the last century and a half to drain the water from the marshy fens and turn the resulting siltfields into some of the richest farmland in England. They stretched in a huge, man-made, geometric web across the landscape, some of them no more than a narrow dyke, others twelve, sixteen, twenty feet wide. They made cross-country travel more difficult but no traveller in these parts need ever die of thirst. Nor need his horses. When Richard returned, Bartram was still asleep, so he removed the horses' hobbles and led them down to drink.

He came back to find Bartram on his feet, panicking. His friend heaved a sigh of relief as Richard and the horses crested the bank and came back down the landward side.

'You scared me to death,' he said. 'I thought you'd made off and taken the horses with you.'

'Thank you very much,' Richard retorted with heavy sarcasm. 'Is that how you trust your friends?'

Bartram was immediately embarrassed. 'Well, no, I didn't mean that, exactly. It's just. . .well, I'd just woken up and all that. I wasn't thinking straight.'

'I'm beginning to wonder if you ever do,' Richard

told him. 'The horses are watered and so am I, and I could eat an ox but I'll make do with Cook's veal pie. She makes a very good veal pie, does Cook.'

The boys were on their way again within the hour, heading north and keeping the Great Ouse on their left. Neither of them knew the road but both of them knew that this way they couldn't possibly miss King's Lynn.

Progress was slow because Bartram insisted that they ride for an hour — at a walk — and then dismount and lead the horses for a further hour. The excitement of the previous day had evaporated into an anticlimactic calm. It would have been a pleasant, peaceful journey if there hadn't also been something a little dispiriting about it. The feeling of adventure had gone and Richard began to feel more strongly than ever that he should have stood firm against Bartram's persuasions. He put himself in India's shoes and tried to imagine what she must be going through. She had been sufficiently concerned for his welfare to leave London, which she had loved, just to get him away from undesirable influences. She must now be tormenting herself with the thought that perhaps she hadn't acted in his best interest after all. Once they reached King's Lynn, he would write to her and, disloyal though it might be to think it, he was disinclined to trust the dispatch of the note to Bartram. He would find a more reliable way.

Bartram, too, was beginning to wonder whether his flamboyant gesture of defiance and independence had been altogether a good thing. Very likely Edward hadn't even realised he was missing yet, though a groom would have told him about the horses. In that case, the Viscount had probably decided he'd gone visiting and had had to stay overnight. Bartram was inclined to think that his decision not to leave a letter had been a mistake. He should have composed one very carefully calculated to hit exactly the right note and leave Edward flattened, humiliated and guilty at his insensitive treatment of his young brother — no, half-brother, Bartram corrected himself. At least Edward would have known. As it was, he probably wouldn't even begin to be concerned until tomorrow, and then as likely as not he would simply shrug his shoulders and bid his brother good riddance. It didn't strike him as at all inconsistent that a young man who was so convinced his brother would care neither about a missing relative nor two extremely valuable horses should be so worried about what would happen when the elder brother caught up with him.

The boys' progress was not only slow, it was silent.

Bartram broke the silence. 'What's that?' he asked.

They were leading their horses at the time. Richard stood still and listened. He could hear a rhythmic sound that was little more than a vibration but he could see nothing. 'I don't know. I'm not even sure I heard anything. Unless it was horses' hoofs.'

'I don't think so. It's more like a drum.'

'Who'd be banging a drum out here?'

Bartram shook his head. 'I don't know.'

They listened more attentively but the sound died away and they soon forgot about it.

Their desire not to be spotted led them to circumlocute any small settlements they came to but they knew it was a wasted effort where more populous villages were concerned and these they rode through; a man on horseback occasioned less comment than one walking because the latter was clearly on a long journey, a question-provoking eventuality in itself.

They had left one such village a mile or so behind them and had dismounted once more when a sudden turn in the road brought them face to face with a small contingent of seamen: a lieutenant, ten men and a powder-monkey.

The seamen stopped, blocked the road and raised their muskets.

'Well, well, well,' said the officer. 'What have we here?'

'Nothing that need concern you,' Bartram said loftily in what he hoped was a fair imitation of Edward's most depressive manner.

The officer was unmoved. 'I can't agree with that. Seems to me you're just what we're looking for: two able-bodied young men. What better to turn into able-seamen? Wouldn't you like to serve King and country in this time of crisis?'

'Not particularly,' Richard said. 'I intend to farm.'

'Do you now? And what about your friend here? What's your ambition?'

'He's on his way to King's Lynn to enlist,' Richard

said, totally unaware of the significance of a contingent of sailors this far inland.

'Now there's a happy coincidence,' the officer said, grinning broadly. 'And what sort of farming are you going to be doing in King's Lynn?'

'None, of course. I'm taking the horses on to Norwich.'

'Ay, yes, the horses.' The lieutenant walked carefully round them. 'Now I'm not an army man,' he said, 'but I'd say these were prime bloodstock and not at all the sort of beasts that I'd expect to come the way of two scallywags like you. Where did you steal them —— ?'

'We didn't,' Bartram interrupted. Unlike his companion, he had a shrewd idea that this was a press-gang, though he'd never encountered one before. The navy suddenly became extremely unattractive. 'They belong to my brother, Viscount Bardolph of Old Fen Hall in Lincolnshire.'

'My, oh, my, a scion of the aristocracy, no less, and trying hard to acquire the manner born. What about you, young man?' he went on, turning to Richard. 'No doubt your father's a belted earl?'

'No, sir. My father's dead. I live with my sister. We returned from India only a few months ago.'

'Did you now? What a fortunate coincidence; after a voyage like that, a life at sea will hold no terrors for you, will it?'

'As a matter of fact, it gave me a profound dislike of the whole thing,' Richard said bluntly.

'The navy'll soon put that right. Now then, we'll do a deal with you; you come with us without any

fuss and we'll make sure you're not picked up as
horse-thieves.'

'But we're not horse-thieves!' Bartram protested.
'I told you, they belong to my brother. He lent them
to us.'

'I thought I'd made it clear that I don't believe
you, and if you could see yourselves you'd understand why. No, we'll take you along to serve your
country and we'll take the horses along, too, until
I've decided what to do with them.'

'If you do anything other than return them to my
brother, it's you who'll be the horse-thieves,'
Bartram said angrily. 'And horse-thieves hang.'

'Something you'd do well to remember. I'd have
thought the navy would be preferable. Maybe I'll
contact this Viscount Bardolph and offer him his
horses back—for a reward. No doubt he'll be glad
to know the thieves have been dealt with.'

Neither Richard nor Bartram commented on this
suggestion but the same hope occurred to both of
them: that any message about the horses should
reach Bardolph before they were at sea. Both of
them had the good sense not to voice this; if it hadn't
already occurred to the lieutenant, far be it from
them to suggest it.

It seemed as if the lieutenant had found some snag
in his own scheme, however, and before they
reached the next village he stopped, had the horses'
tack removed and hidden in a dyke, and the horses
turned loose to fend for themselves.

'Why have you done that?' Bartram asked,
dismayed.

'Don't worry. They'll find plenty to eat and there's no shortage of water. Besides, it won't be long before someone takes them under his wing.'

'I thought you were going to try for a reward,' Bartram persisted.

'Had second thoughts. Wouldn't want anyone to think I came by them illegitimately, would I? Now step out a bit more lively. We don't want to be all day.'

It was the carrier from Downham Market who saw the horses. He drew rein and sat on his cart, and studied them while he sucked on his clay pipe.

'Ther in't many round 'ere like that, bor,' he said, though whether he was addressing himself or his horse was unclear. 'They's the right sort — and the right colour, too,' he went on. 'But wheresa tackle? Thass what I wanssa know.'

He climbed down from his board seat, fished behind it for the iron weight that served as tether when there was nothing else and dropped it on the ground on the end of the tethering rein. Then he looked around him. After that he climbed to the top of the broad bank that kept the river from flooding the lower siltfields on either side and looked along it in each direction. Nothing. He turned round and studied the landscape on the other side. A dyke looked distinctly hopeful and it wasn't long before he found what he was looking for. He hauled the saddles and bridles out of the rushes and turned them over. Under the flap of each saddle, on each girth and stirrup leather and on every separate piece of leather in the bridles, was stamped a 'B'.

'Thass what I was lookin' for, bor,' he said and
lugged both saddles over to his cart and settled them
in among the sacks and bales and covered them with
the tarpaulin. Then he caught the two horses and
tied them to the cart-tail. He climbed back on his
seat and considered his options.

'Now wass for the best?' he asked the world at
large. 'Back to Downham and mebbe catch that
groom and mebbe not and be a day late delivering
and no mebbe about it? Or on to Lynn and ask
around or mebbe find a magistrate.'

Lynn won, despite his natural reluctance to have
anything to do with magistrates. The reward for the
horses mentioned by the groom in Downham was
substantial but it was a gamble at best; people,
especially screw-jawed nobs, had a nasty habit of
forgetting their promises, particularly when they
were made to people in no position to press for them
to be made good. Payment for the delivery of goods
was certain but a day's delay might lose future
business. He climbed down and replaced the tether-
ing-block behind the seat. When he set off again he
was some three hours behind the press-gang and
travelling much more slowly.

India studied herself in the glass. Not bad. Not bad
at all. It was a pity the boots were too big but at
least she wasn't going to be doing much walking.
Richard's cut-away coat fitted her quite well, despite
being a bit tight round the chest. The breeches were
a good fit and the problem of her long hair she had
solved by braiding it from the top of her head and

coiling it round and pinning it so that it was hidden under his high-crowned beaver. From a distance she didn't look at all like a female. She was unsure how readily anyone meeting her at close quarters would be deceived.

A tap at the bedroom door was followed by its cautious opening before India could say, 'Come in,' and Eliza, who clearly expected to find her mistress still in bed, began to tiptoe in, saw India fully, if most indecorously dressed and almost forgot her errand.

'Whatever are you thinking of, madam?' she asked. 'Whatever will you do if someone sees you? Whatever will they think?'

'Are you here to tell me they've brought a horse round?' India asked, ignoring the maid's horrified questions.

'Yes, madam. Leastways, they've brought Master Richard's cob round, seeing as how they had a note from you last night. I nearly sent them packing, what with him not here and all, but I thought if you'd sent the order round — and I remember getting the gardener's boy to take a note for you — maybe you knew what you were doing and I'd better check first.' She looked her mistress up and down. 'And at the risk of being turned off for being pert, madam, I take leave to say you *don't* know what you're doing.'

'I beg to differ,' India told her. 'Now go into the kitchen and fill a bag — one of Cook's hoard of flour sacks will do — with food I can carry: bread and cheese, some ham, some of the replacement pie she made yesterday. Plenty of it because I don't know how long I'll be gone.'

'She'll kill me, madam.'

'Tell her it was my orders and you didn't dare disobey. Tell her she can kill me when I get back.'

'Are you going after Master Richard?'

'Something like that,' India admitted.

'You shouldn't go alone, madam, not dressed like that.'

'I'm dressed like this because that cob Richard rides doesn't take a lady's saddle and neither do any of their other mounts. As for my being alone, I can only reassure you that I haven't the slightest intention of being on my own for very long. Does that put your mind at rest?'

'No, it doesn't,' the maid said bluntly. 'Not when I think of all the possible implications of the remark. What do I tell the household?'

'You'd better tell them something approximating to the truth. Say that I've had some positive news about Richard and have gone to fetch him back.'

'And your clothes?'

'Why mention them? No one but you will know what is or isn't missing from my wardrobe — or from Richard's. Don't answer anything other than the question asked. There's no need to volunteer information.'

'And Cook? She's not going to be satisfied with that.'

India thought quickly. 'The men who brought me the news were hungry and had to be fed. That ought to do. If she queries the sack just shrug and assume either that she counted them wrong in the first place or that Richard must have taken more than she thought. After all, it's not your job to keep track of flour sacks if she chooses to hoard them.'

It was Eliza's sensible suggestion to tell the ostler to tie the cob to the fence and go home, on the pretext that Master Leigh wasn't yet ready. 'He may be nothing but a country boy, madam, but he's not a natural and you'll fool no one else at close quarters.'

India thanked her and looked at the clock. She had plenty of time. Bardolph could only cross the Nene at low water and, while she needed to be fairly close behind him to avoid the turning tide—to say nothing of following his hoofprints for safety's sake—she had no desire actually to catch him up until she was across the river and the rising tide made her immediate return impossible. She guessed that in his eagerness to reach King's Lynn ahead of the boys he would cross at the earliest possible moment. Timing would be crucial for both of them.

Hers was made more difficult by her mount. Richard had often complained about the cob which he apostrophised as a Jerusalem race-horse, a cant expression she accurately deduced to mean a donkey. He was built for stamina, not speed, and would therefore have been ideal for India's present purpose had he not also had a straight shoulder and quite the hardest mouth she had ever had to deal with. The jolting discomfort caused by his forehand construction wasn't helped by her own lack of familiarity with riding astride and getting accustomed to both horse and style took longer than she had planned.

When she reached the river, the far bank was swathed in the mist that the sun had not yet got high enough or hot enough to dissipate. Of Lord Bardolph himself there was no sign but the tide was still firmly out and there were comforting hoofprints in the mud.

India took a deep breath, shortened her reins and put the cob at the barely discernible causeway. She prayed that he was both sure-footed and endowed with a well-developed sense of self-preservation. She had never crossed the river before except by the bridge at Wisbech but she knew how notorious this route was, not only because of the suddenness with which the tide came in and the currents it brought with it, but because it was said the mud in places was enough to suck a man under. Hadn't King John himself and all his baggage-train drowned in these very waters, according to legend? India shivered. These were not the sort of thoughts to encourage except when one was safely on the bank.

The crossing seemed interminable, an illusion created not only by its inherent dangers but by the invisibility of the opposite bank, and India was reassured to discover that the cob was indeed sure-footed and not the least put off his stride when the mud beneath his hoofs became wetter and the prints they were following filled with water that blurred their edges as the passage continued. The tide was turning.

India looked downstream with some alarm and

could just detect those infinitesimal changes that heralded the sea's inexorable advance. She dared not urge the cob to greater speed for fear of his inadvertently putting a foot wrong, and her relief when the mists lifted and she saw the far bank was almost upon them was unbounded. Twenty paces, twenty-five at most, should see them safely ashore but even so the water was fetlock-deep as the cob scrambled up the muddy bank to the safety of dry land.

Now the danger was over and the tide well on its way, India need have no hesitation in catching up with Lord Bardolph. The inaptly named Prince saw no immediate necessity for breaking into a trot and resisted both heels and whip for as long as he could before succumbing and his gait was so uncomfortable that India wasted no time forcing him into a more congenial canter.

The mists were rising rapidly now and ahead of her India glimpsed a horseman heading south-eastwards at a steady, collected canter. Given the superior quality of Lord Bardolph's bloodstock, it was unlikely in the normal course of events that a livery hack would ever gain on him but, fortunately for India's intentions, collection was an equestrian concept unknown to the cob, who thundered stoically along, slowly eating up the distance between them. Such was his single-mindedness, to say nothing of his hard mouth, that he lumbered past the Viscount's half-bred hunter regardless of his rider's efforts to rein him back. By the time she had succeeded in slowing him down, they were so well ahead of Lord Bardolph that she had to stop him altogether and wait for the other to catch up.

Since Lord Bardolph could only have seen her retreating back and was therefore unlikely to have recognised her, India decided that the sooner she made herself known to him the better, and get any unpleasantness out of the way. The alternative would have been to stay behind him all the way to Lynn and have the ensuing scene — for she had no doubt there would be one — acted out in front of an audience of fascinated passers-by.

'Good morning, my lord,' she called out as he approached. 'We seem both to be making good time.'

His head jerked up and only instinctive good horsemanship stopped him jabbing at his horse's mouth. 'Miss Leigh? Surely not?' He came closer and stared more penetratingly. 'Good God, it *is* you! What in the name of all that's holy are you doing here?'

'You have a short memory, my lord. I did tell you only yesterday that I wanted to come with you.'

'And I told you — quite bluntly, as I recall — that you were not coming with me because it would be most indecorous.'

India smiled very sweetly. 'Our recollections don't entirely tally,' she told him. 'That argument was demolished by my drawing your attention to the fact that, as an old maid, lack of decorum didn't enter into it. The clincher — as I recall — was the fact that, although your tack-room contains ladies' saddles, your stables don't contain a horse used to carry them. As you see, I've been able to overcome that objection.'

Lord Bardolph cast a knowledgeable eye over the cob. 'I hope you're enjoying the experience,' he said with heavy irony.

'As a matter of fact, this is quite the most uncomfortable animal I've ever ridden,' she told him frankly. 'Still, it's very sure-footed, it got me here, and I fancy he can go on for mile after mile without wilting, just so long as he isn't asked to do it too fast.'

'Serve you right,' he said cheerfully. A thought struck him. 'Does this mean you crossed the Wash Way?'

'Of course.' Since there was no alternative, India was surprised he should need to ask.

Lord Bardolph scowled. 'You silly little fool. Don't you realise how dangerous it can be? Or have you made yourself familiar with it in your brief stay in the Fens?'

'No, I've never seen it before and, yes, I've heard of its dangers. I used my common sense, that's all.'

'What common sense? You can't have much if you even attempted it. I know it well and gauged my time with care, and when I crossed there was no one else in sight. You must have been some way behind me.'

'I was hidden in the mist, I expect, as you were from me. I guessed you'd cross at the earliest possible moment. When I reached the crossing it was plain someone had just gone over. I simply followed the hoofprints.'

'The tide must have been coming in by the time you reached the other side,' he said shrewdly.

'It was beginning to,' India said. 'I was a little worried for a few moments until the mists lifted and I realised we weren't too far from the bank.'

'"A little worried",' he echoed. 'If you were only a little worried, you must be quite mad. Don't you know how fast the tide can come in over that ford?'

'I have heard but I dare say they exaggerate,' India said defiantly. 'In any case, I made it—and I don't mind admitting I gave thanks for this stolid beast who knew exactly what he was doing.'

'Which is more than anyone can say for his rider,' Lord Bardolph retorted. 'Dare I ask what you intend to do now?'

'I'm coming with you to look for Richard—and Bartram, of course.'

'Dressed like that? You most certainly are not!'

'I thought it was rather a good idea, myself,' India said, outwardly unmoved by either his anger or his sarcasm. 'I can see that you might be concerned at the gossip if you're seen riding with an unchaperoned lady, but no one's going to think it least bit odd to see you with. . .a nephew, for instance.'

'And for how long do you think anyone will be deluded into thinking you a nephew—or any boy at all, if it comes to that? Not once they see you close to, I can tell you.'

'Then we must take very good care they don't get that close. I'll pull my hat further down,' India suggested, doing so.

'I haven't got a nephew,' Bardolph objected.

'You have now,' India said affably.

He put his heels to his horse's side and moved off, closely followed by India, quietly congratulating herself on having won her case.

Her congratulations were premature.

'It won't do, Miss Leigh. You'll have to go back.'

'The tide will be in by now. It'll be hours before the Wash Way is fordable again. Probably not until evening. I should think it was even more dangerous in the dusk, shouldn't you?'

'There's nothing to stop you heading south and crossing the river at Wisbech.'

'Unaccompanied? When I wouldn't get home before dark? Is that more *comme il faut* than dressing like a boy and having your protection? Or were you going to come with me—for safety's sake, you understand—and lose a day in the search for the boys?'

He made no answer and they rode on in silence for some time. When Lord Bardolph spoke, it was in the tone of a man who had been giving the matter a very great deal of thought.

'I think the easiest thing to do in the circumstances—and certainly the most appealing—is to strangle you.'

'You'd hang,' India told him, unmoved.

'I believe the aristocracy is beheaded,' he corrected her. 'It would be a small price to pay.'

'You wouldn't be so sure of that as the axe descended,' India told him confidently. 'Do they keep it sharp these days, or do they have to have several tries, like for Mary, Queen of Scots?'

He gave a short laugh. 'Do you have an answer for everything, Miss Leigh?'

'Not invariably,' she said after giving the matter some thought. 'But I do think you ought to get in the habit of calling me something other than Miss Leigh if there's to be even the slightest chance of our deceiving people.'

'What do you suggest?'

' "India" is sufficiently unusual but I suppose it does have a female sound to it. This is rather fun, you know. It's not often one has the chance to choose one's name.'

'Then for goodness' sake make it something ordinary,' Lord Bardolph warned her.

'You don't like Aloysius?'

'No, I do not. Quite apart from its intrinsic demerits, it's exactly the sort of name to attract attention — and about the only things we seem to be agreed upon is that that would be undesirable.'

'Very true,' India agreed. 'What about Jem?'

'Too ordinary. Besides, viscounts have grooms called Jem, not nephews.'

'Has anyone ever told you you're extremely difficult to please?' India said.

'Frequently. What about Harry?'

India tried to find fault with it and failed. It was perfect. It struck exactly the right note of boyishness, at the same time carrying a hint of having been used in the family for generations. 'All right,' she said. 'I'll be Harry.'

The Viscount grinned. 'Dear me, couldn't you find *any* objection to it at all?'

'I dare say I could if I tried,' India told him demurely, 'but I thought it was about time I let you have the last word.'

They clattered into King's Lynn by the Southgate and Lord Bardolph was immediately accosted by a man who had clearly been waiting for him.

'Gidding!' the Viscount exclaimed. 'I thought you were coming home after spending the night in Downham?'

'And so I was, my lord, but, seeing as how young Master Bartram and his friend was headed out towards Lynn, I thought I'd come on here and see what I could find out.'

'And what have you found out?'

'I think we'd better go somewhere where we can talk, my lord. In private, that is. There's a carrier wants to have a word with you.'

'I'll meet you at the Customs House in ten minutes,' his employer told him. 'That will give me time to hand Phantom over to the ostler.'

'Let me take him, my lord,' said the groom, conscious that it was, after all, what he was employed for.

'You've got to find this carrier,' the Viscount replied. The last thing he wanted was for Gidding, who knew perfectly well there was no nephew, to realise that youth on the cob was not only with his lordship but was also no youth.

As soon as the groom was out of sight, Lord Bardolph beckoned India to follow him and they threaded their way through the narrow streets to an inn which was sufficiently crowded for no one to have enough time to peer closely at young Harry. It seemed respectable enough, if not Bardolph's first choice in normal circumstances. He took the horses into the stables, which seemed well enough run, and engaged a private room, asking that they serve a substantial luncheon.

'My nephew—who will be here in a moment—eats like a horse. I have to go out on business but I'll be back shortly. Just leave him to get on with eating. You know what boys are,' he said.

The landlady said she did, indeed, having raised six of them herself, and what about a flagon of ale?

This presented a small problem: any nephew of Harry's presumed age would be happy with ale and insulted by lemonade but Bardolph doubted very much whether India had acquired a taste for beer. 'Ale for the boy, certainly,' he said. 'Can't stand the stuff myself. Perhaps you'd make some lemonade for me?'

Shaking her head over the eccentricities of the gentry, the landlady said she'd be delighted and Lord Bardolph went back outside to warn India to pour herself half a tankard of ale, so that it looked as if she was drinking it, and to make sure her back was to the door whenever anyone came in. 'I think they're too busy to be curious,' he said, 'but just in case.'

'When you've seen this carrier and listened to whatever your groom wants to tell you, you won't go hareing off without me, will you?' India said anxiously.

'Worried about being abandoned in wicked Lynn?' he chided.

'Not worried, exactly, but I wouldn't put it past you to leave me here while you pursue the search.'

'And if I promise not to?'

'Then I shall enjoy a good meal.'

'I'll be back, if only to tell you what I've learned. That's a promise. Whether I take you with me on the next stage is a matter for discussion when we know what the next stage is. Agreed?'

'I don't think I have a choice.'

'You're learning fast.'

India tried to relax sufficiently to enjoy the plain but plentiful food the landlady sent in. It was difficult because her mind kept straying to Lord Bardolph, where he might be and what he might be doing. Her great fear was that he wouldn't return just to tell her what he had learned, but would choose instead to act upon it, returning only when he could present her with a *fait accompli*. He *had* promised he wouldn't and India was quite sure that promise had been sincerely given. Furthermore, her instinct was to trust the Viscount, despite the fact that they seemed unable to spend more than five minutes in each other's company without falling out.

All the same, when that promise was given, Bardolph had had no idea what might be the nature of the information the carrier had for him and it might well prove to be something she would be happier not knowing. He might therefore break his word in order to spare her. She had no very clear idea what sort of situation this might be, since if it were very bad news indeed she would have to be told sooner or later and sooner must surely be better. So, despite her hunger, she found her appetite had largely deserted her once the door had closed behind her companion. She forced herself to eat because she knew she needed to and because what was on the table was much more appetising than the food that had been jolting across the county tied to her saddle.

When the door opened to re-admit Lord Bardolph, relief flooded her face and she jumped up to greet him.

'You did come back, after all,' she said.

He raised one quizzical eyebrow. 'I told you I should. Did you expect me to break my promise?'

'Not when you gave it,' India said candidly, 'but when you'd gone and I had time to think about it I thought it might be something so dreadful that you'd prefer to deal with it on your own and not tell me anything about it until afterwards.'

He inclined his head in a sardonic bow. 'Thank you for your faith in my integrity.'

India flushed. 'I'm sorry. I didn't mean it in quite that way. It's just that once I was on my own I had time to think and to imagine.' She smiled fleetingly. 'I suppose I gave my imagination too much rein.'

'Much too much, but I'll put it down to a natural anxiety and not hold it against you.'

India's smile was mischievous. 'Until I do it again, whereupon I don't doubt you'll remind me.'

'Of that you may rest assured,' he said, unperturbed. 'And now, if it's all the same to you, I'll repair the damage to my own appetite. He glanced at the table. 'You said you were hungry but you don't seem to have eaten much.'

'I was too worried—and it isn't all the same to me. You can't sit down to luncheon without telling me what happened.'

'I can, however, eat and tell you at the same time, which—if you'll forgive the bad manners involved—will mean saving time by explaining everything to you either before or after the meal,' he pointed out.

'Then let's begin,' India said, pulling up a chair on the opposite side of the table.

Lord Bardolph cut himself a hunk of pigeon pie. 'The carrier, who had been in Downham when Gidding was telling all and sundry there was a reward offered for the recovery of the horses and the boys, found the horses on the road to King's Lynn. Since bloodstock isn't very often found grazing at will on the Fens, he did some hard thinking—his expression, not mine—and decided someone had turned them loose to suit their own ends. He guessed they hadn't strayed very far from where they were released and thought he'd have a look for their tack. He found it more or less concealed in the rushes at the side of a dyke. He was quite positive they'd been concealed, not just put down for later collection. He had enough sense to guess they were marked and when he found the 'B' imprint on the leather he knew he was in line for a reward so he caught the horses, tied them behind his cart and carried on into Lynn with them. He left them at the tavern that baits his own horse, hoping that the magistrate to whom he intended to turn them over would pay the bill and pass on the reward.

'Fortunately, Gidding had taken it upon himself to go on into Lynn instead of doing as he was told and returning home from Downham. By sheer good luck, he happened to see the carrier's cart come into town. He followed it to the tavern and introduced himself. It wasn't really necessary because the carrier remembered him, but Gidding hadn't known that. So both horses and tack are safely back.'

'But what about the boys?' India asked. 'Surely they wouldn't have abandoned the horses?'

'That's the problem. Gidding has checked both animals over. Neither has lost a shoe, neither is lame or saddle-sore, so there's absolutely no reason why they should have been abandoned. I questioned the carrier very closely and he's quite positive that there. . .' he hesitated '. . .that there were no signs of anything untoward having happened.'

'You mean the boys weren't lying in a ditch with their throats cut,' India said baldly.

'Well, yes, but I didn't want to put it quite so bluntly.'

India, who felt the present exigency was far too important to allow for time-wasting euphemisms, said, 'I can't think why not. After all, if I've no pretensions to gentility, my sensibilities aren't likely to be easily offended, are they?'

'Very true. I should have remembered that,' he retorted. 'Very well, as you will. No, Miss Leigh, they do not seem to have had their throats slit or their heads stove in, or, if they have suffered either fate, it wasn't in the locality in which the carrier found the horses. Frankly, that isn't much help in ascertaining just what *has* happened to them. Perhaps your ungenteel mind can offer some thoughts on the subject.'

'No, none at all. Could they have fallen in the river or in a drain?'

'It's unlikely that both of them would have done so and no bodies have been found. Nor does that account for the hidden tack; the horses would have been grazing but they'd still have been saddled and bridled.'

'True.' India grew thoughtful. 'It means we're not very much further forward, doesn't it?'

'I wouldn't say that. We now know for certain what we'd previously only speculated upon: they were heading for Lynn. We now know we're looking for two young men on foot.'

India frowned. 'Doesn't that make it more difficult?' she asked. 'They'll be much less noticeable anyway, and Norfolk must be full of two young men on foot.'

'I'm afraid that's so.'

'So what do you propose we do now?'

'"We" aren't going to do anything. I'm going to retrace the carrier's route to where he found the horses and a little beyond in the hope of finding some trace of them. You will remain here until I get back.'

India shook her head. 'I don't think that's a good idea at all,' she said.

'Then what do you suggest I do? If you've a better idea, I'm happy to listen to it.'

'There's nothing wrong with what *you* plan to do. It's your plan for me that I disagree with,' she said.

'Does that mean you think you ought to come with me?'

'Of course it does! I'm not staying here on my own, worrying myself into a frazzle.'

'I understand that,' he said, his voice unexpectedly gentle. 'But don't you see, whatever's befallen them may prove to be exceedingly unpleasant and it may take unpleasant methods to get them back.'

'Such as what?' India asked, intrigued.

'If I knew, I wouldn't have to speculate,' he said tetchily. 'One thing that has occurred to me, however, is that since both Bartram's family and Richard's are known to be wealthy it isn't beyond the bounds of possibility that ruffians are holding them with a view to demanding a ransom.'

India considered the matter. 'Wouldn't the kidnappers have sent the horses back to you as corroboration of their story?'

'That's why I don't consider that to be the most likely explanation.'

'I see. So you only put that idea forward because you hoped it would frighten me off,' India suggested shrewdly.

He gave an exaggerated sigh. 'I suppose I might have known it wouldn't work.'

'I wouldn't ordinarily describe you as an obtuse man,' India agreed. 'I'm coming, my lord. Action is infinitely preferable to inaction.'

Since this was the Viscount's own opinion, he had no argument to set against it and gave in with at least a semblance of good grace. 'Will you at least give me an undertaking that, once on the road, you'll be guided by me even if you find it irksome?'

'I'll give you an undertaking that I'll try,' India conceded. 'I can't give an *absolute* promise when I've no idea what may arise.'

'I suppose I shall have to be content with that,' he said.

'I suppose you will,' India agreed. 'There is one suggestion I don't think you'll object to. Since you've got the horses back, would it be possible for me to transfer to one of them? Either of them must be a better ride than that cob.'

'I don't doubt it, but very much more difficult to handle, especially in a style of riding with which you're not familiar.'

'I'll cope. Prince has done a pretty good job of breaking me in. Besides, would the nephew of a viscount be riding a job-horse while his uncle was decently mounted?'

Lord Bardolph gave a reluctant laugh. 'I suppose not,' he said. 'At the very least, it may lessen the chances of people looking twice at you. Very well, I'll tell Gidding to saddle Clarion for you.'

'What reason will you give him?'

'That, Miss Leigh, is for me to know and you to wonder.'

'What a very vulgar reply,' India said affably.

'I wanted to be quite sure you understood,' he replied with equal affability and added, his voice serious once more, 'Trust me, India. You can, you know.'

The use of her first name seemed so natural that India did not at first realise it had taken place. 'I'm sure I can, my lord,' she said.

He had left the room to instruct the groom before the use of her given name registered in her conscious mind and she blushed, partly because of its impropriety and partly because she was afraid her own use of the formal address when she answered him might be interpreted as an attempt at a set-down.

If Lord Bardolph had seen it as such, there was nothing in his manner when he returned to suggest it.

'Ready, Miss Leigh?' he asked, apparently quite unconscious that he had ever called her anything else. 'The horses are waiting and I'm anxious to get as far as we can before nightfall.'

Downham Market was well within a day's ride for horses of the calibre of Lord Bardolph's but by the time they left King's Lynn they had only an hour or so of daylight left and both horses had already had a long day's work behind them, thus obliging their riders to take them slowly. India wondered whether it wouldn't have been better to set out early next morning but Lord Bardolph shook his head.

'I can't pretend I'm not anxious about the boys. If there's the slightest chance of finding them this evening, I want to be able to take advantage of it.'

The handful of people they encountered were uncommunicative — strangers riding abroad at dusk were best avoided—but one old man volunteered the information that, while he couldn't rightly claim to have *seen* two boys, on or off horses, he had heard tell that a press-gang had been out that day. Unfortunately, he couldn't rightly say where it had been operating, seeing as how he hadn't seen it for himself, and it might only be a rumour, mightn't it?

'Do you think that's what's happened to them?' India asked as they pressed on.

Lord Bardolph frowned. 'It could be. I can't imagine a press-gang would risk taking two young men who were mounted, especially when their appearance and the quality of their horses would suggest that they had the sort of parents who would be in a position to exert some very unwelcome pressure on the authorities to release them.'

'Can they be released once they're taken?' India asked.

'Legally, no. In practice, it happens. It depends upon who does the asking.'

'You mean it depends upon how rich they are.'

'Quite, though discretion is also needed. Fortunately the navy is very badly paid and their pay is often months in arrears. That's a great incentive to a flexible interpretation of the rules.'

They rode on in silence for a while. 'We don't know when or where or why the boys left their horses,' India said. 'They might not have been on horseback when they met the press-gang—and I should think they were so dusty and dishevelled as to disguise any quality that might otherwise have been apparent.'

'I was hoping that neither of those facts would occur to you,' Bardolph told her.

'Very kind of you, my lord, but I'm really not some delicate flower that needs to be protected from every adverse wind.'

He grinned. 'So I'm beginning to realise.'

Before the last remnants of light filtered from the sky, they stopped at a small inn which regretted that it could only offer one bedroom for the gentlemen but there was a truckle-bed in it that would do his lordship's nephew quite well.

Lord Bardolph groaned. 'The boy needs the comfort of a good bed,' he said. 'He's not used to the heavy riding we're doing, so if it's all the same to you I'll have some clean blankets and a pillow and take myself off to your hay-loft.'

The landlord was horrified. 'My lord, surely that isn't necessary? The truckle-bed is too short for you, I admit, but your nephew'll not have a problem and it's comfortable enough.'

'I'm sure it's admirable,' Lord Bardolph told him. 'Unfortunately my nephew snores. I'll see him settled first. Then I'll be quite happy over the horses.'

He glanced round the little room they were led to and nodded approvingly. 'This will suit you very well,' he told India when the landlord had left them to find some more blankets. 'Make sure you lock the door when I've gone and don't open it until you're ready to come down.'

'I'll have you know, my lord, I do *not* snore,' India told him indignantly.

'I shouldn't think you could possibly know one way or another.'

'No one has ever so much as *hinted* that I do,' she insisted.

He raised one eyebrow. 'Really? Do I infer from that remark that you've been in the habit of sharing your room with a variety of people who might reasonably have been expected to comment?'

'I have no control over what you may choose to infer,' India retorted. 'However, it certainly isn't what I intended to imply. It isn't the case — and I suspect you're very well aware of that and are only trying to provoke me.'

'And succeeding rather well, don't you think?' He laughed and chucked her under the chin. 'Can you think of a better excuse to oblige me to sleep elsewhere?' he asked. 'Or would you have preferred to share the room with me?'

'No, of course not,' India said hastily. 'I just wish you could have found an excuse that didn't make me look ridiculous.'

'Ah, but then the very ridiculousness of it makes it all the more probable that you're my nephew. Now go to bed like a good girl — and lock the door.'

India did as she was told, torn between annoyance at being spoken to as if she were still in the school-room and relief that he was prepared to go to such lengths of discomfort to safeguard her reputation.

She was both disconcerted and more than a little shocked to realise that she didn't actually want him to sleep somewhere else. Lord Bardolph was arrogant, overbearing and unnecessarily rude but he had a dry sense of humour that was more than a match for her own verbal indiscretions and, above all, he induced in her a feeling of absolute confidence that he knew exactly what he was doing and would see to it that she came to no harm. It would be a lesson to her not to make snap judgements on people in future. And on this pious thought, she fell into a deep and dreamless sleep.

They set off as early next morning as India's deep sleep and a hearty breakfast allowed, Lord Bardolph consoling himself for the delay with the thought that at least it meant the horses had had a good night's rest, even if he hadn't himself.

Since footpads might well have hidden the tack once they discovered it was marked but were unlikely to have abandoned horses which could easily have been disguised by the application of dye and a tooth-file, both India and the Viscount accepted that the most likely explanation for the boys' disappearance was the press-gang. Had that been the only explanation, Lord Bardolph would have returned immediately to King's Lynn to seek them out and bring his very considerable influence both as a landowner and a magistrate to effect their release. But there were other possibilties, chief among them some sort of accident to one of the boys which might have led the other to seek help at the nearest cottage, which, in this locality, was not necessarily on a road, much less in a village.

Their journey was therefore a far cry from a straight ride to wherever the horses had been found, and questions asked *en route*. Every outlying cottage

was visited and then their steps had to be retraced
to the road before they sought the next cottage or
reached the next little settlement. By the end of the
morning they were no more than halfway towards
Downham Market and still hadn't reached the spot
where the carrier had found the horses.

Then they had their first bit of good luck — good
luck in the sense that it was word of two boys who
might possibly be Bartram and Richard, that was,
for it was also definite word of the press-gang.
People at Runcton Holme reported having seen it
the previous day 'with two of they poor involuntary
recruits', as one man put it. By the time they had
reached Watlington, the press-gang had acquired
another 'recruit' and was clearly on its way back to
King's Lynn, and the landlord of the tavern confirmed that they had taken the less populated road
along the river, not having been greeted with any
great affection in Watlington.

'Back to Lynn, I think,' Lord Bardolph said. 'And
at the best speed we can muster.'

They took the same road as the press-gang, largely
because they might pick up more detail from the
occasional cottage, but they didn't stop to knock on
doors, only pausing to question people who were in
their fields or gardens and easily hailed.

Calamity struck barely two miles from the town
walls. Clarion cast a shoe.

India dismounted and looked up at Lord
Bardolph. 'You'd better go on, my lord. If you'll let
me have some money, I'll lead Clarion to the nearest
smithy and follow you when he's been shod.'

'Oh, no, you don't, my girl,' he replied. 'There's a hamlet over there. Let's see what it has to offer.'

Sandwiched between the Ouse and the Nar, it offered not only a smithy but an inn, which, though small, was both clean and respectable.

'Leave me here, my lord,' India urged. 'The smith can take care of Clarion and I'll stay at the inn until you return. It's far more important that you trace the boys. I should imagine that the navy gets pressed men to sea as fast as they can to prevent them from running away and, frankly, while that might suit your brother, it won't suit mine. His ambitions lie elsewhere.'

'I don't know about its suiting Bartram,' Bardolph said grimly. 'It would certainly serve him right. You're right, however; I do need to catch up with them as a matter of urgency for precisely the reason you gave but I can't leave you here, unattended and unchaperoned. It's unthinkable.'

'Nonsense,' India said bracingly. 'If I were diffident little Miss Leigh, I'd concede the point, but I'm not. I'm your young nephew Harry. Not, perhaps, old enough or wise enough to be left entirely to my own devices but certainly old enough to be left in charge of a horse with firm instructions not to leave the village until you get back to settle the bill — though I think I'd better have some money for food and a bed in case you're delayed until tomorrow.'

'I doubt if you were ever diffident little Miss Leigh,' he told her, laughing in spite of his concern. 'And I'm not sure you look enough like anyone's young nephew for it to be wise to leave you at all.'

'But all the same, you'd be quite relieved if you felt you could do so,' India said, voicing his thoughts precisely.

'It would be very ungallant to do so, however.'

'Only you and I need ever know about it,' India pointed out. 'And if I promise never to allude to it — or, at least, only under *very* extreme provocation — and if I further promise to be very circumspect indeed while you're away, what harm can there be?'

'You tempt me, but it's against my better judgement.'

'It's my brother as well as yours who's at risk. Please, my lord — you *must* give their cause priority.'

He hesitated but succumbed. 'Very well, but you stay in your room as much as you can and don't draw attention to yourself. Above all, try not to get involved in the sort of conversation that makes people take notice of you.' He chuckled. 'Quite apart from anything else, it will strike them as distinctly odd if they never see you without your hat.'

'I suppose I could hack my hair off,' India suggested helpfully.

'Don't you dare! Will you do as I ask?'

'Yes, my lord.'

'Very well, then. I'll engage a room for you and tell them to send you up some food. That ought to occupy you for a while. I've observed you don't subscribe to the view that you ladies should peck at their food in order to enhance their gentility.'

India chuckled. 'That's probably because I haven't any to enhance,' she said.

'Will you never cease reminding me of one injudicious — and highly inaccurate — remark intended purely as set-down?' he asked.

'I shouldn't think so,' she said cheerfully. 'It gives me that advantage, you see.'

India ate with gusto the meal sent up from the kitchen and then put the tray outside the door so that she could take off her boots and her beaver and lie down. She might have slept very well the previous night but a morning in the saddle and a substantial meal left her quite ready for a nap.

She was awoken by a commotion from somewhere outside the inn. It took a few minutes to register the fact that it was not only outside but a little way off, and then curiosity took her to the window to discover what it was all about. She had to open the casement and crane her neck before she saw the tail-end of what appeared to be a bunch of very angry women, one of whom was brandishing a broom and another a pitchfork.

Intrigued, India pulled on her boots, pinned up her braid more securely and crammed her beaver back over it before running downstairs and out into the street.

The shouting increased as she got nearer and when she rounded the corner she realised that virtually all the women of the village must be there, each of them armed, if only with a rolling-pin. These weapons were being brandished at a small group of uniformed men who were trying to come ashore at the little wooden landing-stage. The seamen were armed with muskets but they were obviously unwilling to use these for anything except inadequate shields against the blows being rained down on them by brooms, shovels, rolling-pins and, in one instance, an expertly wielded riding-crop.

India kept well out of the fracas. It was an entertaining scene even if she couldn't quite make out what it was all about; she wasn't always able to understand the speech of the Fens and when it was uttered by women who were excited and angry and all speaking at once she found it virtually impossible. She leaned against a cottage wall unobserved by the women, trying to make head and tail of what they were saying, and when this amusement palled and she turned away she decided to wander down to the other end of the narrow, straggling street to see how Clarion was coming on before retiring once more to her room.

She might have been unobserved by the women but the press-gang had seen her soon enough. The sight of a youth lounging against a wall grinning at them while the women hurled abuse and declarations that there were no men or boys in the village at all was too much and the officer in charge detached two men with hurried instruction to creep round the back of the village, enter it from the other end and take the insolent youngster while the rest of the party kept the women occupied.

Thus it came about that, as India strolled back towards the smithy, she met two smiling sailors coming towards her. Although she had guessed by now that what she had seen had been a press-gang which had come upriver instead of by road, the implications for herself entirely escaped her. She might be dressed in Richard's clothes but she didn't think of herself as a boy in any sense except the purely superficial one. All the deeper implications had passed her by, largely because she knew her present role was intended to be of extremely brief duration.

So she smiled back and touched her finger to her hat-brim in, she thought, appropriate salute.

She was close to the smithy now and the smith, glancing out, realised the danger his lordship's nevvy was in and called out a warning, but it was too late. Both sailors sprang and seized her 'in the name of the King', bundling her back the way they had come in order to avoid the wrath of the women through whose ranks they would otherwise have to pass. India had time only to shout to the smith to tell Lord Bardolph what had happened before she was being half dragged, half pushed back to the river and the press-gang's boat. The men raised a triumphant cheer as they saw their comrades' success and the young officer with them grinned broadly.

'No young men or boys in the village, eh?' he shouted at the women. 'Now we all know just what a bunch of lying crones you all are.' He gestured to his party to retreat to the boat.

One of the women, whom India recognised as the landlord's wife, shouted out, 'But that ben't a young man — thass Lord Bardolph's nevvy. You take him and his lordship'll have you in chines like an owd dawg.'

The lieutenant had heard far too many excuses for not taking this youngster or that to fall for that one, though he had to admit it was original. 'You tell his lordship to have a word with the captain of the *Pelican*,' he called out. 'That's if he can reach him before she sails.'

'And don't think I won't,' the landlady shrieked back. India blessed her but secretly doubted whether it would do any good.

She had fortunately crammed her hat hard on her head before leaving the inn and now she sat slumped in the skiff with her shoulders bowed so that her face was as much concealed as she could manage.

She thought fast. One way to get out of this predicament was to tell the officer she wasn't what they thought she was. It would be easy enough to prove it but she doubted whether it was necessarily wise to do so at this stage. She could prove she was a woman easily enough, but what sort of a woman? She could hardly blame the seamen if they took her for a lightskirt. Respectable women didn't wear men's clothes. Why, there were even those who condemned the wearing by women of riding-habits with cuffs and lapels in the military mode. The possible consequences of making such a revelation didn't bear thinking about. She had no doubt they would let her go — sooner or later. And in the meantime? They wouldn't be amused at having been so completely deceived, and the longer the deception continued, the greater would be their displeasure, especially when they had been, as now, so close to her. No, she could be reasonably certain that they wouldn't let her go with a pat on the head and an exhortation to be a good girl in future.

If any revelation was to be made, the time to do it was before the *Pelican* set sail. Doubtless the press-gang would suffer gibes about having been at sea too long, but she didn't doubt the captain would get rid of her as fast as he could — and if the *Pelican* was the ship she was destined for, it wasn't beyond the bounds of possibility that Richard and Bartram were also aboard, in which case, even if she was unable to persuade the captain to let them go, too, she would be able to tell Lord Bardolph where they were.

The lieutenant had a notebook out. 'Name?' he snapped.

India hesitated. Truth or falsehood? 'Harry Chelworth,' she said.

'Harry?' he queried.

'I mean Henry,' she amended. It wasn't easy to pitch her voice at a level that wasn't at variance with her appearance and it wasn't going to be easy to sustain it. The fewer words she spoke the better.

'Just Henry?'

She thought quickly. 'Henry Edward,' she said.

He looked at her suspiciously. 'And where are you from, Master Chelworth?'

'Old Fen Hall. It's between Holbeach and the Wash.'

'Is that so? Then you were a long way from home.'

'Yes, sir.'

'I'll tell you, something, Master Chelworth. I

don't believe a word you've said. I don't believe
that's your name and I don't believe you come from
between Holbeach and the Wash.'

Oh, God, India thought, he's realised. She
hunched herself over even more and modelled her
tone on her admittedly limited acquaintance with
Bartam. 'I can't help that,' she muttered sullenly.
'Your not believing it doesn't make it untrue.'

'I'll tell you why I don't believe you, lad,' the
lieutenant went on. 'It's because I've been landing
along these shores and up and down these rivers on
and off for a very long time and in all that very long
time I've never met a local youngster who spoke the
way you do.'

'What's wrong with it?' India grumbled, guessing
that some sort of reply was expected from her.

'Nothing, that's what's wrong with it. No trace of
the local speech, no local words, not even the local
intonation. No, you're not local. In fact, if I were to
go just by your voice, forgetting the state of your
clothes, I'd say you were an educated young man.
Would I be right?'

'Sort of,' India said gruffly.

'And this Lord Something-or-other one of those
harridans was shrieking about. Are you his nephew?'

There was a brief, tell-tale hesitation before India
said, 'Yes.'

'You're lying,' the officer said with the certainty
of one speaking from experience. 'Maybe you
tricked her into believing it. You won't trick me.'

'Beggin' your pardon, Mr Swanmore,' broke in
one of the two men who had captured her, 'but 'e

shouted something to the smith about a-lettin' a Lord Someone know what'd 'appened.'

'Did he now? And what do you think people in a tiny hamlet south of the Ouse know about some nobleman who lives, if this scoundrel's to be believed, some way north of the Nene? Very little, if you ask me. This nobleman — if he exists at all — may be known in King's Lynn among the right sort of people but do you really believe a settlement of illiterate bog-dwellers know him? I take leave to doubt it.

'I'll tell you what I think we've got here, Mr Warsash. We've got the makings of a first-class gammoner. Now it seems to me the best thing for him is going to be a spell in His Majesty's Navy to turn him into an honest man. What do you think, Mr Warsash?'

The sailor grinned. 'I reckon the navy might do the trick, sir — providin' 'e don't get washed overboard or hit by cannonfire or choked by weevils. Yes, sir, in seven or eight years I reckon he'll be a weritable pillar of the community.'

Being totally unfamiliar with flash vocabulary, India had no idea of their precise meaning but she gleaned enough of their drift to be quite sure that it was unfavourable. If Lord Bardolph were here, she could seek enlightenment. She had no doubt at all that he would know what a gammoner was.

If Lord Bardolph were here, she'd have no need of an explanation because she wouldn't be in her present unenviable situation. It was a depressing thought, not made any less so by the fact that he had left her largely at her own insistence and, further-more, that if she had done as she had been told and stayed in her room none of this would have hap-pened. The women would have routed the press-gang—with hindsight India guessed that all the young men of the village had hidden in cellars and barns while their women-folk held the press-gang at bay—and India would not have been spotted. It served her right.

That was likely to be Lord Bardolph's first obser-vation when he learned of this and India thought she would meekly, even cheerfully, accept any objurga-tion he chose to throw at her if only he were there to throw it.

He might well be sardonic, sarcastic and cutting, but he would get her out of this mess first. Right now there was nothing she would welcome more than the sight of his tall, arrogant figure riding along the bank towards them.

The problem with that little pipe-dream was that both banks were now a long way off. The Ouse had widened and deepened as it approached King's Lynn. Their journey downstream had been fast and now the oarsmen needed only the occasional stroke to keep the little boat on course, the river itself doing most of their work for them. Only as the quays themselves hove into view did the sailors swing the skiff closer to the land.

'There she is,' the lieutenant said, pointing ahead. 'There's the *Pelican*, your home for the foreseeable future.'

For the first time since boarding the boat, India

raised her head to see their destination. Anchored in mid-stream—probably, she thought bitterly, to discourage pressed men from leaping overboard— the frigate seemed enormous in comparison with this little rowing-boat, though she was sure it was smaller than the East Indiaman that had brought them back to England.

Another small rowing-boat was in the process of returning to the *Pelican* from the quayside and India's glance involuntarily strayed towards the spot from which it had come.

Two men, their hands tied behind them, were being helped into the saddle by a third who then swung himself on to his own heavy-boned bay. India recognised both man and horse.

Oblivious of the risk to everyone in the little boat, she sprang to her feet and shouted as loudly as she could. 'Bardolph! I'm over here! Bardolph! Come back, Bardolph!'

The sailors grabbed at her coat-tails and pulled her back from a precarious stance which threatened them all. The bystanders on the quay could hear her shouts but they couldn't make out the words. They had little difficulty in interpreting the actions of the youth in the boat and rightly guessed him to be a victim of the press-gang, and one with a bit more spirit than most.

They ambled closer to the edge. This could prove to be good sport and if the lad succeeded in over-turning the skiff. . .well, there would be more than one pair of hands to help him out of the water and into a hiding-place before pleading total ignorance to having seen or heard anything untoward.

Lord Bardolph hadn't heard anything but he noticed the drift away from his own little theatre of activity to something more immediately entertaining and his gaze followed theirs, falling on the tableau in the boat just as India was forced back into her seat.

'Good God,' he breathed. 'Not her as well!' He turned to the two ruffians he had prised away from the *Pelican's* captain on the grounds that they were wanted for horse-stealing and capital crimes took precedence over the requirements of His Majesty's Navy. 'Don't either of you two dare move,' he told them. 'They've got India as well.'

'India!' Richard exclaimed. 'What's she doing here? She ought to be at home, waiting.'

'Don't waste your breath preaching to the converted,' Lord Bardolph snapped. 'Just pray you have a chance to tell her yourself.'

The boat had drawn alongside the *Pelican* now and the crew and their captive were preparing to board it, the latter horribly convinced that her effort had been unnoticed by the very person at whom it had been directed.

Lord Bardolph thought quickly and hastily revised his tactics. He led his 'captives' down a narrow street that was little more than an alley, cut their hands free and passed his own reins to Bartram.

'Keep you hands behind you as if you were both still tied,' he said. 'I'm going to have to try to get India away and I'm not sure the captain is going to fall for the same story twice, particularly not when he realises that it's no youth that's been brought ashore. He'll let her go, of course, but he's going to have his doubts about you two and about my original story. It wouldn't surprise me if he demands to have you back so you need to be ready to leave here fast and in full control of your horses.'

Bartram looked scared. 'Why don't we go on ahead?' he asked. 'You can catch us up with Miss Leigh later.'

'Because it will be easier if she rides pillion behind one of you,' his brother said, his face darkening with anger at this further demonstration of Bartram's selfishness. 'And because I have no intention of letting you get into another scrape from which I shall be expected to extricate you.'

Back on the quayside, a coin acquired the services of a waterman to row him back to the frigate.

'Captain Curdridge, please,' he said to the rating who received him on board.

The captain stood up as his visitor entered his cabin, both men obliged to bow their heads under the low-slung beams supporting the deck above. 'A rapid return, my lord,' Captain Curdridge said politely. 'I do hope those two scoundrels haven't given you the slip so soon.'

'No, Captain, they're quite safe — and have turned suddenly co-operative, doubtless under the entirely mistaken belief it will save them from the noose.'

'Oh?' The captain's interest was more polite than sincere.

'It now appears that there were three of them —

and the third has just been brought aboard by
another of your parties. They claim this one is the
ring-leader.'

'Indeed? May I ask if it's your intention to deprive
this ship of all its crew?'

'No, of course not. I just want the last of this
particular trio.'

'Of whose existence you were hitherto entirely
ignorant,' the captain pointed out, reasonably
enough. 'What guarantee can you offer that he won't
be followed by a fourth or even a fifth horse-thief?'

'I think that's rather improbable.'

'Frankly, my lord, I find it improbable that there
were two and then three. I allowed myself to be
convinced over the two by virtue of the fact that
you're a magistrate as well as a peer of the realm. I
find a third a little hard to take. Perhaps an element
of share and share alike should enter into this.
You've had your first two; now it's my turn to keep
the next brace.'

'At least let me question this one — in your presence if you'd prefer.'

The captain looked at him in silence for a few
moments. 'Yes, I should prefer,' he said, and sent
his midshipman to request Mr Swanmore to deliver
to his cabin the pressed youth just taken.

The lieutenant pushed India through the door and
then ducked in behind her. 'Take that hat off,' he
snapped. 'Show some respect.' And, to force obedi-
ence, he knocked the beaver on to the floor.

A silence fell on the room. In Lord Bardolph's
case, it was due to the need to think quickly. The

captain and his lieutenant were quite simply stunned
and it was the former who collected his wits first.

'Dear me, a mistake appears to have been made,
Mr Swanmore.' He looked piercingly at the younger
man. 'I take it it *was* a mistake?'

The lieutenant blushed scarlet. 'Yes, Captain.
I. . .we. . .had no idea.'

'I can see I shall have to suggest to their lordships
at Admiralty that seamen should have longer ashore
even if they can't have shorter periods at sea. You,
are not, I believe, a married man, Mr Swanmore?'

'No, sir.'

'Perhaps your efforts have hitherto been misdi-
rected.' The captain turned his attention to Lord
Bardolph. 'Were you aware that this third horse-
thief was female?'

'No, I wasn't. It was a detail her confederates
omitted to mention. It makes no difference to
whether or not she hangs, of course, but I suggest,
Captain, that it considerably simplifies your decision.'

'In what way?'

'You can hardly knowingly allow a woman to
serve on board ship. I believe the regulations
expressly forbid it. You'll have to let her go.'

'Yes, I shall, but it only serves to increase my
doubts about this whole story of yours. It was far-
fetched to start with, my lord. I'm more than half
inclined to disbelieve the whole and send a landing
party out to bring those other two back.'

Lord Bardolph grew very still and it seemed to
India that he had somehow, without apparently
moving a muscle, become both haughty and more

than a little menacing. Then he gave a thin-lipped smile and raised his eyebrows as if conceding a point. 'I can't stop you doing that if you insist,' he said and transferred his attention to his fingernails, which seemed suddenly to require scrutiny. 'I wonder how quickly word would get round the fleet that an officer, ten ratings and a powder-monkey, all from the same ship, can't tell a young woman. . .' he glanced at India as if studying her for the first time '. . .a remarkably personable young woman when she's cleaned up, I should think, from a youth? Not even when they've rowed downriver with her in the enforced proximity of a rowing-boat?'

'Below the belt, my lord,' the captain told him.

'Quite, but in prize-fighting it's a matter of no holds barred.'

The captain turned to his lieutenant. 'That will be all for now, Mr Swanmore. Perhaps you'd be kind enough to attend me when Lord Bardolph has gone ashore.'

The lieutenant shot the Viscount a surprised glance and opened his mouth to say something, looked at his captain's face and thought better of it, so closed it again. 'Yes, sir,' he said.

Captain Curdridge sighed as the door closed behind him. 'I don't know what this is all about, my lord, but I've a pretty shrewd and increasingly sure idea you're gammoning me. I know—and so do you—that I ought to get to the bottom of it, but since I'm due to sail on the tide I'm going to let it go.' He glanced at India. 'I'd have had to let her go, anyway. What were the fools thinking of? But I'll be blunt, my lord, and uncivil enough to tell you to your face that I hope I never see you or either of those young blackguards again, least of all on board any ship of mine. And that goes for this female, too.'

Lord Bardolph gave a brief smile. 'I don't think you're alone in that wish.' He took the collar of India's coat in his fist. 'As for you—out!' he said, propelling her through the door ahead of him.

The lieutenant was waiting outside and they heard the captain's shouted 'Mr Swanmore!' as they climbed the companionway to the deck above.

'Did you call him Lord Bardolph?' the lieutenant asked when he stood in front of his captain.

'Yes. Why? Do you have reason to think he isn't?'

The young man shook his head. 'No, nothing like that. It's just that one of the women who tried to stop us landing shouted out that she'd tell Lord Bardolph because the boy was his nephew and the boy—I mean the young woman—also protested that she was. The men say he—she—shouted something to the blacksmith about letting Lord Bardolph know what had happened.' He paused. 'But she can't have been his nephew, can she? I mean, not his *nephew*.'

'And I very much doubt whether she's a horse-thief, either. Mr Swanmore, this business leaves me more confused than a pint of rum. If it's all the same to you, I suggest we regard it as one of the unsolved mysteries of the universe over which we have no control and with which we will therefore not concern ourselves with further.'

The lieutenant grinned. 'Thank you, sir. An admirable suggestion, if I may say so.'

'So glad we concur,' Captain Curdrige murmured. 'You may go, Mr Swanmore.'

CHAPTER FIVE

'THANK God you came,' India said as she was bundled across the quay and down the narrow street towards the horses, under the interested eyes of loiterers playing pitch-and-toss on the flagstones.

'Don't talk. March,' the Viscount replied and India obeyed. The sooner they were out of here, the sooner she would feel safe.

Richard and Bartram stared at Bardolph's companion, momentarily mystified. They recognised India simultaneously, caught each other's eye and promptly roared with laughter.

'If only you could see yourself!' Richard gasped. 'You look a sight!'

'I thought it looked rather. . .becoming,' India retorted.

'I suppose it might have done when you left home,' Richard replied. 'It certainly doesn't now. And isn't that my coat?' he added.

'Your coat, your breeches, your shirt, your cravat, your boots and your beaver,' his sister told him, unrepentant.

'All without so much as a by-your-leave — and they won't be fit to wear when you eventually take them off,' Richard said indignantly.

'I couldn't ask you for them when you weren't

there, and if you had been there I shouldn't have needed them,' India pointed out reasonably.

'I'd be obliged if you two would stop bickering,' Lord Bardolph interrupted. 'Just remember we're not out of the navy's reach yet. I've a suspicion they'll be watching to see how we leave Lynn; whether as a magistrate with three malefactors in tow or as four friends. We're going to have to ride along the quay in full view of the *Pelican*, so we're going back to the waterfront and along the South Quay before turning off again and back into the town. I want you boys to keep your hands behind you as if you were tied, and I'll keep hold of the leading-reins. That will all help to sustain the illusion. I don't think I'm going to put Miss Leigh up pillion behind either of you. She'll ride in front of me, hands apparently tied in front of her. Are we agreed?'

'Do we have a choice?' Bartram grumbled.

'Yes, you do,' his brother told him affably. 'You can do as I say or I'll cheerfully hand you back to Captain Curdridge and allow you to fulfil the lifelong ambition of the last four years to make the navy your career. Is that what you'd prefer or am I correct in deducing that it's lost some of its appeal?'

'I never intended to start off as a pressed man,' Bartram said peevishly. 'I thought you could buy me in as a midshipman at least.'

'Ah.' Lord Bardolph smiled blandly. 'So it was the gold braid that appealed, rather than the sea. I did wonder.'

Bartram flushed with anger. 'That's not what I

meant! There's no future in the service if you start from impressment. No pressed man ever became an admiral.' His tone was scathingly sarcastic but it had little effect on his brother.

'Precisely,' he said. 'And now perhaps we may go?' Lord Bardolph swung himself into his saddle and then leaned down to pull India up before him, a difficult task made easier by utilising his stirrup as a step.

'Ready?' the Viscount asked when everyone seemed to be settled. 'Right — and for goodness' sake look dejected even if you can't manage contrite.'

The little caravan, three of its members looking appropriately downcast, rode back along the South Quay, past a Dutch ketch, the *Amelia*, whose crew were obviously just completing the battening down of the hatches prior to catching the tide and following the *Pelican* into the estuary and on into the German Sea.

So far as Richard was concerned, it was just a ship, bigger than some, smaller than others, but Bartram was a connoisseur to whom no two ships were ever quite the same. He had seen the *Amelia* before, anchored just off-shore in the waters of the Wash.

He was debating how best to draw Richard's attention to it when the necessity of doing so was removed from him by the appearance at the top of the gangway of a familiar sturdy figure about to descend.

There was no mistaking Mr Huggate in his gaiters,

the old-fashioned cut of his coat and his low-crowned beaver. The rest of the party spotted him at the same time and India heard a muffled curse from Lord Bardolph.

'Just the person I least wanted to run into,' he muttered. 'Be uncivil, Miss Leigh. Keep your back to him.'

India had no objection to doing as she was told. She therefore was in no position to observe that Mr Huggate seemed no better pleased to bump into Lord Bardolph than Lord Bardolph was to bump into him. However, since recognition was mutual, neither could pretend otherwise. Lord Bardolph touched his hat. 'Good day, Huggate.'

'And to you, my lord.' The farmer's glance rested briefly on India's back and then travelled on to the two boys, noting the leading-reins and the position of their hands and not, Lord Bardolph prayed, seeing that there was no rope holding them in position. 'Having a spot of bother, my lord?' he asked.

'Boys will be boys,' Lord Bardolph explained. 'This time the mischief's rather more serious and I don't think a bit of public humiliation will do either of them any harm.'

Mr Huggate snorted. 'If they'd had a good thrashing last time they stepped out of line, they wouldn't have had the urge to get up to mischief again,' he said.

Lord Bardolph raised one quizzical eyebrow. 'You think so? I lack your faith in the efficacy of a good beating. Mischief is mischief and, while I can't

applaud it, I'd be very unhappy about any boy who
lacked the spirit to get into it.'

'A view not necessarily shared by anyone on the
receiving end of it.'

'I'm sure you're right. Your servant, Mr Huggate,'
and Lord Bardolph urged his horse forwards and
turned off the quay down the first narrow street that
offered.

As soon as the party had passed through the
Southgate, Lord Bardolph relinquished the leading-
rein and allowed the boys to control their own
mounts. 'What happened to Clarion?' he asked
India.

'He's still at the blacksmith's as far as I know,' she
replied.

'Then the first thing we do is make for there and
collect him.'

They rode in silence for some time and India, now
that her relief at her freedom and gratitude to Lord
Bardolph as the source of it had somewhat subsided,
began to feel a little piqued that his concern for
Clarion exceeded his concern for her in so far that
he had enquired about the horse but had not asked
one single question about what had happened to
her. At last she could stand his lack of interest no
longer.

'You'll be pleased to learn that I'm perfectly all
right,' she told him.

'I can see that for myself.' He sounded surprised,
as if the information was so superfluous as not to
merit being mentioned.

'I thought you might have been worried about what had happened.'

'No. Why should it worry me? You're not my responsibility and if you choose to gallivant about the countryside most indecorously dressed, then you must take the consequences. If my brother hadn't been involved, I assure you I'd have had no part to play.'

'If your brother hadn't been involved, neither would I,' India said sharply.

She had a point but Lord Bardolph was in no mood to acknowledge the validity of it. He was only just beginning to realise how concerned he had been to see her in the long boat and how relieved to find that she had come to no harm. He told himself that he would have felt the same about any female in such circumstances but he had a sneaking suspicion that his concern for any other female, though sincere, would have been entirely cerebral. His concern for India was uncomfortably close to being emotional and he didn't like the implications of that at all. Anger was a convenient refuge.

'What in the devil's name were you doing, anyway?' he demanded. 'I told you to stay in your room. Obviously, you thought you knew better than I.'

'It wasn't like that at all. There was a commotion somewhere outside. I tried to see what was going on from the window but even when I undid the casement I couldn't see anything more than a few skirts and the back of a woman with a pitchfork, so I went down to have a closer look.'

Lord Bardolph groaned. 'How like a woman! Something arouses your curiosity and all circumspection, all common sense, goes out of the window.'

No more was said for some time but it was the Viscount who spoke first because India, unable to think of an immediate riposte and unwilling to acknowledge any justice in his comment, deemed it wiser to say nothing. 'What *was* going on?' he asked suddenly.

India smiled to herself in the moonlight through which they were now riding. 'Female curiosity, my lord?' she asked.

'Not at all. An entirely laudable request for englightenment.'

She nodded wisely. 'A very different matter altogether,' she agreed and retailed the events leading up to her capture.

He heard her out without comment and lapsed into thoughtful silence when she had finished. It was not, however, an unfriendly silence and it seemed to India that the anger she thought she had sensed had somehow slipped away as the daylight had a short while ago. She was glad to be sharing a horse, to have his strength behind her and to feel his arms around her. She knew this was reprehensible, that she should be both shocked and embarrassed at this degree of intimacy; very likely she should ask to be transferred to her brother's horse. But India didn't care. Bardolph would almost certainly despise her for not raising the objections to this mode of travel that any woman with pretension to gentility would raise, but she needed to be realistic. This was as close as she was ever going to get, in any sense of the phrase, to Lord Bardolph, who she knew already regarded her as trade, having money but not refinement, pert-tongued and rashly indecorous and, since she *was* trade and pert-tongued and nothing in her behaviour would have led any man to think she was other than impulsively indecorous and lacking in any ladylike qualities, there was nothing she could do about his opinion of her. She would make the most of what there was and try to think no more about it.

The trouble was, there had been moments when it had seemed as if they were on the verge of reaching a level of understanding that would at least have enabled them to continue as friends, but every time such a moment arrived something happened to put their relationship back several notches. And sometimes, she admitted reluctantly, it was that very same pert tongue of hers that was responsible.

Lord Bardolph had no hesitation in continuing through the early part of the night. There were sufficient of them not to attract the attention of footpads and nothing more sinister was likely to be encountered on these roads. There was a full moon and the road was easy enough to follow. He was anxious to reach the village where Clarion had been left, and not out of any concern for the horse. It would suit his plans very well if they were to arrive at night. He couldn't stop the landlady talking, though he thought a surreptitious guinea or two would ensure that lady's discretion.

Accordingly, when they reached the inn, he instructed the others to wait outside while he found out what accommodation they could offer for themselves and their horses.

The landlady had been dreading his arrival and the explanations he was likely to demand as to the whereabouts of his nephew, and her husband, no less apprehensive than she, stepped forward before Lord Bardolph had so much as opened his mouth.

'Now, my lord, I takes leave to tell you, you in't got no call to blame me or the owd woman for what 'appened 'ere earlier on. Yer 'oss is orright but as fer yer nevvy, well, there weren't much as anyone could do — and they did try.'

They were a little disconcerted that Lord Bardolph — who might reasonably have been expected to demand to know what they were talking about — merely drew off his gloves and laid them neatly on the counter.

'Landlord, my nephew is a young fool and deserves everything he got. He was told in no uncertain terms to stay in his room. He chose not to. Very well, then let the navy teach him to do as he's told.'

The landlord gasped and his wife stared openmouthed at Lord Bardolph. Of all possible reactions they had considered, this was not one. What was more, it looked as if no explanations were necessary: his lordship plainly knew what had happened to the boy.

'I've come back for my horse,' Lord Bardolph went on, 'and I'd appreciate a quiet word with your good lady — a matter of some delicacy, you understand.'

'Of course, my lord,' the landlord said, though he

didn't. 'Er—will you be wantin' a room, or shall I send to the farrier to bring the 'oss round?'

'No, I'll settle with him in the morning. I'd like two rooms for tonight, stabling for three horses and a private parlour if you have such a thing.'

The landlord shook his head regretfully. Largesse such as this betokened rarely came their way, and in circumstances least likely to produce it. 'No private parlour, my lord, but if it's a meal yer wantin' the owd woman can serve it in the bedroom.'

Lord Bardolph looked past him to the landlady and bestowed on her his most charming smile. 'Perhaps we could first have that quiet word, Mrs——?'

'Mrs Ramsey,' she confided. 'If you don't mind stepping this way, my lord.'

My lord stepped, and must then have left the inn by the back door because when the landlady reappeared she was alone, bustling with intrigue and on her face an expression big with importance.

Outside, India did not receive news of Lord Bardolph's plan with anything like Mrs Ramsey's approval, but that might have been due to the fact that Lord Bardolph made no attempt to use charm. On the contrary, he was arrogant, peremptory and high-handed.

'No, my lord, I will *not*,' she insisted. 'For one thing it's totally untrue.'

'Don't come the self-righteous pillar of veracity with me, my girl,' the Viscount retorted. 'If riding around the countryside dressed as a boy isn't living a lie, I don't know what is.'

'That's quite different. It was forced on me by circumstances. And I am *not* your girl.'

'You should be eternally thankful you're not,' he told her. 'The fact that you are nothing to do with me except by the accident of fate that made you decide to settle in the Fens at least relieves me of the obligation to demonstrate the full extent of my disapproval. As for your dress being forced on you by force of circumstances, well, so is this slight adaptation of the facts.'

'Your brother is only sixteen.'

'Oddly enough, I'm aware of that fact, Miss Leigh.'

'You're perhaps not aware that I'm three-and-twenty.'

'I should never have guessed from your immature behaviour that you were so old. I must congratulate you.'

'On what?' India asked suspiciously, aware that she was laying herself open to some cutting comment but unable to squash her curiosity.

'On having lived so long without anyone having felt the need to strangle you.'

'In any case, the landlady won't believe it — she'll recognise me.'

'She won't see you until you've done as I say. I very much doubt she will remember you. Dressed as a youth you look a great deal younger than you do in women's clothes.'

'All the more reason why she won't believe it; she'll take one look at me and one look at Bartram and realise it's nonsense —— '

'I'm not too happy about this myself,' Bartram interrupted. 'Who's going to believe that I eloped with a. . .' dismay drove courtesy out of his head '. . .with an old maid?'

'Thank you, Bartram,' India said with heavy irony. 'That was just what I wanted to hear.' She turned back to his brother. 'All the same, he's right. No one is going to believe a woman of my age would elope with someone who still ranks as a schoolboy.'

'Women—especially a certain class of women— will do almost anything to acquire a title,' Lord Bardolph pointed out with some relish.

'Bartram hasn't got a title,' India retorted. 'Not unless you count Honourable, and that doesn't convey any rank on his wife.'

'True, but you see, Bartram is at present heir to my title and you've heard that I'm not generally expected to live very long.'

For a moment, India thought he was referring to some genuine rumour. She paled. 'Why? What's wrong with you?' she asked.

'Something to do with my dissolute lifestyle, I believe.'

'Really? I hadn't realised you were so interesting!'

'Thank you, Miss Leigh. Whenever I need my opinion of myself boosted, I shall know where to come.'

India chuckled in spite of her annoyance. 'I hadn't observed you to suffer very much from that complaint,' she said and then added, more seriously, 'But you really can't expect me to admit to a *tendre* for Bartram, my lord. It goes beyond the bounds of credibility.'

'I agree. Only your greed for a title lends it any credibility at all, and then only in the estimation of those ignorant of these things. Use your common sense, India: if you're dressed as a boy they will recognise you as my "nephew" and will be close enough to realise you're no such thing. Now I've disposed of Harry; he was taken by the press-gang — as they already know — and so far as I'm concerned it serves him right for not doing as he was told and staying in his room. I have to account for needing women's clothing. Having inveigled Bartram in eloping with you, you dressed as a boy to avoid remark and make the pair of you less easy to follow.'

'And Richard?'

'He was sent by your family to accompany me; they didn't want to leave you to my notoriously untender mercies.'

'I see. And have you also thought of a good explanation as to why, if we're eloping to get married — which has to mean Gretna Green — we happened to be travelling in the opposite direction?'

It was clear that that salient point had escaped Lord Bardolph's notice. 'It has to be attributable to something more convincing than poor geography,' he said doubtfully.

'The villagers may have some idea where you and Bartram live, my lord,' Richard broke in. 'They don't know where we do. Bartram — and I suppose you as well — were staying in our locality. India

ensnared him in a very short time,' he added
helpfully.

'You see?' Lord Bardolph said triumphantly.
'Between us we have a foolproof story. Now will you
go upstairs and put on the dress Mrs Ramsey will by
now have put out for you?'

'She'll see me go in and recognise me,' India
objected.

'No, she won't. I've stressed the importance of
discretion and she'll be in the taproom making sure
no one slips out and accidentally catches sight of
you. I suggest the sooner you go, the more likely she
is to have been successful.'

India knew he was right. She had also realised
that if she changed into women's clothes now it
meant she and Richard could ride straight up to
their own front door without the fear of undesirable
gossip. So she swung her leg over the horse's neck
and allowed Lord Bardolph to catch her by the waist
and lift her down. Once on the ground, he did not
immediately let go and she found herself looking up
into his grey eyes and thought she detected a warmth
there, but it was difficult to be sure in that light; it
might be nothing more than wishful thinking.

'Believe me, India, this is for the best,' he said
quietly.

'I know, my lord,' she replied with uncharacteristic meekness. 'It's just that you're so. . .
provoking.'

His finger flicked her cheek. 'Only because you
rise so delightfully to the bait,' he murmured.

India whisked herself out of the remnants of his

hold and hoped the moonlight hid her blush. She ran quickly into the inn, refusing to rise to that particular bait, if such it was.

When she reappeared she was wearing a dimity frock that had originally belonged to Mrs Ramsey's eldest daughter, a mob-cap, and some ill-fitting shoes. She was aware how unfashionable she looked. She did not realise how well the simple dress became her.

Lord Bardolph unfastened his cloak and placed it round her shoulders. 'No woman travels without a cloak,' he said.

India glanced down at it and smiled. 'And capes are such a noted feature of women's cloaks,' she commented.

'You hope to set a fashion,' he told her.

They entered the inn by the front door and the curious stares they encountered were due as much to the reappearance of a man who had not been seen to leave as to any curiosity about the rest of his party.

On the Viscount's instructions, Mrs Ramsey had cleared and laid a table for them in the corner of the taproom, Lord Bardolph having been of the opinion that, in the absence of a private parlour, it was preferable for them all to be seen eating in public than to congregate in one or other bedroom away from the common gaze.

They ate well, but it had been an exhausting and trying day for all of them; the night was well advanced and Lord Bardolph wanted to make an early start in the morning in order to reach the Nene at the best stage of the tide. India was the first to beg to be excused and neither of the boys raised even so much as a token objection to Bardolph's suggestion that they, too, should get what sleep they could for what was left of the night.

He was not far behind them, delayed only by Mrs Ramsey, shaking her head in disbelief.

'Who'd 'a' thought it, my lord?' she said, waylaying him on his way out. 'Such a genteel-looking lady, too, and him no more than a lad. Who'd 'a' believed it?'

'Who, indeed, Mrs Ramsey?' He leaned over confidingly. 'Mind you, if she'd been too obvious in her wiles, I think the boy would have seen through her, to say nothing of the rest of the family. Why, I was as much duped as anyone else!'

Mrs Ramsey was shocked. 'And I take leave to tell you, my lord, that you in't no flat, not by a long chalk.'

'I flatter myself that's true — which just goes to show how very clever she is.'

The landlady nodded. 'A good thing you found out in time, if you asks me.'

'A very good thing, Mrs Ramsey. A very good thing indeed.'

'You'll take good care she don't run off with your brother again, I'll wager.'

'I think I can safely guarantee that whoever that young woman marries, with or without eloping first, it won't be my brother. Goodnight, Mrs Ramsey.'

* * *

Although Lord Bardolph awoke looking, if not necessarily feeling refreshed, the same couldn't be said for his companions. Clarion was fetched from the smith and a lady's saddle, somewhat the worse for neglect, obtained, which the horse accepted with surprise but without animosity.

Lord Bardolph viewed it apprehensively. 'I'll be lucky if it doesn't give him saddle-sores,' he commented. 'Miss Leigh, will you be very much offended if I keep him on a leading-rein initially? I mean it as no insult to your horsemanship but he's never carried a side-saddle before, let alone anyone on it, and neither of us can have any idea how he'll behave.'

The same worry had occurred to India. 'I'd be grateful, my lord,' she said.

They crossed the Ouse by way of one of the small bridges to the south of King's Lynn and set out across the network of droves that would eventually bring them to the Wash Way. On one stretch, where there was room to ride several abreast, Bartram drew level with his brother and Richard, with whom he had been in close converse, drew alongside his sister.

'What do you think Huggate was doing in Lynn?' Bartram asked.

'How should I know?' Lord Bardolph replied. 'I wish he hadn't been. I'd as lief not have it spread about the locality that your behaviour is such that you have to be brought back home in fetters.'

'Hardly fetters!' Bartram exclaimed indignantly.

'Rest assured that "fetters" is how Huggate will

retail the story—and it will lose nothing in the telling. You've made an enemy there, Bartram, and for no better reason than your immature behaviour.'

'But what was he *doing* there?' Bartram insisted. 'Doesn't it strike you as odd that he should be so far from home?'

'No odder than our being so far must have seemed to him. He's an astute businessman. I dare say business is what brought him to Lynn. It's brought me often enough over the years.'

'But you're different. You're a major landowner with interests in a number of ventures.'

Lord Bardolph laughed. 'Don't fall into the trap of thinking that because a man farms just a couple of hundred acres he has no other interests. From what I know of Huggate, I'd be prepared to wager that he has fingers in a great many more pies than I can lay claim to.'

'Pies involving Dutch ketches?'

'Why not? Business is business and there are plenty of Dutchmen who'd rather do business with the English than with their French masters.'

'Do the French allow them to?' Richard asked.

'I think you'll find that merchantmen are quite skilled at evading men-o'-war when they choose to,' Lord Bardolph told him. 'And the French are not yet in a position to risk an attack in English waters.'

'You make it sound as if the Dutchman's a smuggler,' India suggested, and caught a warning glance from her brother.

'That wasn't necessarily what I meant to imply,' Lord Bardolph said. 'I can't say I'd be altogether surprised if I were told he ran a little contraband from time to time. Most of them do.'

'For a magistrate, you sound remarkably unconcerned,' India said, ignoring Richard's increasingly anxious expression.

Lord Bardolph laughed. 'As a magistrate, I have more than enough to do without initiating searches of every ship that docks on the off-chance that they've contraband aboard. Besides, we have tidesmen to supervise that. Magistrates just deal with the consequences of what they find.'

'Don't you have any power to initiate action?' India asked.

'I've the power of any other citizen who suspects contraband is being run. I can alert the proper authorities to my suspicions. I'd have to be very sure of my facts, though. Riding officers are already stretched to breaking point.'

India pondered this for a while before pursuing it a little further. 'So if anyone thinks contraband is being run, they should tell Customs, not a magistrate?'

Lord Bardolph shrugged. 'It would certainly be a quicker route to the same result,' he said.

'You sound as if you have a reservation,' India commented.

'I suppose it's true to say that if you were able to convince a magistrate of your story and persuade him to alert the authorities his word would be more likely to be believed and it would be difficult for the relevant officer to ignore the warning——'

'But you'd run the risk that the magistrate might

be involved himself,' Bartram interrupted, rather smugly, India thought.

His brother frowned. 'It's not unknown for magistrates to be involved themselves to a greater or lesser degree,' he admitted. He gave India a penetrating glance. 'Why all these questions, Miss Leigh? Do you suspect someone?'

India caught Richard's imploring expression. She had no right to expose the boys' over-fertile imaginations to Lord Bardolph's scathing tongue. They were in enough trouble as it was. She shook her head. 'No. I was just pursuing the idea to its conclusion.'

'Dear me. Are you always so dogged?'

'Terrier-like,' she assured him.

'Thank you for the warning. I prefer bird-dogs, myself.' He glanced down at her and smiled. 'They have softer mouths, you know.'

As a statement it was unarguable but India had the uncomfortable feeling it meant something else, something that any delicately nurtured female would find offensive. Obviously, she wasn't a sufficiently delicately nurtured female, a fact of which Lord Bardolph was all too well aware and to which he had never been reluctant to draw her attention. She would pretend not to have noticed the innuendo. 'How long will it be before we reach the Nene?' she asked.

He laughed and India had the disconcerting impression that he knew exactly what had been going through her mind. 'Another hour or so. We should have time to rest the horses while we wait for

the tide to fall far enough. Will you be able to bear
with me that long?'

'I shall make a truly valiant effort,' she told him,
and was rewarded with a genuinely amused laugh.

'Then I undertake to make an equally determined
effort not to provoke you further — not today, at any
rate.'

India chuckled. 'I'm glad you're honest enough to
recognise your limitations,' she said demurely, but
Lord Bardolph refused to be drawn and only
laughed once more.

When the little party drew rein outside the Leighs'
house, India heaved an audible sigh of relief. 'Thank
goodness,' she said. 'I was beginning to think that
"home" was a figment of my imagination.'

Richard dismounted from the hired cob to help
his sister to the ground and India immediately made
to unfasten her cloak. Lord Bardolph held up a
prohibiting hand. 'Wear it till you're indoors,' he
suggested. 'The dress you have on underneath is
sufficiently unlike your usual style to occasion comment. If you've no objection, I'll call tomorrow and
collect it.'

'There's no need for that,' India assured him. 'I'll
send someone round with it.'

'Does this mean my visit would be unwelcome?'
he asked.

India coloured with confusion. 'No, not at all. I
didn't mean to imply anything of the sort.'

'Good, then you may expect me.' He looked her
steadily in the eye. 'If I didn't wish to visit, I could
always send one of my own servants, you know.'

'Till tomorrow, then, my lord,' she said. 'And I must thank you for your efforts on behalf of Richard and myself — we are both indebted to you, and most grateful.'

Lord Bardolph leaned down towards her, an amused smile on his lips. 'May I venture a piece of good advice, Miss Leigh?' he asked.

'Of course!'

'Go in and lie down before this excess of civility gets the better of you. I trust your spirits will be restored by the morning. *Au revoir*, Miss Leigh.'

India turned from him with something precariously like a flounce and went up the garden path as quickly as she could without actually running, her indignation fuelled by the chuckle that followed her progress.

'Tea,' she announced to the startled Eliza. 'Master Richard will be here as soon as he's returned the cob to the livery stable.'

Eliza relieved her mistress of Lord Bardolph's cloak and considered the ill-cut, old-fashioned dress beneath with disapproval. She shook her head. 'Not an improvement, madam,' she said.

'I assure you, it's a great improvement over Richard's breeches,' India told her.

'I take leave to hope you didn't exchange the one for the other,' the maid went on.

'What else? I was in no position to carry half of Richard's wardrobe around with me.'

The maid shook her head again. 'You had a bad bargain, madam. Master Richard won't be too pleased, either; you took his best habit.'

'Then he will have to regard it as a small price to pay for having run off like that.' India caught sight of herself in the large glass hanging in the hall. 'On second thoughts, the tea can wait until I've had time to change. You're right, Eliza. This may be more appropriate but it isn't an improvement. Ten minutes will suffice.'

India went early to bed that night and fell asleep straight away, such was her exhaustion. Her sleep was deep and dreamless and, as a consequence, she woke up in the early hours of the morning, wide awake and superficially refreshed. Such had been the events of the preceding days that it would have been scarcely surprising had her thoughts been full of them, and in particular of the very different outcome that could have been expected had anyone — and particularly any member of the press-gang — discovered her true sex. But these considerations were only peripheral to her thoughts. The centre ground was firmly occupied by the tall, arrogant, opinionated and downright uncivil form of Edward Chelworth, Viscount Bardolph.

She exonerated him — with reluctance, but one had to be fair — from her original charge of pomposity: the pompous had, by definition, no sense of humour; Bardolph did have. It was dry, sardonic, frequently self-mocking and usually sarcastic, but it was there. India thought it quite likely that many who were subjected to the whiplash irony of his tongue offered no retaliation but, metaphorically at least, crawled away to die. India was made of sterner stuff. She had a perverse streak that would give no one — and least of all Viscount Bardolph — the satisfaction of knowing they had struck home. She would do her best to give as good as she got and it was in Bardolph's favour that he took a successful set-down with the outward appearance of good grace. In fact it had become almost a positive pleasure to thus spar verbally with a man who never took refuge in a charge of 'feminine logic' when he was worsted in an exchange.

When India had first made his acquaintance, she had not been at all surprised to learn that his intended bride had come to her senses in the nick of time. Now her sentiments had undergone a complete change and she could only pity a woman with so little perspicacity. Lord Bardolph was provoking, even annoying, but India sensed there was no real malice behind his ascerbic wit; apart from that initial confrontation, he had never passed any remark that she wasn't perfectly capable of responding to in kind, and she had asked for that initial set-down by uttering a far more unkind one herself.

Behind the irony, Lord Bardolph had proved himself to be a man upon whom she could depend. He had gone to enormous trouble to rescue the boys. A cynic might have pointed out that, since one of them was his brother, he could hardly have been expected to do otherwise, but India was sure that, had only Richard been involved and had she sought the Viscount's help, he would have gone to just as much trouble. He had tried to discourage her accompanying him but when she had done so his recriminations had been minimal and he had acted throughout in a manner best calculated to preserve her reputation. When he had issued her with instructions, they had been the right ones for the circumstances and only when she had ignored them had she found herself in jeopardy.

India had been brought up to think for herself. She regarded herself as an independent woman and privately acknowledged her good fortune in being in a financial position to be able to indulge that independence. Now, for the first time, she began to see that there might be advantages to having someone else — a man — take many of the decisions, especially if that man should be one whom she had learned to trust. A man like Lord Bardolph, for instance. She tried to think of some other man of her acquaintance who fitted her criteria, and failed. It irked that same spirit of independence to feel that Lord Bardolph was unique: there must be other men capable of filling the gap of whose existence she had hitherto been entirely unaware. There probably were, but since she wasn't acquainted with any of them it was a purely academic exercise even to consider the possibility.

The truth was that Lord Bardolph was the only man she had ever met — apart from her late father, who could hardly be said to count — with whose company she wasn't totally bored within half an hour. Not only did he talk like a sensible man, but managed to do so with humour and without treating her as if she were of lesser intelligence. He never patronised her, and that was a rare accolade.

All of this India was prepared to acknowledge

without reservation. It was more difficult to be equally frank with herself about other feelings. Her head played a large part in her assessment of his character. It played no part at all in accounting for the rest of her feelings towards him.

Apart from the ride to pick up Clarion, when he had been obliged to put his arms round her and had done so in an unobjectionably matter-of-fact way, he had touched her only three times: a flick of her cheek, a finger under her chin, and his arms on her waist when he helped her from the saddle. Small gestures, an essential service, but none of them perfunctorily performed—or so it had seemed to her.

Perhaps she had been deluding herself that there had been an unusual warmth in his eyes and a tenderness in the apparently careless brush of a finger. The fact remained that those superficial intimacies, simple as they were, had made her heart beat faster and brought a colour to her cheeks, making her feel as bashful as any schoolgirl in receipt of her first compliment. She wished the boys had not been there and wondered whether, had that been so, Lord Bardolph would have been less circumspect. India chided herself for so unladylike a thought but it persisted and with it came a longing that they should have an opportunity to be together without the presence of anyone else. This longing was in no way eased by the reflection that, were they alone, Lord Bardolph was far too much of a gentleman to make even such innocuous gestures as he had so far.

And there lay the whole nub of the problem. Lord

Bardolph would always be the perfect gentleman. India Leigh, on the other hand, was not only harbouring very unladylike thoughts at this very moment, but had on several occasions recently been guilty of unpardonably vulgar taunts and hardly less vulgar behaviour. The fact that the taunts, at least, were the result of provocation from his lordship was no real justification, and India knew it. Lord Bardolph could have very few illusions about the sort of woman she was, since she had made no particular effort to behave as she ought. It was hardly surprising therefore if, when he himself was provoked, he made it clear exactly what he thought of her. It was a lowering reflection that an opportunity to be alone with him would do absolutely nothing to promote her intense longing to be taken in his arms, to be loved and cherished. If he behaved like the gentleman he was, he wouldn't put her in so compromising a position, and if he did it could only be because he was so convinced of her lack of gentility that he felt free to treat her accordingly.

India, tossing and turning in a vain attempt to sleep, found it ironic that, with so many eligible men in India with whom she hadn't been able to contemplate a life together, she should now have come all this way to fall in love with a man who, while indubitably eligible, was possibly the least likely to seek such a union. Well, she admitted with a surge of unhelpful honesty, not a legitimate union, at any rate, and she didn't think she was sufficiently independent or unconventional to consider the alternative. Not yet.

CHAPTER SIX

THE morning was well advanced before India woke up, heavy-eyed and not at all refreshed, as Eliza observed when she put her head round the door to see whether her mistress was awake yet.

'I'll bring your breakfast up to you,' she said, pulling back the heavy curtains that cut out the clear Fen light as well as the strong Fen winds. 'And if you takes my advice, you'll indulge yourself in the luxury of a day in bed. You looked half dead when you came in and I can't truthfully say you look very much better this morning. I'd have thought you'd have slept like a log.'

'So did I. I spent too long in the saddle and even though I was lying down it felt as if I was still riding,' India told her. It wasn't a lie. She merely omitted to add that this well-known physical phenomenon was swamped by other, less freely admitted results of her recent escapade. 'Breakfast in bed will be most welcome,' she went on and was about to add that the rest of the day in the same place would be equally so, when she remembered that Lord Bardolph had said something about calling to collect his cloak. Eliza could perfectly well be entrusted with the task of giving it him, but it was unthinkable that the Viscount should leave without being thanked for his kindnesses of the past days, and who better to thank him than India? 'But then I'll get up,' she said instead.

'Very well, madam,' Eliza replied, not at all surprised at her mistress's decision; no one could ever accuse Miss Leigh of indolence. 'I'll put out your fawn cambric.'

'I think not,' India told her. Her fawn cambric did all very well around the house. It was a useful dress but by no stretch of the imagination a becoming one. 'Not fawn. My spirits need lifting. The apple-green lawn will do very well and perhaps you'd put out one of the silk shawls we brought back with us. Isn't there one of a darker green which tones in well with that gown?'

Eliza agreed that there was and took the dress down to be pressed while India ate her breakfast.

Any fear the household might have had that India might be sickening for something vanished when it was seen that she had demolished a very hearty breakfast indeed, and if Eliza thought it at all strange that Miss Leigh should be *quite* so particular that her hair was arranged just so when, so far as the maid knew, she was going nowhere, she knew better than to comment.

When Lord Bardolph sent up his card about an hour later, Eliza smiled to herself. Who'd have thought Miss Leigh could be so very close?

India rose as he came into the room. The borrowed cloak, sponged and pressed, lay carefully folded over the back of a chair. India smiled.

'I'm so glad you were able to come by,' she said, extending a hand in greeting.

Lord Bardolph returned the smile appreciatively. Since the inference that he was just passing had not been one that could have been drawn from his words of the day before, he guessed they were for the maid's benefit and doubted very much whether they would have their intended effect of eliminating speculation. He took the proffered hand and raised it politely to his lips. 'Your servant, Miss Leigh. I'm glad to see you've recovered from the exertions of the last few days without ill effects.'

India watched the door close behind the maid before answering. 'Since my mirror tells me I look positively haggard,' she said with some asperity, 'I beg leave to tell you that that remark leaves me torn between questioning your powers of observation and doubting your veracity, my lord.'

'Dear me, and I thought it was nothing more than a social commonplace,' he said, more amused than taken aback.

India flushed. 'And I had vowed to be nothing but courtesy itself yet here I am already being impolite.'

'And on so little provocation, too. I dread to think what reply I could expect if I set out to be provoking.'

'At least as good as you gave,' India told him. 'If it weren't, it wouldn't be for the want of trying! But I really do apologise, my lord. I had intended this meeting to be entirely affable; I was going to return your cloak and thank you for your good offices on Richard's behalf, to say nothing of the care you took of me.'

'Perhaps you'd prefer me to go away and come

back tomorrow at a previously arranged time — I undertake to be punctual — so that you can have your polite phrases of indebtedness all neatly polished and tripping off the tongue. I, on my part, will polish up a selection of appropriate responses which I shall endeavour to make as bland and inoffensive as I can, though, since you will be working from a text and I shall have to improvise, I must apologise in advance if they don't quite fit.'

'Don't be absurd, my lord. You might just as well suggest we sit down now and construct the dialogue prior to enacting it tomorrow!'

'Miss Leigh, your brilliance overwhelms me! A scheme of such originality bears witness to a quite remarkable imagination. Just think — you could double your fortune by assembling a collection of unexceptionable conversations to fit all situations. Men and women alike would buy the volumes — I feel sure they would run into the plural — and learn their parts in the privacy of their own homes. They would emerge equipped to cross all the minefields of social interchange without fear of a *faux pas* and would hail you as their saviour.'

India put her head on one side and looked at him speculatively. 'I don't think I'm the one with the remarkable imagination,' she said. 'Mind you, I'm not saying you're wrong. I should think there are a great many shy, unconfident people who would jump at the chance to learn their way through the shoals of social converse.' She chuckled. 'I think you've just given me a capital way to occupy the long winter evenings. Should I use a *nom de plume*, do you think?'

'Undoubtedly—and, since we're both determined not to annoy each other, I'll refrain from drawing your attention to the fact that you are not necessarily the person best qualified to construct inoffensive conversations.'

'And in order to maintain my part of that resolve, I won't make the cutting reply that I might otherwise have done.'

'Which really means you couldn't think of one, because I don't believe you could have resisted the temptation.'

India laughed with genuine amusement. 'In the interests of accord I'll neither acknowledge nor deny your accuracy, my lord.' She took the cloak from the back of the chair. 'This is what you came for, sir. My thanks for the loan of it.'

Lord Bardolph took it gravely. 'I could perfectly well have sent my man for it,' he told her. 'There was something I wanted to put to you if you can spare me a few minutes.'

India indicated a chair. 'Then I see no need to continue standing. Shall I ring for some refreshment?'

He shook his head. 'Please don't bother. I've already stayed longer than I'd intended. If we're not careful this visit will give rise to unwelcome speculation, which I imagine you'd like no more than I. Miss Leigh, whatever opinion I may have on your action in following me in the search for our brothers, I observed that you're a very competent horsewoman. You said something about your not riding because the livery stable had nothing suitable and, since you obviously enjoy riding, I wondered if you'd allow me to furnish you with a mount.'

'I thought nothing in your stables would carry a lady's saddle?' she said.

'That's true. Clarion has given that the lie. Either he's been trained to it before he came into my possession or he's a natural. I've told Gidding to do some work on him, using a properly fitting saddle instead of that thing we had to make do with. He will then be at your disposal every day. You have only to send a message over to the Hall, and I'll have him sent round. You'll be able to ride with Richard.'

'Thereby keeping both him and Bartram out of further trouble, you mean,' India suggested.

'Believe it or not, that was not only not my intention but I can truthfully say it hadn't even occurred to me. In fact, I was going to make quite a different suggestion.'

'Yes?'

'I wondered whether you'd allow me to escort you, at least to start with, until we're quite sure of Clarion. You'll get quite a different view of the Fens from horseback and it would give me pleasure to show you.'

She glanced up at him from beneath her lashes. 'Despite the unwelcome speculation it might incur?'

'If that worries you, I'll have Gidding ride a discreet distance behind.'

'That would probably be best,' India agreed,

privately cursing the conventions that made it necessary.

'Good. Gidding reckons, given Clarion's aptitude, he can have him ready in a week. If you're agreeable, we'll ride out seven days from now.'

India's eyes sparkled, and not entirely at the prospect of an enjoyable ride. 'I shall look forward to it, my lord,' she said.

If Lord Bardolph chose to put an extremely valuable hunter at Miss Leigh's disposal on the altruistic grounds of taking pity on her for being able to find nothing else suitable, it was not within Gidding's terms of employment to tell his master that the other one had bells on it, tempted though he was. It was a very long time indeed since his lordship had mounted a lady—in the equestrian sense, that was, as the groom pointed out to the valet—and if his lordship asked Gidding's opinion he could do a lot worse than Miss Leigh, for all she wasn't strictly speaking gentry.

'You mark my words, Mr Folksworth,' he said over a tankard of ale in the pantry, 'that's a young woman as can bring him to heel, if ever I saw one.'

The valet was less convinced. 'She's not Our Sort, Mr Gidding, and you're not telling me his lordship won't be the first to recognise that fact. Now I'll agree he normally plays away from home, and that makes this one different, but it's not as if she's a local, after all.'

Gidding stuck to his guns and considered his opinion vindicated by his lordship's insisting on his accompanying them. Lord Bardolph had issued no particular instructions to his groom beyond that basic one and it was left to Gidding to decide how to interpret his precise degree of accompaniment. Through villages he was simply a length behind. Away from them, he kept well beyond earshot and, since the Viscount made no comment upon either, he reckoned he'd judged it about right.

India revelled in the pleasure of riding a good horse again. Clarion was a far cry from the delicately boned Kathiawaris with their extraordinary ear-carriage. He had power rather than speed and was undeniably better suited to the often water-logged going than those agile descendents of the Mogul emperors' Arab horses would have been.

Lord Bardolph was on his best behaviour. That was to say, at no time did he utter any remark that could conceivably be interpreted as provoking. It seemed to India that this was the result of a conscious effort on his part and it behoved her to respond in kind. Quite apart from any other considerations, it would do no harm to demonstrate that she was capable of behaving in a conventional way. It didn't occur to her that Lord Bardolph's motive might be to preclude the sort of dispute which would make it difficult for her to continue to use one of his horses in a pastime she so demonstrably enjoyed.

The consequence was that the atmosphere between them became the relaxed one of old friends and eventually she decided that she could broach a subject that still rankled slightly without jeopardising their current good relations.

'How well do you know Mr Huggate?' she asked one day as they rode side by side along one of the substantial broad-topped banks that separated drains from siltfields.

'"Know" is not the word anyone can honestly use about Huggate,' he said. 'I've been acquainted with him all my life and watched him prosper but I can't claim to know him.'

'You surprise me. In such a close-knit community, I'd have thought it impossible *not* to.'

'Huggate lives in some isolation and doesn't welcome visitors. He's something of a recluse and I suspect is not at ease among people. It's not uncommon in isolated farmsteads, you know. The villages are, as you have observed, close-knit to an extraordinary degree. I doubt if in any other part of the kingdom you would find a group of village women acting so concertedly, not just to fail to co-operate with the press-gang but actively to thwart them — and remember, there's nothing illegal about impressment; it's been England's way of filling the army and navy since the thirteenth century. But that sense of community doesn't necessarily extend beyond the villages.'

They rode on in silence for a while — in silence because the Viscount was clearly deep in his own thoughts and it was he who spoke first. 'I've not been entirely fair to the Fenmen,' he said. 'In one sense, Huggate isn't a part of the community; he prefers to be left alone and people are perfectly happy to respect that wish, but if there were a dispute between him and an outsider they'd take his part to a man, even if he were in the wrong. Why this sudden interest in him?'

'It isn't sudden. I'm not even sure it really qualifies as an interest. Richard is still smarting under what he calls Huggate's injustice.'

'Was he unjust?'

'I don't know; I wasn't there, but Richard has always been truthful. He says they weren't around the outhouses but a large barn which is too far from the farm to qualify as such.'

'In Richard's estimation.'

'True. Anyway, he also says they weren't trying to set straw on fire and Huggate's degree of anger was out of all proportion to the offence.'

'Does he deny they were on Huggate's land?'

'No.'

'Or that they were in close proximity to one farm building or another, under whatever name?'

'No.'

'Did they have a spy-glass?'

'I gather so.'

'Then personally I think Huggate had every right to be angry, whether or not they were trying to set fire to his straw — which I feel bound to say I always considered very unlikely. Look at it this way; how would you feel if you caught a couple of boys — or young men, since both of them are old enough to know better — skulking in your garden with a spy-glass?'

India thought about it. 'Angry,' she said. 'Angry and frightened, I suppose, but then, it's a very small garden.'

'I don't imagine Huggate was afraid, or at least not for his personal safety, but I think he had every right to be angry. The boys had no right being on his land at all unless he had given his permission. Had it been simply a matter of riding circumspectly through, I doubt if he'd have made any objection, but if they want to play around outhouses — or barns, for that matter — they can play around mine.'

'Put like that, you certainly demolish Richard's case,' India admitted. Lord Bardolph's argument was so entirely reasonable that she couldn't bring herself even to mention Richard's more bizarre speculations about the farmer's activities, as she had been in half a mind to do.

'Your partiality to your brother's cause is understandable and very much to your credit, Miss Leigh,' the Viscount said. 'Don't let it blind you to a less partial view.'

'I'll try not to,' she agreed with a meekness that earned her a sharp glance. She looked up at him sideways from beneath partly lowered lashes. 'My lord, may I say something. . .perhaps a shade indelicate?'

'What man could possibly say no to a request such as that?' he exlaimed. 'You intrigue me, Miss Leigh.'

India laughed. 'Well, at least that's a friendlier response than telling me you were wondering how long my good behaviour would last,' she said bluntly.

'The thought never crossed my mind. This. . . indelicacy. . .?'

India blushed. 'It's just that. . .well, a couple of

times when we were trying to catch up with the boys, you called me India. It sounds so much more friendly than "Miss Leigh", don't you think? I wondered if you'd have any objection to. . .to using it more often.'

Lord Bardolph looked straight ahead between his horse's ears. What India could see of his expression was stern and only he knew how great was the effort with which he prevented his lips twitching.

'I hadn't realised my tongue had slipped,' he lied. 'Please accept my apologies. I hope it didn't cause you any distress.'

India wished the earth would open up beneath Clarion's hoofs. Why, oh, why couldn't she learn to keep her mouth shut? She had taken advantage of the easy relationship that had seemed to exist and with what result? All she had done was to reinforce his belief in her basic vulgarity. 'No, my lord. No distress. On the contrary, I rather liked it.' I may as well be hanged for a sheep as a lamb, she thought defiantly, though there was no defiance in her tone.

'You do realise that it would be. . .most improper?' he went on.

'I was assuming it would only apply when we were alone together—not in company,' she said miserably.

'I'm not at all sure that that doesn't make it even worse,' he commented thoughtfully. He glanced down at her contrite face and guessed with an accuracy that would have surprised India what was going through her mind. He had been teasing her long enough. 'On the other hand, friends—

especially true friends — are few and far between, so how can I spurn an offer of friendship? I'll call you India, but there's one condition attached to it.'

'What's that?'

'You return the compliment and call me Edward.'

India studied his face. He seemed to be perfectly serious but with Bardolph one could never tell. It wasn't beyond the bounds of possibility that he was just leading her on into further indiscretions to underline the opinion he already had of her. Besides, she hadn't thought that far ahead.

'I don't think I could, my lord.'

'Dear me, am I so formidable?'

'No, not at all. It's just that. . .it isn't something I'd even considered.'

'Then consider it now.'

India did, in silence and for several furlongs. 'It doesn't seem natural, somehow,' she said at last.

'Yet "India" does?'

'Yes.'

'Don't you think you're being just a shade illogical?'

'Maybe, but it still wouldn't feel right.'

'Then I'm afraid we're destined to remain on formal terms until your feelings undergo a change.'

'If your tongue doesn't slip first. It has done in the past,' India pointed out.

He chuckled. 'Rest assured I shall be watching it like a hawk, night and day, from now on.'

India opened her eyes very wide in obviously feigned surprise. 'Will that be necessary, my lord? Night and day, I mean? I know I suggested it should only apply when we were alone together but I wasn't envisaging that eventuality occuring at night. I'm afraid you've been reading too much into my words.'

'A slip of the tongue,' he conceded. 'Still, slips of the tongue can be surprisingly revealing, you know. Perhaps that one disclosed my true wishes.'

The colour flooded into India's cheeks. So that was what he thought of her! She had had enough hints in the past. Now she had been told in so many words. She pursed her mouth.

'I think, my lord, we should confine our converse to the expectations of this year's harvest.'

'Very wise, Miss Leigh. Do you know anything about harvests?'

'Not a thing. I'm relying on you to tell me what opinion to hold.'

'I'll try not to disappoint you.'

The ride continued in silence apart from the occasional courteous suggestion from the Viscount that they go this way or take the left fork, suggestions to which India was too miserable to object even had she wished to. She had only herself to blame. She had laid herself open to misinterpretation and Lord Bardolph was the last person to turn down an opportunity to take advantage of it. She had thrown away, in a few unguarded moments, any hope she might have had of him revising his opinion of her.

Had India but known it, Lord Bardolph was equally unhappy. He had handled badly a situation which India had already indirectly warned him was delicate. He flattered himself that he was normally adept at avoiding misunderstandings. He certainly hadn't proved so on this occasion. What was it about India Leigh that prompted some inner demon to put the worst possible construction on anything she said — and let her be aware of it?

He had offered her the use of Clarion for several reasons, about some of which his motives were unclear even to himself. True, he had guessed that it would give India a great deal of pleasure, and so it had proved. Nor had he himself been unrewarded: he had had the pleasure of her company and, if he had sometimes missed the stimulus of crossing verbal swords with a worthy opponent who neither burst into tears, as most women did, nor became surly, as did many men, that had been compensated for by the easy relationship that had grown up between them. That had been destroyed in a few ill-advised exchanges. He should have known better. She thought he was pompous and arrogant. He had been at considerable pains over the last few weeks to prove her wrong. Nothing would give him greater pleasure than to hear her call him by his given name. He should have agreed to use hers without comment and without conditions. Had he done so, there was every chance she would sooner or later have slipped into the unconscious use of his own name, in much the same way as he had dropped his guard and used hers. Now, no matter what amends he made, they were back on a rigidly formal footing which would make it impossible for any informality in address to slip in by the back door. Henceforth the use by either of them of the other's given name would have a significance that might have been avoided.

There was one thing that could — and must — be avoided. It would be unforgivable if his tactlessness led India to feel that she must discontinue these rides, which so obviously gave her pleasure. Her continued use of Clarion must be salvaged even if all else was lost.

Accordingly, when they drew up outside the Leighs' house, he helped her from the saddle and, instead of remounting his own horse, said, 'Would you be kind enough to invite me in, Miss Leigh?'

It was the last request India expected and her surprise was evident. 'Of course. This way, if you please.'

Both horses were handed over to the groom. 'Take them home, Gidding,' Lord Bardolph told him. 'I'll walk.'

India led the Viscount into the front parlour and invited him to sit. 'Shall I send Eliza for some tea, or would you prefer some other refreshment?'

'None, thank you.' He waited until the door had closed behind the maid. 'Miss Leigh, I've been cursing my confounded tongue for the past half-hour. I've embarrassed you and offended you and I intended neither. Will you forgive me?'

She smiled briefly. 'There's nothing to forgive, my lord. I was out of order.'

'No,' he replied, shaking his head. 'I should have accepted your request as it was meant and not made a tease out of it.'

'Is that what you were doing?'

'Yes, and have subsequently regretted it very much.'

'It's very kind of you to put it like that.'

'Kindness doesn't enter into it. That's how it is.'

'Thank you, my lord. I don't think apologies come easily to you. This one has all the more value on the account.'

'You think this is just an apology, offered out of the kindness of my heart to make you feel better?'

'Isn't it?'

'No — yes —— Good God, was there ever a more provoking woman?'

'That sounds a bit more like you,' India observed without rancour. 'Shall we leave it there?'

'No, because that isn't what I came to say. Miss Leigh, I'm aware that I've made it more difficult for us to regain the easy friendship I thought we had. I don't want to see your pleasure in riding sacrificed on the altar of either your pride or mine. If you wish to take your revenge by offending me in return, you will decline to ride Clarion again.'

'Wouldn't that be cutting off my nose to spite my face?' India enquired.

'Yes, it would, but I'm not at all sure you wouldn't do that if you thought it worth it.'

'If my spite was great enough, you mean.'

'No, I did *not* mean that,' Lord Bardolph said firmly. 'Plain speaking, Miss Leigh: I believe you enjoy riding Clarion. I should like you to continue to have that pleasure. Ideally I should like to be able to continue to accompany you, but if you would prefer to have only the company of Gidding or

Richard I shall entirely understand and the horse is still at your disposal. I hope you will accept this as meaning precisely what it says.'

India smiled — a little wistfully because she couldn't quite see how they might ever return to the pleasant friendship that had existed before, a friendship which was the most she felt she could hope for and which her own thoughtless tongue had damaged, if not completely destroyed. 'I'd like it above all things,' she admitted.

'Good. That's settled. Clarion is at your disposal.' He hesitated briefly. 'And so are his owner's services as a guide, should you wish to avail yourself of them.'

There was nothing wistful about India's smile this time. It was warm and generous. 'Who better to teach me a true appreciation of the locality in which I've chosen to live?' she said.

So the rides continued whenever the weather permitted, which, in the Indian summer so typical of the Fens, was most days. India was loath to miss an opportunity, not only of riding but of doing so in the company of the man with whom she most longed to be. She hadn't yet experienced the driving rain and biting winds that everyone told her — with an unnecessary amount of glee, she thought — characterised Fenland winters, but if the tales she heard were only half true riding would be out of the question and, with it, Lord Bardolph's company.

She drank in avidly all the information the Viscount imparted. She recognised the hovering flight of the marsh harrier and the melancholy pleading of the curlew's call. She learned to spot the heron waiting for his lunch, as stationary as any lead replica beside a garden pool. She learned to judge when the outmarshes could support a horse and when the tide was far enough in to render the apparently sound grey-green grasses unsafe. By the same token, she knew when not to be surprised that vessels stayed in the deeper channels at the limit of her vision and when to expect to see them close enough to be able to count the men on deck.

As a consequence, she knew enough to be surprised to see a ship at anchor, sails furled, dangerously close to land, though not enough to recognise it.

'Is she aground?' she asked, pointing seawards.

'I doubt it,' Lord Bardolph replied. 'She's on an even keel, as if the master knows exactly what he's doing. The channel there is narrow and dangerous but for those who know it it's deep enough.'

'But why stop there at all?' India persisted. 'Why not go on round to Wisbech or to Lynn?'

'Why, indeed. I imagine she'll get under way with the tide and be gone.'

'It still seems very odd. My lord, may I borrow your spy-glass?'

He took it from its saddle holster and handed it to her, and if there was a slight reluctance to do so India didn't notice it. When she handed it back to him, she looked puzzled. 'Do you think they could be wildfowling?' she asked.

'Most unlikely at this time of day,' he said, surprised. 'Why?'

'Some seamen have rowed towards the shore—
there must be a channel out there leading across the
mudflats—and I can't think what else they'd be
doing.' She watched him put the spy-glass back in its
case. 'Aren't you going to look?' she asked.

'I don't need to. I'd already noticed it and, yes,
there is a channel just about there, running quite a
long way towards the shore.' He hesitated, as if
unsure whether to say more. 'You didn't recognise
the ship?'

'Should I have done?'

'You've certainly seen it before.'

India looked out to sea. 'The *Pelican*?' she suggested. 'I would have said it was bigger than that.'

'You'd have been right. No, not the *Pelican*, the
Amelia.'

India couldn't immediately place the name. 'The
Amelia?' she echoed.

'The Dutch ketch berthed at Lynn. Perhaps you
were too relieved to have escaped the navy's clutches
to notice anything else.'

'Of course! That was the ship we saw Mr Huggate
disembarking from. At least, you all saw him. I had
to keep my back to him, if you remember.'

Lord Bardolph chuckled. 'I'd forgotten. I remember wishing him at the devil and cursing the need to
acknowledge him. Maybe it was a fortuitous encounter, after all.' He lapsed into silence and they rode
on without speaking, the Viscount obviously deep in
thought. When he spoke again, it was with an
uncharacteristic tentativeness. 'I don't suppose it's

occurred to you that Huggate's land begins just beyond where that channel ends?'

'I don't see how it could have done since I have at best a very hazy idea of the limits of his land and none at all that there was a channel there.'

'Do you feel inclined to pay a social call on Mr Huggate, since we are, in a manner of speaking, passing by?'

'Now why didn't I think of that myself?' India wondered. 'What a marvellous opportunity to demonstrate that at least one member of the family is neither a fire-raiser nor a felon to be brought back in chains. I should perhaps draw your attention to the fact that our respective brothers are firmly convinced Mr Huggate is in league with smugglers.'

'Our respective brothers have too vivid a corporate imagination for their own good,' Lord Bardolph said repressively.

'I know, but you must own it adds a *frisson* of excitement to what will probably turn out to be an exceedingly tedious visit.'

The Viscount reined his horse in. 'Miss Leigh, you will watch your tongue, won't you? For God's sake don't breathe a word of our brothers' stupid suspicions.'

'Of course not,' India replied, surprised. 'I want to mend fences, not smash them altogether.'

'Good. Please bear that in mind.'

They rode down the sea-bank and could see the Huggate farm buildings huddled among their sheltering trees not very far off.

'Mr Huggate will be able to see us coming,' India pointed out to her companion.

'I should hope so, too. You don't imagine I hide behind banks or skulk in dykes when I pay a social call, do you?'

'How silly of me! There's bound to be a simple explanation, after all.'

'And in all probability an exceedingly dull one. Just remember that, Miss Leigh.'

'Of course, my lord,' India said demurely, and pretended not to notice the sharp, suspicious look cast in her direction.

A large barn lay apart from the rest of the farm buildings and India deduced that this must be the one that had so interested her brother. There were men around it, not in itself an unusual occurrence on a farm. India did think it somewhat odd that they should disappear when they caught sight of the approaching riders. Lord Bardolph, more familiar than India with the innate curiosity of the English countryman, considered it most peculiar, though perhaps no more so than the sight of farm workers going about their agricultural business in waders. He said nothing and betrayed no undue interest in the barn as they rode past it and on to the house.

India had never met Mr Huggate before but she knew his reputation for being reclusive and taciturn. She was therefore entirely unprepared for the effusiveness of their welcome.

'My lord Viscount, this is indeed an honour. And this is Miss Leigh from India? A privilege to welcome you, Miss Leigh, and, if an old man may be permitted to say so, that continent's loss is our gain. I dare say there were broken hearts left behind when you sailed!'

'You're too kind,' India murmured, both over-whelmed and taken aback by this reception.

'You'll take refreshment with me, of course,' the farmer went on and raised his voice to call over his shoulder, 'Ned, take his lordship's horses and bait them while I bait their master,' and he slapped his thigh at appreciation of his heavy joke.

A farmhand appeared from somewhere behind the house and took the reins of both mounts after respectfully touching his forelock to the Viscount. ''Mornin', me lord,' he said.

'Good morning, Goldham. How's your wife?'

'Not too bad just now, me lord, though the winter do play hell with her joints, if you'll pardon me sayin' so.' And he led the horses off to the stables so that his employer could lead their riders indoors and out of sight of things they shouldn't see.

'I dare say Miss Leigh would like some tea, and what about you, my lord? I can offer you a glass of Madeira or perhaps you'd prefer good English ale?'

'Ale would fit the bill very well indeed,' Lord Bardolph told him. 'I think Miss Leigh would prob-ably prefer Madeira to tea; we've been riding for some time and I think the warmth wouldn't come amiss. Miss Leigh?'

'Madeira would be perfect,' India agreed, unsure whether to be surprised or gratified that he had so accurately read her mind.

Their host poured the wine from a fine crystal

decanter and handed the glass to India with a little
bow, saying, 'I take leave to tell you, Miss Leigh,
that you'll not taste a better Madeira this side of the
Canaries, and that's a fact.'

'Paid duty, has it?' the Viscount asked jocularly.

Mr Huggate tapped the side of his nose. 'You can
inspect my cellars to your heart's content, my lord,
and I guarantee you won't find a single bottle or a
single cask that hasn't paid full duty.'

'I'm sure that's so — and I wish I could be equally
sure about every other cellar in the district,' Lord
Bardolph replied.

'Aye, I don't envy you the job of magistrate,' Mr
Huggate said with such heartfelt sympathy in his
voice that India found herself disbelieving every
word.

She wasn't warming to their host. Even had she
not known of his reputation for taciturnity, she
would have found his present effusive garrulity
uncomfortable. She liked him less and less, and was
more and more inclined to believe that Richard and
Bartram might unwittingly have hit the nail very
accurately on the head. She could only be relieved
that he was more intent on engaging Lord Bardolph
in conversation than her, which at least left her free
to glance around in the intervals between smiling
politely at his ponderous witticisms.

The parlour in which they sat was old-fashioned
and might have been comfortable had it not had the
indefinable air of a room rarely used, and then for
funerals or, evidently, visits from the local aristocracy. The furniture was solid, the walls dark and the

flags uncarpeted. If the boys' theories about Huggate's activities were correct, there was no evidence in this room that he had a substantial alternative income to farming. If he did, it sat in the bank or, more probably, went back into the farm. She had already observed that the farm buildings were in excellent repair and had thought little of it; anyone worth his salt made sure that the tools of his trade were in good condition before attending to his own creature comforts, which was not to suggest that Mr Huggate went short of much. There was simply no outward show of the wealth the boys attributed to him. That might be a point in his favour but it might also mean he was far too clever to provoke gossip.

The room had just one window and the view from it was restricted by an old yew hedge that cut the worst excesses of the winter winds. India could, however, just make out the shape of the infamous barn — and something else, as well. It would never do to be staring too determinedly out of the window so she had to make do with seemingly casual passing glances. On one of the first of these, she spotted three men running from the barn and, since they were then cut off from her sight by the bulk of the barn itself, she concluded they were heading seawards. That glimpse had been a fortunate one because on every subsequent occasion the limited view was devoid of human life.

All right, her common sense told her. What would you expect on a farm if not workers making use of a barn? There are fields between the barn and the sea.

Why shouldn't they be going there? But even India's limited acquaintance with English farming was enough to tell her that there had been no stock and no crops other than grass on those fields. Lord Bardolph might be able to explain what the men might have been doing. She would ask him when they were alone again. She brought her attention back with a jolt to the visit in hand, suddenly aware that their host had turned his attention to her.

'So you're the sister of that young rapscallion I caught with his lordship's brother near my barn a few weeks ago,' he said with a joviality far removed from the report she had had of his attitude at the time.

'I'm afraid so,' she said, forcing herself to smile. 'I must apologise if he gave you cause for concern.'

'Think nothing of it. Boys'll be boys and there's not a lot the rest of us can do about it.' He turned to the Viscount. 'I'll be bound you got up to a thing or two in your young days, my lord.'

'Undoubtedly. They did not, however, include setting fire to a barn,' Lord Bardolph replied frostily.

'Well, no, and I didn't mean to imply. . . Still, no harm was done, when all's said and done, so what say you we forget all about it?'

Lord Bardolph inclined his head politely. 'Between the three of us I think that would be an admirable policy. However, I suggest that neither Miss Leigh nor I should convey that agreement to our respective brothers. I don't think anyone's interests are best served by letting them think they've been absolved from criticism, least of all theirs.'

'I can see you're a wise man, my lord,' Mr Huggate gushed, 'and I dare say that's reflected on the Bench.'

'I certainly don't endeavour to be foolish,' Lord Bardolph replied tartly and stood up. 'And now, if you'll excuse us, I think we should be on our way. Miss Leigh will be feeling the strain of a long morning in the saddle if she isn't home soon.'

'And here's me thoughtlessly rabbiting on,' the farmer said. He stuck his head round the door. 'Edith!' he called down the flagged hall. 'Tell Ned to bring his lordship's horses round as fast as may be.'

When they made their farewells, Mr Huggate pressed India's hand in a manner that she decided she had better regard as fatherly and peered at her intently. 'Are you sure we haven't met—apart from the odd glimpse in church?' he asked.

'Quite sure,' India said positively. 'I'd have remembered.'

Mr Huggate smirked. 'Flattered, I'm sure,' he said. 'All the same, I can't help feeling there's something familiar about you.'

'There's absolutely *nothing* familiar about me—unless, of course, you've been to Bangalore,' she said firmly.

He sighed. 'That pleasure's been denied me. Still, it's very odd.'

'I don't think I've ever been called odd before,' she said reflectively, as if she were trying to recall such an occasion, and she was rewarded by his

embarrassment at being misunderstood. This had
the advantage of enabling them to get away without
any further delay, Mr Huggate being clearly desirous
of avoiding any further misunderstandings.

'That was unkind of you,' Lord Bardolph said
when they were out of earshot.

'Yes, wasn't it?' India agreed affably. 'It got us
away, though, didn't it? Why, the man's the most
appalling toad-eater I've ever met!' She glanced up
at her companion. 'Is that the effect being a viscount
usually has on the lower orders?'

'It didn't have that effect on you,' he pointed out.

'I am *not* a lower order,' India said indignantly
and then corrected herself. 'Well, I am, of course,
but I've never toadied to you like that.'

'Very true,' Lord Bardolph murmured. 'You need
to learn the trick, you know; the Prince Regent
would be deeply offended if you treated him like an
equal.'

'Since I'm hardly likely to meet him, I don't think
I'll worry too much about that,' India replied.

'Still, bear it in mind. You never know what the
future might bring.'

India considered this statement but she could
detect no hidden significance so she dismissed it.
'And another thing, my lord. I am *not* feeling the
strain of a morning's riding.'

'Would you have preferred our visit to be
extended?'

'No, of course not! It was well-nigh intolerable as
it was!'

'It was, wasn't it?' he agreed cordially. 'One might

almost suspect that he was trying to keep us there as long as possible.'

'Especially since he's not supposed to welcome visitors and to be particularly close-mouthed,' India said.

'Precisely. It makes one think.'

'Did you notice those men?'

'What men?'

'Yes, I thought he was occupying your attention too efficiently to allow you to glance out of the window. You could see that barn, you know.'

'Not from where I was sitting. I'm not totally unobservant. All I could see was yew hedge.'

'I could see the end of the hedge and the barn beyond. Early on in our visit I saw some men. They seemed to come out of it and then ran round the back and disappeared. That would be seawards.'

'Or fieldwards,' he pointed out.

'I thought of that but there was no stock in those fields and no crops that would require attention.'

'My compliments, Miss Leigh. You learn quickly.'

'Do you think there might be something in the boys' ideas about Mr Huggate's activities?'

'Smuggling, you mean? It's not impossible but it seems most unlikely—and especially in broad daylight.'

'Do you have an alternative explanation?'

Lord Bardolph needed to consider that for some time before answering. 'Not at the moment, but that doesn't mean there isn't one.'

That was unarguable but although India, too, gave it a great deal of thought she couldn't think of another explanation, either. She changed tack. 'Did you believe what he said about there being nothing in his cellar that hadn't paid duty?'

'Implicitly.'

'Isn't that rather naïve?'

'Miss Leigh, I'm a number of things, but naïve isn't one of them. Good God, girl, use your head! If the boys's suppositions are correct — and yours, too, for you seem increasingly inclined to endorse them — just about the last place there would be any contraband liquor would be in Mr Huggate's cellar.'

'Perhaps that's exactly what you're *meant* to think,' India suggested. 'Now, if it were me, I'd put the contraband in the cellar and have strange seamen skulking around my barn just to convince people like you that it was there, when in fact the barn would be full of straw or fleeces or something equally innocuous. You should have asked to see his cellar.'

'You can't pay a courtesy call and insist on seeing a man's cellar. Not even if you're a viscount,' Lord Bardolph pointed out in some exasperation.

'But a magistrate can,' India objected.

'A magistrate can issue a warrant for a riding officer to investigate but before he does so he has to be convinced there are good grounds. I'm by no means convinced that there's anything wrong at all.'

'You were sufficiently interested to go there in the first place,' India reminded him.

'A mistake,' he said shortly.

'You disappoint me, my lord.'

'I'm sure I do,' he said harshly. 'I take comfort

from the fact that disappointment is something from which one generally recovers.'

Nothing more passed between them until they had been riding along the sea-bank for some time. India pointed out to sea. 'Is that the *Amelia*?' she asked.

'It certainly looks like it,' he agreed and utilised his spy-glass. 'Yes, that's the Dutch ketch. Did you recognise it or was it an intelligent guess?'

'The latter — I'm no Bartram. To me a ship is just a ship. Doesn't that rather confirm the boys' suspicions? We saw the seamen heading inland and as soon as we appeared on the scene at Huggate's farm they disappear and are now putting back out to sea.'

'Nonsense. I told you they'd leave on the tide and that's precisely what they have done. Of all the reasons they may have anchored just there in broad daylight, smuggling is the least likely but, whatever their reason, it would have been the height of stupidity to stay there any longer than they had to.'

India sighed with exasperation. 'You're an intelligent man, my lord. Why do you persist in thinking in straight lines? It's the same as the cellar — what better to throw the revenue men off the scent than to work in broad daylight?'

'You don't think the revenue men have spy-glasses of their own? You don't think they would take an interest at least as keen as yours in what an isolated ship was doing, anchored in a deep channel at low tide for no apparent purpose? Perhaps you should try thinking in straight lines for a change, Miss Leigh. Your life would certainly become a lot less complicated.'

He had made a valid point and India was annoyed with herself for not having seen it. She had no desire to cross swords with Lord Bardolph and yet, try as she would, she always seemed to end up doing just that. At the same time she had the unaccountable feeling that there was something behind his argument other than a wish to put her straight. Gentle irony was one of his more effective weapons and all that would have been necessary, yet he had preferred heavy sarcasm. It was, as her father might have said, like taking an elephant gun to kill a fly, and that wasn't Lord Bardolph's usual way.

When they drew rein outside her house, the Viscount helped her from the saddle, as he always did, but, instead of releasing her waist as soon as her feet were on the ground, he held her a little longer and his voice was gentler than it had been at their last exchange.

'I mean no offence, Miss Leigh, when I say that I think you've fallen under the spell of our brothers' imagination. I can't deny that smuggling goes on around these coasts but it really is a very subtle, surreptitious affair. If it were as open as you seem to think, the revenue men wouldn't have half the difficulty catching the perpetrators as they do. I would advise you to put it from your mind. At the very least, you'll sleep easier in your bed.'

India opened her dark eyes wide in genuine surprise. 'I assure you that thoughts of smugglers on the outmarshes don't keep me awake, my lord.'

'Perhaps not, but don't you think every horse-hoof you hear is the gentlemen riding by?'

'To tell you the truth, I sleep too soundly to be woken up by a mere horse. Besides, wouldn't they muffle the hoofs?'

He laughed reluctantly. 'You're right, of course. You wouldn't hear twenty sets of iron shoes clattering over the cobbles. You confuse me, Miss Leigh; I can't quite decide whether you're an immensely practical, sensible woman, or a romantic with a vivid imagination. It's an intriguing dilemma.'

India glanced up at him through her lashes. 'Thank you, my lord. Every woman likes to be considered intriguing—and now, if you don't mind, I think you ought to let go of me. We wouldn't wish to attract gossip, would we? And that's my sensible side coming out,' she added helpfully.

He smiled wryly. 'I hoped you hadn't noticed,' he said, letting go.

'Even if I hadn't, you may be sure those behind the twitching curtains had.'

Lord Bardolph sighed. 'I wish I could decide which I prefer.'

'My lord?'

'Common sense tells me I should prefer your practical face but the reprobate in me has a pronounced hankering to see more of the romantic.'

India whisked the skirt of her habit out of the dust and chuckled. 'I leave you to grapple with your dilemma, my lord,' she said and made her way up the garden path without a backward glance.

CHAPTER SEVEN

INDIA had a great deal to think about when she was back in her room. Eliza took her habit to brush the dirt out of it and press it for its next use and this left India to sit before her glass, brushing her hair but so sunk in thought that the action was automatic. She might be facing her reflection but she saw nothing.

Lord Bardolph's parting words had lifted her spirits out of the depression his previous rebuke had caused. They might almost have been considered flirtatious and for the first time in her dealings with the Viscount she felt she had neither made a fool of herself nor set up his back. She smiled to herself. A flirtation with Lord Bardolph might be very enjoyable, the more so since she had already decided that a more serious relationship was out of the question. It began to look as if he might be rather adroit at it, which surprised her. She had never entirely abandoned her early impression of humourless pomposity. That was to say, she had firmly acknowledged that he was far from humourless, but he was inclined to stand upon his dignity—which, in India's estimation, was very close to being pompous—and flirting, by definition, involved unbending to a degree that India would not have expected of him.

His attitude to the smugglers bothered her. She knew as well as the next man that smuggling was rife

all round the coast of England—and Wales, too, in
all probability. Something had not been right at
Huggate's farm; there had been no plausible explanation of seamen—presumably Dutch seamen—
heading for the barn. Yet Lord Bardolph had
seemed singularly unconcerned even though, as a
magistrate, he must surely be one of those most
deeply concerned to wipe out illegal practices. A
large part of the population felt the law was quite
simply wrong and a sizeable proportion turned it to
their financial advantage but that didn't absolve
magistrates from their duty to enforce it. The
Viscount didn't strike India as the sort of man to
turn a blind eye or not to care, and he had certainly
been interested enough in Huggate's visitors to ride
over for a closer look, yet he dismissed her ideas
with some scorn as being the figments of Richard's
imagination—which, she had to admit, to some
extent they were. They had learned nothing and had
merely been subjected to the farmer's effusions.
India had thought these very odd but Lord Bardolph
seemed to find nothing unusual about them. She
could only conclude that he was so accustomed to
being treated like that that it struck him as being in
no way remarkable. And if that were so, it would
certainly destroy India's contention that such
uncharacteristic behaviour had any sinister
connotations.

Nevertheless, it continued to niggle at the back of
her mind and when Richard left his books to join
her for a belated luncheon she said, 'Richard, what
sort of a man was Mr Huggate?'

Her brother grinned. 'A very angry one.'

'Understandably, by all accounts, but that isn't what I meant. Forget the anger if you can and tell me what sort of a man he was behind it.'

'All I saw was anger,' Richard pointed out reasonably. 'Bart says he keeps himself to himself and doesn't talk much even when he's among other people — at market, say. He doesn't normally have two words to string together. That's what Bart says but he didn't have any problem finding them when he caught us, nor when he let loose about us to Bardolph.'

'How did he treat Lord Bardolph?'

'How would you expect? He didn't have any grudge against *him*, only against us, and he had his temper under enough control for that to be apparent.'

'But he didn't toad-eat him?'

Richard considered. 'I wouldn't call it toad-eating, exactly. He was very angry, you see, and I suppose he had to be careful not to contradict himself since he wasn't telling the truth in the first place, so he was fairly forthright but that was mixed with a sort of obsequiousness that made me feel a bit sick, to tell the truth.'

'What sort of obsequiousness?'

'Oh, you know — your lordship this and your lordship that, never risking letting Bardolph think he'd forgotten his rank and the deference due. Quite nauseating, really, because, to give Bardolph his due, I've never thought he wanted to be addressed like that. Mind you, Bart says that's how a lot of people address him.'

'So he expects it?'

Richard shrugged. 'I don't know what he expects. I only know what Bart says he gets. Bart himself says Bardolph doesn't like it above half, but if you ask me Bart's a bit piqued about it. I think he'd rather like it if being an Honourable gave him the right to some sort of similar address.'

India recalled Bartram's discontented face and thought her brother had probably summed it up rather well. 'I know Bartram's a friend of yours and he's told you quite a lot about farming and the Fens, but the more I hear about him and see of him, the less I like him. I do wish there were someone else with whom you could be friendly.'

'He's a bit childish,' Richard admitted, 'and very stubborn when he's set on something and, of course, he doesn't much like Bardolph, but that's envy as much as anything else. It's not just the title. Bardolph's got the money and the self-confidence — which isn't surprising, given how much older than Bartram he is — but he's all right really. All the same, I shan't be sorry to go to Cambridge and make a wider acquaintance.'

It was a remarkably adult view for a fourteen-year-old, and India wondered whether life in a colony where Englishmen assumed authority was theirs by right had contributed to her brother's undoubted precocity. It didn't leave her much further forward in her attempt to understand Lord Bardolph.

*   *   *

She was awoken from her usual dreamless sleep by a sound which she at first took to be an unexpected downpour of rain. As her sleepy brain cleared, she realised that it was too intermittent to be rain and the sound wasn't quite right. Leaves rustling against the window? No, there was none close enough to reach, not even in a gale.

The sound came again, heavier this time, and India sat up. Someone was throwing gravel at the window. Who on earth could want to wake her up but not be prepared to knock on the front door like a reasonable human being?

She climbed out of bed and carefully parted the heavy curtains that hung at the room's other window. Glancing down at the angle forced on her by the desire to disturb the curtains as little as possible, she could make out the foreshortened form of the Honourable Bartram Chelworth, his face expectantly upturned.

India let the curtain fall, confident that he hadn't seen her, and frowned. It didn't take much thought to realise that Bartram had mistaken her room for Richard's, which was across the landing and on the other side of the porch. The big question was why? What did he want—and was it his intention to get the two of them involved in some other mischief? Worse, was it a pre-arranged signal which had misfired only because Bartram had picked the wrong room?

Since the only way to find out was to tackle Bartram himself, India threw on a wrap and her slippers and went swiftly downstairs to unbolt and unlock the door. Locks, bolts and hinges being in first-class order, this was quickly accomplished and the door was opened just before Bartram had time to realise what was happening and make his escape. He clearly hadn't expected anyone to open the front door, much less India.

'I think you'd better come in,' she said. 'I want to know why I've just been woken up in so clandestine a manner. Or were you hoping to elope with me and my fortune?'

His expression was one of pure horror. 'Elope with you? Good God, no!' His eyes strayed to the other windows on the floor above. 'I thought I'd found Richard's room.'

'Come in,' India commanded. 'I shall try to overcome my disappointment — indeed, my dismay — that you haven't come to rescue me from the shelf, but I give you fair warning; I intend to know what this is all about.'

A shamefaced Bartram followed her into the front parlour. 'I didn't mean that I didn't *want* to elope with you, Miss Leigh. I mean, it's not a thing that's ever crossed my mind.' It seemed to strike him that, true as this might be, it was hardly the most felicitous way of making amends for an instinctive reply which had been somewhat uncomplimentary. The trouble with Richard's sister was that, as with Edward, Bartram was never entirely sure when she was joking.

'Stop floundering, Bartram,' India told him. 'I believe it's customary for elopements to be planned by both parties in advance — though I suppose you

might have been intending to abduct me. No——'
and she held up a hand to check his horrified protest
'—I'm only teasing. Was Richard expecting you?'

'If he had been, I'd have taken jolly good care to
make sure which window it was,' Bartram said
sulkily.

'That would certainly have made sense,' India
agreed, relieved that at least she hadn't stumbled on
some juvenile conspiracy. 'What's this all about?'

'I'd rather talk to Richard, if it's all the same to
you.'

'It isn't.' She noticed that he was wearing a
greatcoat and boots. 'Is one of Bardolph's horses
standing out there in the cold?' she demanded.

'No. He locks the stables these days.'

'Very wise. Maybe he should lock bedroom doors
as well. You look as if you're dressed for a journey
rather than for a night's poaching.'

'I'm not a poacher!' Bartram protested
indignantly.

'I'm glad to hear it. I dare say Bardolph will be
quite relieved, too.' She saw that he had started to
tremble despite the coat. 'I think perhaps a glass of
wine would do you no harm,' she said more kindly.
'Come into the kitchen with me. There'll be some
warmth left in the range and I'll see what I can find.'
She pushed him ahead of her down the hall and lit
the oil-lamp that served the kitchen. Instead of wine,
she poured him a brandy. 'On second thoughts, I
fancy this will do you more good. Sit down and drink
it. You look to me like someone who has stoked

themselves up for something and suddenly finds the fire's gone out.'

Bartram grinned in spite of himself. 'Not a bad way of putting it.'

'Something to eat? Cook makes a rather splendid cherry cake.' India was not unfamiliar with the weaknesses of young men who weren't quite as grown up as they liked to think.

'That sounds good.'

India watched him devour a large portion of tomorrow's cake, knowing that it would fall to her to placate Cook in the morning. 'Well?' she said, when she judged he had had time to collect himself. 'What's going on?'

'I'm running away.'

'Again?'

'There you are, you see. I knew you'd make fun of me.'

'In view of the fact that it's only a few weeks since you last ran away, I think it was an entirely reasonable reaction,' India pointed out.

'If you say so,' Bartram said with a studied politeness intended to convey that he didn't believe a word of it. 'This time I'm serious.'

'Are you telling me that last time you weren't?' India demanded. 'I wish you'd let everyone know. We wouldn't have felt obliged to put ourselves to very considerable inconvenience to get you back. Do I take it you expect Richard to go with you again?'

'No, you don't. At least, I wouldn't mind if he did

but I've a shrewd idea he'll tell me not to drag him into it.'

'You've no idea how much that acknowledgement eases my mind,' India told him. 'Why try to wake him up, then?'

'I don't have any money left and I thought Richard would lend me some.'

'Lend?'

'I intend to pay it back. Though I can't be sure when,' he added honestly.

'Is this another attempt to join the navy?'

'Sort of — eventually. I decided that going in at the bottom, whether through impressment or volunteering, is probably not going to suit me very well. I'll have to buy myself in, but I've no money — and I don't expect Richard to help me with more than my coach fare to London. That's where I'm going and I'll find some work and save until I've enough to buy myself in as a midshipman.'

'I think you'll find it takes you a very long time,' India told him. 'You won't earn much and you've got to live. Surely it would be more sensible to try to persuade your brother that you're really serious. He doesn't think you are, you know. He thinks you imagine it will be like one long cruise on his yacht.'

'That's stupid,' Bartram said scornfully. 'I'll admit that's what gave me a taste for the sea, but I'm not a complete half-wit. I do realise that the navy won't be half so much fun. In fact, I don't think it'll even be very pleasant most of the time, but it's what I want to do.'

'Then convince Lord Bardolph,' India repeated.

'He's the one who can find the money — and the contacts to get you on the right ship.'

'I've tried, but he won't listen. I tried again this evening, but he just told me it was time I grew up and, anyway, he's already arranged for me to go to this old college and there's an end to it.'

'He wants you to go into the church, I believe,' India said.

'He always did — he said it was the best place for younger sons. Then when he realised I was set on the navy he changed his tune a bit and said I was to go to Cambridge first and then we'd see.'

'That sounds a perfectly reasonable compromise to me,' India told him. 'I can't see that a few years at university can do anything other than good.'

'You don't know Edward,' Bartram said bitterly. 'Not really know him, that is. All he's doing is buying time. He thinks I'll have changed my mind by then and he can push me into the church after all.'

The more India saw of Bartram, the less suited she thought him for the career his brother was supposed to have planned for him and she was only surprised if Bardolph himself hadn't yet realised it. She was inclining to the view that, while she couldn't see what attraction the navy held for Bartram, it might be good tactics to suggest that he pursue his studies at Cambridge with the promise that then, if he still wanted the navy, no obstacles would be placed in his way. It was not, however, a suggestion that was best made by Bartram, so she kept it to herself.

'Be that as it may,' she said, 'I can't see that running away is the answer. I think you'll find life in London very different from what you imagine and your brother will worry about you.'

Bartram snorted. 'Edward? Worry about me? Rubbish! He'll be glad to be rid of me.'

Correctly diagnosing the first hints of self-pity in this reply, India adopted a suitably bracing tone. 'He was worried enough last time to set out after you — and to have his people scouring the countryside to find out where you'd gone.'

'He was worried about his horses. If we hadn't taken them, we'd have been welcome to go. Well,' he amended, 'I would. I shouldn't think he cared much either way about Richard.'

'You're forgetting that I was with him. I can assure you you're mistaken. I dare say we'll never agree on that so I think we'd better decide what to do for the best tonight. Richard, happily, is sound asleep and I'm not having him woken up just to lend you money. Nor am I lending you any at this time of night. It's extremely dangerous to wander about the countryside at night, as I'm sure you're very well aware, and you'll have to tramp into Wisbech to find a coach. I suggest you spend the night here and have a good breakfast and then the three of us will put our heads together and decide what to do for the best. How does that strike you?'

Aspects of it, notably the thought of a warm bed followed by a filling breakfast, were definitely appealing. 'You won't send a servant over to the Hall to tell Edward where I am?'

'The servants are all sound asleep and I'm certainly not waking them up just to run over there with pointless messages — after all, Lord Bardolph presumably doesn't even know you've gone yet, so why wake him up to tell him?'

'But I'll wager you'll send someone over there first thing,' Bartram insisted.

India had no intention of frightening him away from the safe haven of the Leigh household, nor did she want to wake up and find he'd gone from here, too. 'I promise I won't let him know until after we've had a chance to discuss it thoroughly. Will that do?'

Even Bartram could see it was the best he could hope for, so he agreed, albeit grudgingly. India gave him one of Richard's nightshirts and showed him into a spare bedroom. She handed him bedlinen and blankets.

'Here you are,' she said. 'Have you ever made your own bed before? No? Well, you'll certainly have to do so in the navy, so you may as well get some practice in. I'll see you're called in the morning.'

She went out and closed the door behind her. As a hostess she felt quite guilty at such perfunctory hospitality but she had a shrewd idea that the last idea she needed to convey to Bartram was that he was in any way an honoured guest, and being obliged to make his own bed — which, if he'd never done it before, would be bound to be an uncomfortable onc — was as good a way as any she could think of achieving that object.

India had closed his door behind her. She was

about to close her own but thought better of it and left it half-open. She was a heavy sleeper but the landing and stairs creaked. If Bartram, upon reflection, decided he wasn't happy with the scheme he had grudgingly agreed to, at least there was a chance she might hear him tiptoeing past.

'Did you know you slept with your door open?' Eliza demanded when she brought India's morning chocolate.

'Did I? Oh, yes. That's right. It was intentional.'

'And Cook's in none too good a humour, either,' Eliza went on, throwing back the curtains. 'She says the cherry cake she made for today has had half of it eaten and since the back door was securely locked and bolted she supposes Master Richard felt hungry in the night and would you be so good as to have a word with him.'

'Oh, dear, she's discovered it already, has she? It wasn't Richard, it was me.'

'*Half* a cherry cake, madam? You've never been one to peck at your food, I know, but half a cake. . .'

'Was it as much as that? It didn't seem it. Give my apologies to Cook. Actually it wasn't me, precisely. It was my idea but the eater was Bartram Chelworth. He's in the blue room in Richard's nightshirt. Someone had better take him up some water and wake him. If he's still there,' she added doubtfully.

'But the bed's not made up in there, madam. We weren't expecting anyone.'

'Don't worry, I gave him the bedlinen and told him to make it himself.'

'You told him to. . .? Dear God, anyone would think you'd been brought up in the gutter!'

'It was entirely calculated, I assure you. Now please be so good as to let Cook know there'll be a third for breakfast—after you've apologised about the cake, of course—and then see to it that both boys are down at about the same time. I don't want them putting their heads together before I've had a chance to talk to them both.'

'Like a Dutch uncle?' Eliza suggested.

India grinned. 'More like a spinster aunt, I think.'

Her plan of waiting until the boys—and Bartram in particular—had been comfortably fed and were consequently in a favourable humour before discussing what to do for the best was destined to be thwarted. Bartram was tucking into his second helping of kedgeree when the sound of the heavy brass door-knocker reverberated down the hall and into the breakfast-room at the back of the house.

'Funny time to be calling,' Richard remarked.

'It doesn't sound like someone paying a morning-call,' India agreed, and her heart sank. If it were whom she thought it was, an unpleasant interview was likely to ensue.

Bartram went pale. 'It's Bardolph,' he said.

'Nonsense,' India told him, even though she thought he was probably all too accurate. 'How would he know where you were?'

'He has ways of finding things out,' Bartram said darkly.

Their common suspicion was verified when Lord Bardolph entered the room on Eliza's heels, before the maid could announce him.

'I knew it!' he said. 'I was right!'

'How gratifying for you,' India said coldly. 'That will be all, Eliza. You may leave us.' She turned to her visitor. 'And you, my lord, will sit down like a civilised human being and take three deep breaths before you let your temper get the better of you.'

'You're impertinent, madam,' he retorted.

'Quite possibly, but very sensible. You've remarked upon it yourself. Nor am I a toad-eater. Do, please, sit down. It makes my neck ache to look up at you and Bartram here looks most uncomfortable.'

'Not half as uncomfortable as he will when I've finished with him,' his brother said grimly. 'And no, Miss Leigh, I will not sit down. This isn't a social call.'

'Do you know, somehow I didn't think it was?' It was an effort to speak equably but India was determined not to be pushed into answering him in kind.

'Would you be so kind as to explain to me what justifies your undermining my authority?' he demanded.

'In what way am I doing that?'

'By harbouring my very foolish brother,' he said.

'"Harbouring"?' India repeated. 'Isn't that what one does for criminals? I'm sorry, I didn't know. I thought I was just offering a bed to a friend of Richard's.'

'With his own home less than a mile away, why should he need it?'

India smiled. 'You have me there, sir, but I'm sure you're going to tell me.'

'He ran away—again—as I'm sure you very well know. And you were stupid enough to take him in instead of sending him straight home.'

'And how was I supposed to do that?' India turned to the boys. 'Richard, take Bartram upstairs and stay there until I've had a chance to talk to Lord Bardolph. And I mean stay there—I expect you both to be there when I've finished. Is that clear?'

Richard, who had no idea what this was all about except what his intelligence suggested, agreed but Bartram became even more petulant.

'If you're going to discuss me, I've got a right to stay and listen,' he said.

'Don't talk to me about your rights,' his brother snapped.

'I really think it would be better if you weren't here,' India suggested. 'Now be a good boy, do, and go with Richard.'

Bartram looked suspiciously from one to the other. 'This is something you've cooked up between you, isn't it?' he said. 'I reckon you sent a servant over to the Hall first thing. How else did he know where I was?'

'I made an intelligent guess,' his brother said, exasperated. 'It wasn't difficult. If you ever used such intelligence as you possess you'd have realised this was the first place I'd think of.'

'This is getting us nowhere,' India pointed out.

'Bartram, I did not send a message to the Hall, though I have to say I'm not nearly so surprised as you seem to be to see your brother here. Now go with Richard. He has some Greek translation to do. You can help him with it.'

This suggestion was greeted with a snort of good-humoured derision from Richard and an expression of incredulity from his friend, but they both went.

'And now, my lord,' India said as the door closed behind them, 'perhaps you will sit down after all, and let me pour you some coffee.'

He hesitated as if seeking some hidden meaning in her offer, decided to take it at face value, and did as she bade.

'What time did he arrive?'

'I've no idea. I didn't look at a clock, but he woke me up. You may count yourself lucky that he mistook my room for Richard's, so it was at my window he threw handfuls of gravel.' She chuckled. 'I asked him if he wanted to elope for the sake of my fortune. I don't think I've ever seen such a look of pure horror on a man's face.'

'I can imagine,' he said grimly, totally unaware of how this reply might be interpreted by his audience. 'You said I might count myself lucky. In what way?'

'His plan was to persuade Richard to lend him some money—enough for the coach to London. I gather that, after the last little escapade, you were unreasonable enough to keep the stables locked, so he had to walk.'

'I wish I'd locked the bedroom door, too,' Lord Bardolph said savagely.

'I thought of that,' India said. 'I decided if I did he'd only go by way of the window if he wanted to escape. Besides, what useful purpose would be served by keeping a boy of that age a virtual prisoner?'

'Peace of mind. Mine.'

India hesitated. Disagreements within the Chelworth family were nothing to do with her. In so far as she had been dragged into them, it had not been at her instigation. Both prudence and good manners dictated that she should not get any further involved. That said, it seemed highly unlikely that Lord Bardolph and his brother were going to reach any accord without some kind of outside mediation and she was as well placed as anyone to be that mediator. Perhaps she shouldn't speak, but she would.

'My lord, I know you had your heart set on Bartram's going into the church and I dare say it's an idea of some standing. Perhaps it was originally your father's wish and you're simply anxious to see it fulfilled, but hasn't it struck you as the years have passed that he's really quite unsuited to such a career?'

Lord Bardolph's mouth set in a thin, humourless line. 'You feel the navy would suit him better, do you?'

'Frankly, I can't see why anyone should want to join the navy—or the army, if it comes to that, but then, I've never understood the workings of the male mind.'

'No, you haven't.'

'It's not that I think he should join the navy, even though that seems to be what he's set his heart on. I simply don't think you should insist on his entering the church.'

'I wasn't aware that I had insisted on it.'

'Bartram seems to think you have.'

'Much as it grieves me to call my own brother a liar, the fact remains that if that's what he's told you, then that's what he is. As a matter of fact, Miss Leigh, I had come to precisely your own opinion some time ago. I have suggested to him several times that he should go to Cambridge and then we'll think about his future again.'

'He says you want him to go because you hope he'll have dropped the idea of the navy by the time he leaves.'

'Then he's shrewder than I gave him credit for. His experience of life is quite limited. The Grand Tour, which would have put that right, is out of the question. University will educate more than his brain. It will enlarge both his circle of acquaintance and his understanding of life, if not of the world, and all without being under the disapproving eye of an elder brother. Yes, I hope the outcome of that would be a change in his ambition and I'd be lying if I said anything else.'

'In short, the church.'

'No, Miss Leigh. Not at all. It's most unlikely that he would come round to considering that as a possibility, but there are other choices, you know. I confess I can't quite see him as a scholar—unlike your own brother—but there's the law, there's farm-

ing, about which he's a great deal more knowledge-
able than he chooses to admit. There's even
business; if he displayed an aptitude, I can see no
reason why he shouldn't go abroad—India is the
obvious choice, of course—and see what sort of a
success he can make of it.'

'But you wouldn't want him going into business in
this country?'

'I think the opportunities for success are greater
elsewhere.'

'To say nothing of the fact that a peer of the realm
would prefer not to have to admit to a brother in
trade.'

'There is always that, I suppose.'

This conversation was not going quite as India
would have wished. In pursuing her well-intentioned
goal of mediating between the brothers, she had
now heard two things of which she would have
preferred to remain in ignorance. She steered the
converse back on course.

'Bartram thinks that you'll still try to insist on the
church,' she said.

'I'm well aware of that, Miss Leigh. I had a far
from enjoyable evening yesterday being told so in a
variety of intemperate ways. I have made it as clear
as I possibly can to Bartram that such is not my
intention but I can hardly force him to believe me.
Now I'm telling you. You're an irritating female but
you don't lack intelligence or common sense so I
hope I can convince you that I mean precisely what
I say.'

India flushed. 'Your compliments unman me, sir.'

'Do they? Then make the most of them for they're likely to be the last you get—from this source, at least. I take leave to tell you that I resent your interference in the private affairs of my family and I'd be much obliged if you'd keep your meddling fingers in your own pies and leave mine alone.'

India kept her temper with an effort. 'I was only trying to be helpful,' she said.

'Oh, I'm quite sure your intentions were of the best,' he retorted scathingly. 'That doesn't alter the fact that they were unnecessary and unrequested.'

'This was the house to which Bartram came for help,' India pointed out.

'No, this is the house he came to for money. And by your own admission it was from your brother he intended to ask it, not you. If you did anything at all, it should have been to send him straight back home.'

'He wouldn't have gone.'

'You have servants. One of them could have accompanied him.'

'My servants need their sleep and, besides, they wouldn't have had any authority over him if he had decided to run off. I kept him here because I thought that after a good night's sleep—what was left of it—and a good breakfast, I could make him see sense and come home of his own accord this morning.'

'My complaint exactly; you meddled.'

'If you're determined to see it like that, my lord, there's nothing I can do about it. All I can say is that it was intended for the best. Obviously I erred.'

'Obviously.'

India stood up, knowing that by doing so she brought this difficult interview to an end. 'How extremely pleasant to know that we agree on one thing,' she said. 'You'll want to take Bartram back with you, I imagine.'

'I shall. I have to tell you, Miss Leigh, that, while he has never been a particularly easy boy, his behaviour and his attitude have deteriorated since the onset of his acquaintance with your brother. Richard's has not been a good influence. I wish them to have nothing more to do with each other.'

'I'll be sure to pass your wish on to Richard as soon as you've gone.'

'And you will forbid their meeting?'

'No, Lord Bardolph. I shall make it clear that *you* forbid it. I've no desire to spark off in my own family the sort of problems your high-handed demands have engendered in yours. Good day, my lord.'

'Good day, Miss Leigh.'

When the breakfast-room door had closed behind him, India sank back on to her chair, trembling with impotent anger at his unreasonableness. She had been trying to help. She had been hoping that the friendship so painfully established over the preceding weeks was sufficiently solid to permit her to step outside the bounds of conventional good manners in order to help. She had been mistaken and the direct consequence was that they were back where they had been after that first confrontation all those weeks ago.

In the course of their disagreement she had learned quite a lot, none of it to her liking. Lord

Bardolph found her irritating, regarded her as a meddler and had, above all, made his views on those engaged in trade perfectly clear. It was acceptable only if it were done abroad and it was something with which a peer of the realm preferred not to be associated. That told her very clearly where she stood. The fact that she had previously worked it out for herself was no consolation. While it had been in her head, there was always a barely acknowledged possibility of error. But Bardolph had confirmed it. Very well. At least she had been careful never to let him guess that her feelings for him had gone deeper than was proper. That meant she could hold her head up and appear unmoved by the coldness that must now inevitably descend between them. She wondered briefly whether he would do as once before he had done, and come with an olive-branch. She decided not. This time the breach was both wider and deeper. She was left with the sole satisfaction of not having lost her temper. It was a very small consolation.

Richard burst into the breakfast-room. 'Bartram's gone,' he announced. 'My, wasn't Bardolph in a fury? Did you and he have one of your battles?'

'We weren't entirely in agreement,' India admitted.

'That's what I thought. He had a face like a thundercloud. I'd have guessed you'd fallen out even if we hadn't been able to hear you.'

'You heard us?'

'Good grief, India, I should think the whole village heard you!'

'So you know what it was all about.'

'Not exactly. I mean, we couldn't make out the actual words, though we tried—short of coming downstairs and putting our ears to the keyhole, that is. Bartram was all in favour of that but I told him it wasn't on.'

'I'm relieved to hear it.'

'He told me why he came here last night. What a hoot him catching the wrong room! Not that it would have done him much good if he'd got the right one because I'm out of funds till my next allowance is due. Well, not *entirely* out of funds,' he added punctiliously, in case India thought he was about to touch her for more, always a sore point between them. 'But too low to be able to lend him any, and certainly not the coach fare to London. Do you know what I think?'

'About Bartram? No, tell me.'

'I think if he isn't very careful he's going to become a dashed loose screw. I'm not surprised Bardolph gets annoyed with him. I don't like Bardolph above half but give him his due, he's a gentleman through and through.'

'I'm glad you can recognise that fact,' India said and wondered whether the life stretching endlessly ahead of her might not have seemed so featureless had Bardolph been less of a gentleman.

'Did Lord Bardolph say anything to you before he left?'

Richard shook his head. 'No. He semeed more concerned to get Bartram home. You know, if

Bardolph let up a bit, I don't think Bartram would do half the silly things he does.'

'Well, at least he left it to me to broach in my own way,' India said.

'Broach what? No, don't tell me. Let me guess. He wants Bartram to stay away from my evil influence and since he doesn't seem able to stop Bart doing exactly what he wants he expects you to make me promise not to have anything to do with him. Right?'

'Masterly. I was going to try to phrase it more diplomatically. You've saved me the bother.'

'So much for what Bardolph wants. Do you agree with him?'

'It seems to me that the bad influence, if there is any, is all on Bartram's side, but maybe I'm just as biased as Lord Bardolph. In any case, that isn't really the point, is it? There's no denying that the two of you do seem to have a genius for getting into mischief and perhaps it wouldn't be a bad idea not to see each other for a while.'

Richard grinned. 'Until Bardolph's calmed down, you mean.'

'No, that's not what I meant, but it'll do to begin with.'

'Are *you* forbidding it?'

India thought about that. 'I suppose I ought to. It's certainly what Lord Bardolph expects me to do but, no, I think not. If it's not forbidden, there's no challenge to be taken up, is there? Let's say I'd prefer you not to see him for the sake of good relations with our neighbour.'

Richard hooted. 'What good relations? If Bardolph's the neighbour you're talking about, I shouldn't think relations could be much worse.'

'You may be right. I'd rather not risk discovering that you're wrong. What do you say?'

He shrugged. 'Why not? Bart's good company when he's in a good humour—and very knowledge-able about the countryside and horses, but he spends so much of his time grumbling about his brother and how nothing's fair that it really becomes a bit tedious. In any case, I think I'm better able to find my own way around now. The people know who I am. They don't treat me like one of them, the way they do with Bart, but they don't become all silent and stolid any more. In fact, old Micah, down by the estuary, offered to take me out plover-netting some time. I'd like that. I don't think it'll bother me, not for a while, anyway. Mind you, it could be a bit difficult if Bartram decides to disobey his brother, and he's very likely to.'

'I'm afraid you're right. You'll just have to deal with that if and when it arises. Do you still want to be a farmer?'

'As a matter of fact, I do. Why? Afraid you're turning into a female Bardolph?'

'Nothing of the sort,' India said indignantly, refus-ing to admit that he had been disconcertingly accu-rate. She had found herself wondering whether there was any great difference between the Viscount's refusal to sanction Bartram's ambition and her simi-lar refusal to accept Richard's. They went about it differently but the underlying principle wasn't so different. 'Would you rather do that and not go to college?' she asked.

'Oh, no. I shall enjoy Cambridge. Besides, I can't see that it hurts to be an educated farmer.'

'Very true.'

'Does this mean you've changed your mind?'

'It means I'm thinking about it. I'll certainly be a lot happier at the prospect if you've had a good education first.'

'You sound like Papa,' Richard commented.

'Is that so surprising? I'm trying to take his place — and Mama's, too.'

'I suppose you are. I've never thought of it quite like that before.' He slapped her on the back. 'You're not doing too bad a job of it, either.'

'Thank you. I'll remind you of that some time.'

'Well, you're making a better job of it than Bardolph,' Richard said in qualification.

'I rather think that constitutes damning with faint praise,' his sister said wryly. 'Now be off with you, I have to make my peace with Cook.'

India had no difficulty making her peace with Cook. Making it with herself was another matter. She had handled the interview with Lord Bardolph badly. She must have done or they would still be on friendly terms. Yet she was uncertain what else she could have done. The only thing that would have met with the Viscount's approval would have been for her to drag Bartram back home in the middle of the night, wake up the Viscount's household and hand him over. Leaving aside the sheer physical difficulty of compelling an unwilling sixteen-year-old to go a mile in one direction when he was intent on going a hundred in the other, would any rational person really expect a woman to get dressed and traipse through the streets at dead of night? Of course not, as Lord Bardolph must surely recognise when his anger had subsided. She had done what she could by keeping Bartram there until morning and she had been entirely confident of her ability to persuade him to go home of his own accord. Lord Bardolph's arrival had pre-empted that plan. He had been angry that she had been meddling in his family's business, and India accepted that it would have been better had she not been, but it was his brother who had embroiled her in it and she couldn't, for the life of her, think what else she could have done in the circumstances.

She had more than half hoped that the Viscount would seek her out when he had calmed down and, without necessarily apologising, make it clear that he knew he had been unjust. As the days passed and no such approach was made, India realised that his pride, or perhaps it was his family pride, was too offended. He neither came nor wrote. When they met in church, there was nothing more from him than an icily polite inclination of the head, to which she responded in kind. She might have her origins in trade, but he would see she could be every bit as high in the instep as he. The almost daily rides ceased. India told herself these would soon have come to an end anyway, with the onset of winter, but there was no denying she missed them. She wasn't sure whether it was the rides themselves she missed the most, or the company in which she made them.

Some of the blame must surely lie with Lord Bardolph, who had apparently not known her well enough to realise that she had acted with the best of intentions. She had known him to be arrogant but perhaps she had underestimated his pride. It was at best a great pity things had turned out as they had but she must learn to live with it. They would stay here until the spring and then, if it was still too painful only to encounter the Viscount in this cold and distant manner, she would suggest to Richard that they would be happier elsewhere.

There was every sign that Richard was keeping his word and not seeing Bartram. India wasn't sure that this was altogether an improvement. He was acquiring a repertoire of skills of whose existence she had previously been totally ignorant and all of which seemed to necessitate crawling across mud-flats or wading in muddy dykes in the hours before dawn. He learned to set plover-nets and eel-nets, to go punt-gunning and ferreting, to catch moles and set rabbit-snares, all good Fenland pursuits that endeared him to the villagers if not to the servants who had to clean up the mud he trailed through the house. India sighed, said nothing except to suggest that he use the back door and wipe his feet before he came in, not afterwards, and was quietly grateful that he also spent some time on his studies. It began to look as if he had been successfully weaned off his friendship with Bartram, and India hoped Lord

Bardolph was observing the same change in his brother.

Her complacency was jolted when Richard announced that he had bumped into Bartram on his way back from the salt-marshes that morning.

India tried to appear unconcerned. 'Indeed? It must be some time since you've met. Did he have anything much to say?'

Richard helped himself to three large slices of sirloin before answering. 'Much as usual. Bardolph won't let him do anything. Bardolph keeps him on a short lead. That sort of thing.'

'Not so short that he can't go to the salt-marshes in the early morning,' India remarked drily.

'That's what I said, but you know Bartram — nothing's ever right and Bardolph's only out to do him down, though why he should want to I've never been able to make out.'

'The sort of person who makes it feel as if the sun has just gone in,' India suggested.

'That's it exactly. Half an hour with Bartram's enough to throw anyone into the doldrums. He's still going on about old Huggate and the smugglers, you know.'

'Don't let yourself be lured into another escapade like the last one, I beg you,' India said.

'I don't intend to. Not unless he can find rather more convincing proof. He's decided Bardolph's involved.'

India's teacup halted halfway to her mouth. 'Bardolph? Involved with smuggling? Nonsense.' She thought about it. 'I can't think of anyone less likely to be involved. For one thing, he's a magistrate.'

'That's what I told Bart. He said there's plenty of magistrates who are, and a lot more who just turn a blind eye in return for the odd cask of brandy.'

'That may be so,' replied his sister, who had heard much the same herself. 'I can't believe Lord Bardolph to be among their number.'

'That's what I said, but Bartram won't have any of it. In fact, he says it's a lot more than just turning a blind eye. He says Bardolph's up to something. He says they've had some rum visitors from time to time who come to see the Viscount but who come and go through a side-door—not even the kitchen where they'd have to account for themselves.'

'You don't think this could conceivably be a case of Bartram's imagination reading far more into it than is really there?'

'Probably—and fuelled by his dislike for his brother, as well, I don't doubt. All the same, it *is* odd even if it's only half true. Old Huggate *was* up to something—still is, if Bart's to be believed—and Bardolph refused to take it seriously, or even to go through the motions of getting the authorities to look into it. It does make you wonder.'

'Just so long as wondering doesn't lead you into more mischief,' India said flatly. 'Are you sure you've had enough? You wouldn't like me to send out for another side of beef?'

He grinned. 'No, thank you, I'll have died of starvation before it's cooked. I've got some work to do. If it's all the same to you, I'll take a chunk of this Dundee cake to tide me over. You can send Cook my compliments, if you like.'

He left India a prey to mixed thoughts. If ever there was a case of the devil finding work for idle hands, it was Bartram Chelworth, who seemed to spend his spare time — a time which appeared to constitute all his waking hours — developing grudges and then finding evidence on which to feed them. When it came to accusing his own brother of having something to do with the smuggling that Bartram alleged to be centred on Huggate's barn, he was being downright malicious, and malice was unforgivable.

Then the uncomfortable thought occurred to her that it might be malicious but that didn't necessarily make it untrue. She was able to discount the episode involving the boys and the barn. Lord Bardolph had been understandably angry and, while that might be due to the discovery that the boys were looking into something he preferred to see kept secret, it was much more likely that he was angry because, if Huggate was to be believed, they had been behaving in a thoroughly irresponsible way and because his pride couldn't tolerate having to apologise to the likes of Mr Huggate.

The visit he had paid with India was much more puzzling. There was no denying his interest in the Dutch ketch's activities and they had ridden over to the farm presumably in order to see what was going on. Yet when she had reported some of the odd things she had seen, he had dismissed them and derided her theories. Had he gone to the farm because he didn't want her to think he was dismissive of activities that were possibly illegal? Or had he done so knowing full well that their open approach would result in any evidence — including the presence of foreign seamen — being hidden? There would have been plenty of time to do so. All Huggate had to do was to keep them talking — or, more accurately, to hold them captive to his own volubility — while the seamen got away to catch the tide. He did it very well. India had presumed Lord Bardolph found it tolerable only because he was accustomed to such effusiveness, but what if the real reason was that he knew very well its purpose and was perfectly willing to encourage it?

India shivered. She wouldn't have believed Lord Bardolph capable of such duplicity. It seemed totally out of character. She didn't *want* to believe it, and yet. . .and yet. . .

She slept restlessly that night and awoke miserable and depressed. Her friendship with Lord Bardolph might have regressed into nothing more than a cold and impersonal acquaintance but she found it very hard to believe his worst fault was anything more than pride and arrogance, reprehensible as those might be.

Perhaps she should advance her plans to move away from here; to dig up now the first slender roots of whose thickening and strengthening she had gradually become aware and to do so before it became too painful. She would have preferred to go with her conviction of Lord Bardolph's integrity intact but the seed of doubt had been sown and, so far as she could see, nothing now could totally eliminate it. The recollection of what had been, the dreams of what might have been, would always henceforth be marred by that small, insidious question mark.

CHAPTER EIGHT

'I can't, Bart. I promised India.' Richard Leigh tried to sound as determined as he knew he ought to be but his friend caught the hint of doubt and worked on it.

'How old are you? Fourteen? Don't you think you ought to be out of leading-strings by now?'

'I am,' Richard protested indignantly.

'No, you're not. You're just tied by longer ones. If your sister won't undo them, then cut them yourself. Or don't you want to grow up?'

'It's not that. It's just that she'd be furious if she knew what we—you—were planning. And I'm not very happy about it myself,' he added frankly.

'Just because she's forbidden you to see me. Well, Edward's done the same, and how much notice do I take?' Bartram said with the triumphant air of one clinching an argument.

'As a matter of fact, the one thing she *hasn't* done is forbid me to see you. She said she'd prefer it if I didn't because it causes bad feelings between the families. That makes it much harder to go against her wishes, that's all.'

'So your sister is a lot cleverer than my brother, isn't she? She realises it's much easier to disobey a flat prohibition than an appeal to one's better nature. I bet she'd be furious if she knew we met the other day.'

'She does know, because I told her, and she wasn't, but what you propose is a horse of a very different colour.'

'But there's got to be more than one of us.' Bartram was almost pleading now. 'It's a matter of safety. There's got to be one who can go for help in an emergency.'

'Doesn't it occur to you that if it's potentially that dangerous—and I'll not deny it is—we'd be better advised to be sleeping soundly in our beds?'

'Where would be the fun in that?'

'It sounds to me as if it could be about as much fun as being taken by the press-gang. That may not have bothered you, but it did me and I'm not ashamed to admit it.'

'It wasn't quite the way I'd intended to enter the navy, either. But this is quite different. No one's going to take us captive and ship us out to sea for a few years.'

'No,' Richard said bitterly. 'This lot will just bundle us overboard in the German Sea with or without slitting our throats first.'

'All the more reason for us to be very, very careful. And all the more reason to see them brought to justice,' Bartram added altruistically.

'If you're right, one of them's your own brother.'

'Yes, but I'm not sure he isn't clever enough to slide out of it at the end.'

Richard shook his head. 'I don't like it. It'll be

exciting and I suppose you can argue that it's one's duty and all that, but I don't like it a bit.'

'But you'll come?'

'Before I decide, I want to be quite clear about what we're going to do.'

'We're going to spy on them, that's all. We're not going to tackle them or anything foolish like that. Just watch them so that we can each verify what the other says when we take the evidence to the revenue men in Wisbech.'

'Wouldn't it be wiser to tell them our — your — suspicions and leave it to them?'

'They wouldn't take them seriously. They'd say it was too much imagination and send for Edward to take us home — and that's something I couldn't face.'

Richard was inclined to agree with him on both counts.

'Can you get horses?' he asked.

'No. Edward keeps the stables and the tack-room locked. In any case, we want to be able to lie low and horses would get in the way of that. We'll have to walk.'

'But it's miles!' Richard protested.

Bartram shrugged. 'So we have to leave that much earlier.'

It was Richard's bad luck that the enforced early departure coupled with his sister's troubled mind meant that she was only drifting on the outer edges of sleep when he closed his bedroom door and made for the stairs. He was as quiet as he possibly could be but, even so, the click of the bolt slipping back into its mortice was dismayingly loud. He comforted himself with the thought that all sounds seemed louder at night and probably no one had heard it, and prayed that the same should be true of the creaking board across the landing—which he had tried to avoid but miscalculated—and three creaking stairs in succession.

His prayer was unanswered, though he continued in blissful ignorance of that fact. India heard the click. To be more precise, a small, sharp sound penetrated her sleepy haze sufficiently deeply to make her wonder whether she had heard something. The creaking board told her she had, woke her up completely, and sent her mind racing over the possibilities, of which burglars headed the list. They were there only briefly. No one had been in her room—she hadn't been sufficiently soundly asleep for them not to have wakened her—and there was nothing in Richard's room worth stealing, and it must have been Richard's door she heard.

She listened briefly to the creaking stairs and guessed that Richard was on his way out of the house. But why? Quickly, she swung her legs out of bed and crept across to the window where, as on a previous occasion, she stood to one side and parted the curtains just enough to enable her to see down the garden path. She had already dismissed the idea that Richard might leave by the kitchen door: its locks and bolts were old and clattered heavily whenever they were moved, certainly enough to wake at least one servant. The front door had modern, well-oiled hinges and a smooth lock. Even the bolts slid more easily and almost silently.

India strained her ears, and even though she was listening for the sound of the front door, and even though it was immediately below her, she only just heard it. The slim figure that slipped out and along the muffling grass bordering the path was unmistakably Richard's.

She wasted no time assuming he was off fishing or wildfowling for the very simple reason that he always told her so that, if she heard him leave, she wouldn't worry. No, this was something else, and, since he had said nothing to her about it, it was reasonable to conclude that she'd disapprove.

Therefore it was something she ought to know about.

In that case, she'd better find out.

The only way to do that was to follow him — and quickly, while there was still a chance of picking up his trail.

She opened the wardrobe and reached inside for her habit and then had second thoughts. Richard had no access to a horse at this time of night and if she again borrowed some of his clothes she'd be able to move much more quickly. It wasn't as if there was anyone to see her. She guessed that Richard must be planning to be home before morning because otherwise he would surely have given her some story to account for his possible absence.

She snatched breeches and boots and tucked her voluminous night-chemise into the former. It wasn't comfortable but it was warm and, in any case, she didn't have time to fiddle with shirts. She grabbed a coat and was still pulling it on when she reached the stairs. Since she had no desire to draw to herself the attention of any of the neighbouring houses, she, too, closed the door as quietly as she could and kept to the grass beside the path, though this was as much to prevent the sound of her footsteps reaching Richard as for any other reason.

India slipped out of the gate and stood under the overhanging branches of a laburnum so that she could have a good look in either direction with a minimal chance of being spotted herself. She was just in time to see Richard disappear round a corner at the far end of the village street, a corner that she knew led only to the marshes. She hastened after him, instinctively making what use she could of any trees, and found this was just as well, because when she was about halfway to the turning another young man came stealthily out of the cobbled street opposite, crossed the main road and followed Richard up the grassy track.

Bartram? Of course it was Bartram, she thought bitterly. Now what are they up to? Surely he hasn't persuaded Richard to run away with him again? No, said her common sense. Not on to the marshes. They're playing some other game.

Lord Bardolph dismounted and signalled to the men behind him to do the same. It had been a long and difficult ride, made worse by the need for concealment. They had set out in the darkness before the sliver of moon was in any position to cast even its thankfully inadequate light over a landscape which night rendered not only flat but also featureless.

They had been obliged to avoid roads and habitations; their bridles had rubber bits and their horses' hoofs were muffled; all the men wore dark, enveloping greatcoats with buttons that matched rather than the fashionable mother-of-pearl or bone ones that such coats usually sported; they communicated by hand-signals instead of words — not easy to spot in the poor light and therefore requiring a part of each man's concentration to be on the dim shapes ahead, while another part watched the possibly treacherous saltmarsh underfoot.

There were fifteen of them, a paltry enough number but all that could be spared, and Lord Bardolph comforted himself with the knowledge that at least the fewer there were the less became their chances of being noticed. He and the riding surveyor beside him glanced seawards. They were unlikely to be spotted yet, even had there been a ship out there. If there was, it showed no lights and their keen eyes, accustomed to detecting objects far out to sea, could see nothing. It was a little early yet. The tide wasn't quite right.

The danger was greater from the landward side. They weren't going to be the only horsemen abroad tonight. It behoved them to find their cover before the others dispersed themselves along the creeks and runnels of the marshes. They needed to be sufficiently far back to remain unobserved until it suited them to move, yet sufficiently far forward to see what they wanted to see and to be able to cover the ground before the others could flee. It was a nice problem.

The riding officers knew the terrain, but only in a broad, general sort of way, far removed from the minuteness of Lord Bardolph's familiarity with it, and the surveyor knew that their success depended largely on his presence with them, allied to a large chunk of luck. They therefore moved inland, partially hidden by the banks of a muddy defile, at his signal and then took the necessary risk of leading their mounts over the sea-bank and quickly down the other side. There was less cover on the out-marshes, but they contained the remains of another bank, intended to hold back the sea in the old days, before the systematic drainage of the Fens rendered it obsolete. It provided cover of a sort, albeit inadequate, but it had the advantage of being sufficiently far from the anticipated scene of operations for the horses to remain there with little likelihood of being detected. Stakes were driven into the soft, fertile soil; ropes were stretched between and each horse was tethered to it. Then the riders moved forward, crouching low so that they presented no recognisable shape should someone catch a glimpse of them against the sky. Even a moonless night wasn't totally dark. Even on a moonless night some things were a denser dark than others and this was no moonless night—it was cloudless and the thin sickle-blade of the moon was approaching its zenith. Very little remained hidden for long from those actively searching.

It was the riding surveyor who first spotted the ship, a lightless form moving softly, slowly against the lighter sky. He touched Lord Bardolph's sleeve

and pointed. The Viscount nodded. Both men knew
the master steered a dangerous course so close to
land in channels that were deep enough but narrow.
Both knew that a seaman must be taking soundings
on each side of the bow and the captain must be
praying that there had been no great shifting of the
mud- and sand-banks since his last visit.

Without a sound, by touch and signal, the news
passed along the attenuated line of riding officers
that at least one part of their information had proved
correct: a ship had come; a master had risked a
channel that few would have chanced in daylight.
No captain did that unless the rewards were worth
the risk. And men prepared to take that sort of risk
were unlikely to be too squeamish about the welfare
of a few revenue men. It was a wonderful incentive
to keep the senses alert.

Bartram, keener-eyed than his companion, spotted
it, too. 'Out there,' he whispered fiercely. 'I told you
so.'

Richard nodded, but with a sinking heart. He
hadn't been altogether convinced by Bartram's
story, which had seemed to him to have a strong
element of imagination in it. He didn't think
Bartram was lying; on the contrary, he was quite
sure his friend had convinced himself of the truth of
his imaginings. This reservation had been in his mind
when he had agreed to join the older boy. Now it
began to look as if Bartram might not be so fanciful,
after all. Richard couldn't compete with him when it
came to knowledge of ships and the sea, or with this

stretch of water in particular, but he was intelligent, he had spent the last few weeks in the company of men who might be unlettered in a bookish sense but whose minds were packed with information about the Wash, its mudbanks, creeks and marshes, and even he now realised that no master in his right mind sailed his ship up that channel at the present state of the tide except for a very strong incentive. Such as money. Danger had hitherto been something to think of lightly because it was unlikely to happen. That had changed with the arrival of the Dutch ketch — for, although Richard didn't know enough to recognise it, he had no doubt that they were looking at the *Amelia*.

So intent were they that neither boy heard the rustle of sedge behind them and both spun round, wide-eyed with fear, when a discreet cough told them they weren't alone.

It was several seconds before they recognised the newcomer.

'India?' Disbelief permeated Richard's whisper.

'What on earth do you two think you're doing?' she asked, whispering, not because she thought there was any need to, but because it seemed entirely natural to answer one whisper with another.

'Go home,' Richard said. 'Go home and go back to bed. I thought you were sound asleep.'

'I thought you probably did. You were mistaken, so I decided to see what you were up to. You know you're not supposed to meet. Lord Bardolph won't be pleased if he gets wind of this.'

Bartram snorted. 'I don't think we need worry

unduly about what my dear brother thinks,' he said. 'Please go home, Miss Leigh. You could spoil everything.'

'I have a feeling that spoiling everything might be the best thing to do. Tell me what it's all about. I can see that, whatever it is, it's both clandestine and secretive, otherwise why should we be whispering? So either you tell me, or I'll jump up and down singing "Lillibullero".'

Bartram stared at her, dismayed. 'You wouldn't.'

'Are you willing to take the risk?'

He shifted uncomfortably. 'I think you're bluffing.'

He could feel rather than see India's smile. 'There's one way to find out,' she said.

'She will,' Richard broke in. 'We'll have to tell her. You keep watch while I explain. It's Huggate and the smugglers, you see,' he offered.

'Not entirely. You'd better elaborate.'

'Bart says that Dutch ketch has been here several times, both during the day and at night. He reckoned they'd be due tonight—and he was right; she's out there now. So, in order to have a witness before telling Customs what's going on, he asked me to come along, too.'

India decided against letting them know that at least one of the ketch's daytime visits had been seen. Better to play devil's advocate. 'If it's been here during the day, why hasn't it been boarded and searched?'

'Those visits were just ruses so that tidesmen got used to seeing her in that channel.'

'Don't you think that possibility has occurred to them?'

'If it has, they've done nothing about it,' Richard said. 'Bart wants to present them with evidence they can't refute.' He hesitated. 'And that's not all.'

India groaned. 'Go on.'

'Well, since you're not friends any more, we can tell you. Bart's convinced his brother's one of them.'

India felt her stomach lurch. This was not something she wanted to hear. 'What? A Dutch smuggler?' she asked, deliberately obtuse.

'No, of course not. Involved at this end — not just turning a blind eye to what goes on but actively helping them.'

'Aren't you forgetting he's a magistrate?'

'He wouldn't be the first,' Bartram hissed over his shoulder. 'Hurry up, you two. We shouldn't stay here much longer or we'll be too late.'

'And just what evidence does your friend have to back up this bizarre story?' India demanded.

'He says that at first he didn't think it amounted to much more than turning a blind eye, but when he was forbidden to see me he was at a bit of a loose end so he started shadowing Bardolph, and he found he was meeting with some very rum coves — peculiar individuals,' he amended hastily, knowing his sister's objection to cant.

'And all this time Bardolph never suspected he was being followed?' India asked sceptically.

'So Bart says — and he's very good at being unobtrusive when he wants to be,' Richard added.

India resisted with difficulty a gibe about being

sly, underhand and deceitful. Members of the same family often shared characteristics, and hadn't she already had a suspicion that Lord Bardolph was less than entirely open? It wasn't a reflection that gave her any comfort. She had no intention of letting either boy get wind of her feelings on that score and if there were any truth in Bartram's story they were putting themselves in an extremely dangerous position.

'This amounts to the biggest cock-and-bull story I've ever heard,' she said finally. 'Richard, you're coming home with me. Bartram may do as he pleases since he's not my responsibility, thank God. If he's got any sense at all, he'll come too. If he's right, you're running into considerable danger and if he's not you're going to make fools of yourselves.'

'Well, I'm staying,' Bartram said. 'You can run home with your big sister if you want to be a baby. I keep forgetting you're only fourteen.'

'It's about time you remembered it,' India snapped. 'Richard?'

'Do I have to? I don't want to. After all, if Bart's wrong the three of us are the only ones who'll know what fools we've been, and if he's right we'll be doing our public duty, and you can't object to that.'

'Very noble,' India told him. 'I'm not convinced that in this case it's worth the risk.'

'In any case,' Richard said, ignoring the argument of common sense, 'I don't quite see how you're going to drag me back if I don't want to go.'

His point was unarguable but India knew she couldn't, having found out so much, go home and back to bed and leave them to get on with it, yet the last thing she wanted to do was to stay and take any part in the rest of this expedition. The choice was denied her.

Bartram turned his head towards them. 'Come on, or we'll be too late. They've just launched the long-boat.'

India glanced out to sea but could see nothing new. 'How do you know?' she asked.

'I saw the white foam when it hit the water,' he replied impatiently. 'Come on. The gentlemen'll be waiting. We'll have to go cautiously.'

Caught up in the excitement of things happening, Richard forgot his earlier misgivings and followed Bartram. India, after a brief hesitation during which she was sorely tempted to go home and leave them to it, followed close behind. She hadn't been able to stop them. At least she must stay with them. It was probably just as well that she didn't stop to ask herself what she could possibly do if they were caught because she wouldn't have had the slightest idea.

Bartram soon proved that he could move a great deal more quietly than either of his companions and India was forced grudgingly to admit that he might very well have been able to follow his brother without the latter's having any inkling of it. There were fields in which such skills might have their uses but she didn't think they were ones which a viscount would consider more acceptable for his younger brother than the navy.

A hand-signal from Bartram had them lying flat

on their stomachs. He breathed an instruction to India to button her jacket to the neck, and she realised that the white of her chemise would be like a beacon to anyone who caught sight of it. She did as she was told.

'Over there,' Bartram whispered, pointing to their left.

India's gaze followed the direction of his out-stretched arm but at first she could see nothing. Then it was as if a denser part of the darkness stirred. People? Something about the movement made her think not. 'Horses?' she whispered.

Bartram slithered back towards them from the tussock from behind which he had been peering. 'It must be the pack-horses waiting to be loaded,' he whispered. 'If they are, their hoofs will be muffled and that can only work to our advantage. We'll have to keep on the alert for signs of the gentlemen. They can't be far and they could be very close indeed. What I propose we do is creep up behind them and take the horses. That leaves them with the problem of carrying away their contraband, while we have the evidence of the horses. Not only that, but all those horses must have owners so we indirectly identify others who are involved.'

India had an uncomfortable suspicion that this was one of those ideas which sounded easier than it proved. 'We're going to have to be very careful,' she offered.

'Haven't I said as much? I can't see anyone placed to guard them but that doesn't mean there isn't someone and the moment they spot us. . .' Despite the dim light there was no mistaking Bartram's gesture of drawing his finger across his throat. India shivered and wished herself almost anywhere else.

They made slow, crouching progress towards the tethered horses and had covered half the distance when Bartram held out a hand to stop them again. This time he pointed away in front of them and when they had concentrated for several minutes on the dark landscape ahead his companions could make out the occasional movement that this time did resemble that of humans rather than horses.

'They're a good way from their animals,' Bartram murmured. 'If we don't run into a guard, it should be quite easy.'

If. . . India thought, but it seemed that luck was with them. As they approached the stake-line there was no sign of anyone's having been left on watch.

The horses stirred restlessly as they came closer but this only served to reveal their muffled hoofs, firm evidence of the accuracy of Bartram's assumptions. Coiled ropes hung from their saddles, further evidence of their nefarious purpose. It was Richard who raised a brief objection.

'These aren't pack-ponies,' he said. 'And they're not carrying panniers. Are you sure you're right?'

'Of course they're not carrying panniers — that would give the game away to anyone who happened to see them on the way here,' Bartram replied. 'The ropes are more than enough to lash barrels alongside, and they're all of them pretty sturdy animals.'

This was true enough. They might all be riding-horses but with one exception they weren't what any gentleman would want in his stables. It was the exception that attracted India's attention. She knew it well.

'Bartram,' she whispered urgently. 'Isn't this your brother's horse?'

'It is, by God! I knew he was involved! I knew it!' India had the distinct impression that if his life hadn't depended upon remaining concealed Bartram Chelworth would have danced a victory jig on the spot. She enjoyed neither the implications of the horse's presence here nor the light Bartram's reaction threw on his character. She wished more than ever that she had stayed in bed. There were suspicions she would have preferred to see allayed, not confirmed.

'Right,' Bartram went on. 'There's no time to waste. Let's take them——'

'Hold on a minute,' Richard interrupted. 'There's five or six horses each here. We can manage three each: one to ride and one led on either side, but how can we manage more?'

Bartram hesitated, but only briefly. 'No good turning them loose—they'll be spotted before we've got far enough away. We'll have to tether each horse to the saddle rings of the one in front. If the reins aren't long enough, there's always the ropes.'

The plan was sound enough. Unfortunately for their peace of mind, it was also a time-consuming one and the fear of being discovered conspired with the horses' restlessness to make fingers behave like thumbs and the task take twice as long as it might otherwise have done in broad daylight and without the sense of urgency.

It was accomplished at last and the trio by tacit agreement resisted the impulse to mount up immediately and get as far away as possible. Instead each led a string of horses away from the staking rope as stealthily as possible and only when several hundred yards had been covered without any alarm being raised did they pause to mount up.

It was difficult to believe their luck was holding and when faint but unmistakable sounds of distant uproar floated across the still night air towards them they knew with awful certainty that the horses had been missed. They also knew that, with four or five horses in train behind each of them, it was out of the question to increase the pace; time spent untangling the inevitable confusion of ropes and reins would use up more time than any increase in speed would save.

'They can't follow us on foot,' India said, 'but how quickly will they be able to find fresh horses?'

'Huggate might be willing to lend one or two,' Bartram conceded. 'Otherwise they'll have to go to the Hall, Edward's got enough in his stables. But there's no need to worry. They'll let us go.'

Neither Richard nor India shared his complacency. 'Not if they can be identified by their horses,' Richard said bluntly. 'And if India could recognise Bardolph's, other people won't have any difficulty either with that one or the others. They'll be after us and they won't waste their time. We need to get these to customs as soon as we can.'

* * *

The attention of Lord Bardolph, the riding surveyor and his officers was fixed so intently in front of them on the different shades of dark that the landscape had become that they simply didn't hear any sound from their horses even though the abduction was far from silent. They had concealed them a good way back, horses being larger and less biddable objects than men, and since they had seen no sign of their adversaries' ponies they assumed they had done the same.

Like Bartram, they spotted the spurt of white that signalled a boat hitting the water and they concentrated their attention in two directions: on the incoming boat, which they couldn't hear and could no longer see, and on any signs of movement on the marshes that might give them a clue as to the whereabouts of the receivers.

Only when the boat, with another close on its heels whose launching they had failed to spot, could be detected in the winding creek in front of them to the right did they also spot the first signs of movement on the landward side. Now every man's hand went instinctively to the pistol tucked into his belt and his grip tightened on the cudgel that was likely to prove the more useful weapon of the two.

All knew the importance of judging their assault with precision. Too soon, and the boats' crews would be able to push off and rejoin the ketch; too late and many of the receivers would be too widely scattered to be rounded up effectively. The success of this expenditure of men and horses would be judged on the number of smugglers and the quantity of contra-band apprehended.

The first boat had come as far inshore as it safely could. The crew were in the shallow water of the small creek. The goods were being unloaded. Pre-viously invisible figures grew out of the marshes and ran forward to help and soon the second boat was close behind the first and its crew, too, was over-board and at work.

Lord Bardolph's optimism leapt three notches higher. The first boat would be forced to wait until the second had unloaded before it could return to the mother-ship because the creek was too narrow to allow it to do anything other than follow the hindmost out. Their chances of catching both crews were greatly increased and that, in turn, meant that any attempt by the ketch's captain to weigh anchor would be handicapped by a shortage of seamen. A revenue cutter should by now be approaching the channel where the *Amelia* lay. That, however, was not Lord Bardolph's immediate concern. It was more important to concentrate on the job in hand. It wasn't going to be easy. There must be all of thirty or forty people out there now, and many of them would be his own tenants and neighbours. That couldn't be helped.

The right moment came. Lord Bardolph exchanged glances with the riding surveyor and the latter nodded briefly. It would be a gamble to wait for a better opportunity. A hand-signal passed down the line and the revenue men ran forward, cudgels flailing, shouting and yelling to create the impression of a much larger force. Some of them spread out to the rear of the landsmen, thus further enhancing this illusion.

The ensuing uproar—which India and the boys heard and misinterpreted—was proof that the smugglers were taken totally by surprise.

Few shots were fired, the revenue men preferring to lay about them with cudgels, weapons which had the advantage of not needing several seconds to reload after every use. Only when a man's cudgel was struck from his hand did he reach for a pistol and a cutlass. It no longer mattered if the thin moonlight caught the blade.

Some of the landsmen deserted their comrades and fled for their homes before retribution could identify them for future punishment. This considerably reduced the opposition and by the time some five-and-twenty smugglers lay clutching broken heads and slashed arms only two of the revenue men were similarly out of action, one of them dead.

Lord Bardolph sent a man for the ropes while the others rounded up the walking wounded and encircled them until they could be brought to justice. The punishment for those among them with sea-going experience would be impressed into His Majesty's Navy. The rest would be lucky to escape with hard labour, especially since a customs official had been killed in the mêlée.

'They've gone!' came a shout from behind as the man sent to fetch ropes ran towards them, leaping tussocks as he came. 'The horses have gone. All of them,' he panted.

'You sure you looked in the right place?' the riding surveyor said sharply.

'He's a local man,' Lord Bardolph interrupted. 'He knew where they were.'

'The stakes are still there—and the stake rope, but that's too thick for tying men. They've gone all right,' the young man replied.

Lord Bardolph looked about him and frowned. He would have sworn their enterprise had been a complete surprise. How, then, had someone taken the horses? 'You're sure they haven't just slipped their tethers?' he asked.

The man shook his head. 'No, my lord. The tethers are all there. They've been unclipped. There aren't any horses wandering about, grazing, either. They've been stolen.'

The Viscount could think of only one explanation. Someone—possibly someone arriving later than planned, had come up from the rear and, seeing the horses and guessing what they betokened, had simply abducted them. The horses would have told him the strength of the force was heavily outnumbered by the smugglers. That would mean its defeat and the loss of the horses would make it impossible for any survivors to escape either to sound the alarm or bear witness at a later date, and bodies were easily enough disposed of in these waters.

One man alone couldn't have done more than set the horses loose. Two would have had great difficulty leading them all away. Three could have managed it and four would have found it relatively easy.

'There must be three, maybe four horse-thieves,

then,' he said. 'I want them, and when I get them they'll be prosecuted to the full extent of the law.' He turned to one of the smugglers. 'I know you, Coldham,' he said. 'I knew you were a fool but I never guessed you were such a big one. You've a wife and how many children? Seven? Eight?'

'Seven, me lord,' the man said sulkily.

'Then do yourself and them a favour by telling me where the ponies are to shift these goods inland. You'll save your neck and I'll see the family doesn't starve.'

The man hesitated only briefly. His sound arm pointed. 'Over there, me lord. About three hundred yards back.'

Lord Bardolph turned to the surveyor. 'How many men can you spare?'

'We'll tie this lot with their own belts if there aren't any ropes on their ponies. That done, I can let you have four or five.'

'Better than nothing. Let's get on with it. God alone knows how much of a start they've got.'

The horse-thieves found their escape fraught with anxiety because of the impossibility of making any speed. They guessed pursuit was inevitable and even a man on foot could catch up with a string of horses obliged to keep to a walk. If the smugglers got a couple of cobs from a helpful farmer—or even a plough-horse, for that matter—they would be over-taken very quickly. They were continually glancing back over their shoulders, a vain exercise in the darkness: any pursuer would be upon them before they spotted him.

'It isn't your eyes you need to use,' Bartram scoffed as India looked fearfully back for the hundredth time. 'It's your ears. You'll hear them long before you see them. Listen for the sound of hoofs. They won't be muffled.'

'If they've got horses,' Richard said. 'We don't know that they will have. It'll be much more difficult to hear them if they're on foot.'

'And it'll be much more difficult for them to catch us up,' Bartram replied.

They were on the embankment now. It offered smoother going than the marshes and, while it was a longer route than riding across country, it wasn't intersected by dykes as the farmland was and therefore no time need be wasted riding along a dyke in the search for a bridge across it. A rider with only one horse to consider could jump the intersecting dykes, even at night. It was impossible when one was leading a string. It was worth the disadvantage of the extra distance, especially since the distance saved cross-country would probably have been consumed by the necessary detours. Less easy to accept was the fact that they were much more visible.

They were able to lead their retinues across the Westmere creek with no greater difficulty than that caused by the balking of one or other of the horses in each string and were on their way towards Cross Keys House. This stood at the junction of the track along the embankment and the road from Boston of which the treacherous Wash Way was an extension.

They could just make out the chimneys of this landmark when Richard, the last of the three, called out, 'Whoa!' and then, 'Hush!'

'What is it?' Bartram called in a loud whisper.

'Horses, I think. Listen.'

They did, straining their ears through the sighing wind to catch the thud, thud that Richard had detected.

'More than one,' Bartram guessed. 'Coming fast.' He looked down at the estuary stretching away on their left. 'It's a risk but we'll have to take it,' he said. 'They'll be just too far behind to chance following us.'

'Are you suggesting we ford the estuary?' India demanded.

'Don't worry. I know the path. You've only got to follow me,' Bartram told her. 'I think we'll have to let the extra horses go, though. Saving our own skins is more important than evidence right now.'

'But the tide's already turning!' she exclaimed.

'Then let's stop dithering,' Bartram said with a decisiveness India had never heard before.

'We were going to Wisbech,' Richard objected. 'This way we'll find no customs officers before King's Lynn.'

'Good God, man, if they catch up with us, we won't live to reach Wisbech, Customs or no Customs. Can't you hear them?'

'They can't have seen us yet,' India protested. She didn't at all fancy another crossing at the most dangerous point of the tide. 'Why not just turn the extra horses free and make for Wisbech at a good gallop?'

'If they haven't seen us, it works to our advantage,' Bartram pointed out. 'We'll be halfway across before they spot us and we'll have plenty of time to get to Lynn. Come on. Follow me and you'll be safe enough. We've wasted enough time.'

Without looking to see whether they were following his lead, he released his string of led horses and put the big bay he was riding into a canter that would bring him to the ford in minutes. His companions hesitated only briefly before following his example.

When they pushed their mounts into the river, their hoofs were already splashing in water just level with their iron shoes but India remembered how rapidly it deepened once it was on the move.

'We're too late, Bartram,' she called out.

'Not if you keep at him,' Bartram called back. 'Use your heels. Drive him on. He'll do it.'

It was easy for him, India thought, mounted on his brother's horse which had both size and stamina, neither, she suspected, strong points of the two she and Richard were riding. She glanced back. They could see their pursuers now. Maybe they'd drown. Perhaps that was a fate preferable to having one's throat slit. She and Richard drove their heels into their horses' sides and followed Bartram's lead as precisely as they could. It wasn't easy when water swirled over the hoofprints and wiped the mud clean.

Lord Bardolph and the riding officers drew rein at

the ford and watched, aghast, as the three horses ahead of them ploughed through water that was already hock-high.

'The poor beggars'll drown,' one of the customs men said.

'Serves them right,' Lord Bardolph replied savagely.

'Isn't that your horse in the lead, my lord?' said one of the others.

The Viscount stared. Even in that dim light there was no mistaking the outline. It was well ahead of the other two. 'It is,' he said grimly. 'And if any of them survives this crossing, it'll be that one — provided his rider doesn't lose his nerve.'

The first grey hint of dawn was lightening the sky ahead of them now and when one of the riders glanced over his shoulder Lord Bardolph thought he caught a glimpse of a tail of hair. He stared intently into the distance and groaned.

'Oh, my God, no!' He rode his pony down to the water's edge and raised his voice. 'India. For God's sake come back! You'll drown! India!'

India turned again at the sound of voices. She neither recognised the voice nor could she distinguish its words but she had a shrewd idea such urgent tones must be framing a warning and quite likely a request to turn back. She glanced down and her heart sank. They were already halfway across and it was at least as dangerous to return as to go on. She had very little faith in either being successful. Ahead of her, it looked as if Bartram on the strongest horse might very well make landfall.

Richard was in the same boat as herself — and looked as frightened as she felt. The horse beneath her was increasingly unhappy, too. India knew all horses could swim, but not all were too willing to try, especially with a rider increasing their weight.

'Come on!' she shouted, urging him forward. 'Come on! You can do it! You can!'

Back on the shore, Lord Bardolph leapt from the saddle, tore off his coat and his boots.

'We've made a terrible mistake,' he shouted as he strode into the water. 'These aren't smugglers. Find a dinghy and get the boy over there.' He pointed towards Richard. 'I'll swim for the other one.'

'And the third one, my lord?' someone called out.

'The horse will get him across, God willing.'

Then he was striding into the water until a combination of in-flowing current and the depth of water obliged him to swim. It wasn't easy to maintain his course and keep an eye on India, whose horse was now floundering badly.

He reached her at last and trod water as well as he could. 'Let go the reins,' he commanded. 'Give him his head. Swing your leg over his neck so that you're in the water.'

'I can't swim,' India protested.

'Then it's a good thing I can. When I've caught you, do as you're told and go quite limp. Don't struggle and don't try to swim. Just relax. Do you understand?'

India didn't but she nodded just the same. She was conscious of two contradictory thoughts. One was the depressing one that here was her proof that

Lord Bardolph was involved with the smugglers; the other was a certainty that at least in his hands she was unlikely to have her throat slit. All the same, it took courage to relinquish her mount, the only security she seemed to have in these terrifying waters, and only the confidence in Lord Bardolph's ability to extract her from difficult situations that she had learned in the past could have persuaded her to do so.

She was conscious of a moment of sheer panic as she relinquished all contact with the horse and felt him surge away from her, free at last of her hindering weight and—to him—confusing aids. Then she felt strong hands under her arms and was dimly aware of the strong, rhythmic propulsion of Lord Bardolph's legs through the water, fighting the current that would otherwise carry them both upstream until they had to contend with the conflicting river currents flowing in the opposite direction.

Long before they reached the bank, cold, fatigue and fear conspired to render her unconscious. She was oblivious to the fact that a dinghy had rescued Richard and then, having deposited him safely on shore, returned to take first her and then Lord Bardolph from the water.

'You'd better wake them in the house,' the Viscount said when they were all ashore. 'There's three of us at least in need of warm, dry clothes.'

'You know them, my lord?' one of the riding officers ventured.

'I know them all right—and a constant scource of trouble they are.'

'The third one, too?'

'The third one, unless I'm very much mistaken, is my misguided younger brother.'

'Then I hope he got across safe,' the man said respectfully.

'Do you? Then you're a great deal kinder than I am. I hope the horse did, certainly. I've mixed feelings about Bartram.'

One of the other men had been trying unsuccessfully to rouse India. He lifted his head and looked across at the magistrate. 'My lord, I think this one's a lady.'

Lord Bardolph smiled grimly. 'A woman, certainly,' he said. His tone did not invite clarification.

CHAPTER NINE

INDIA was only hazily aware of the next few days. She spent most of them in bed, warm and cosy and being cosseted by Eliza, whose motherly instincts came to the fore so that she not only looked after her employer's physical well-being but also defended her against the local gossip. In this respect, Eliza had the advantage of not being local and therefore not subject to conflicting loyalties.

It was hardly likely to have escaped remark that Miss Leigh had been brought back to the house in the early morning — but not early enough to have been unobserved — by his lordship and several of the hated revenue men. Nor did it escape the sharp eyes of those who saw her return that her hair was in its night-time pigtail and she was wearing men's boots; there was even a rumour that, when the greatcoat covering her had slipped to one side, she was seen to be wearing breeches, but this wasn't altogether believed.

Eliza, totally ignorant of the circumstances preceding her mistress's return, dealt roundly with the questions and speculation.

'And what would you expect her to do when her brother's off on one of his escapades except go after him and bring him back? It was just their good luck that there were revenue men on the river at the time or I don't think we'd have seen either of them alive again. What was Lord Bardolph doing there? How should I know? I doubt if Miss Leigh or Master Richard'll be bothered about the whys and where-fores. Just grateful he was is my guess.'

So the villagers had to be satisfied with answers like this and speculate among themselves as to why Lord Bardolph and the riding officers, who had descended on an old-established smuggling route in such force and with such ferocity, also happened to be several miles away at the Nene at precisely the right time to haul the Leighs to safety. 'Mark my words,' they said to one another, 'there's more to this than meets the eye.'

India was oblivious to all this, her time being largely divided between sleeping interspersed with shorter bouts of eating the delicacies that Cook sent up to tempt an invalid appetite.

'Not that she's an invalid, exactly,' Eliza com-mented to Cook as she relieved her of a tray bearing a coddled egg, wafer-thin slices of bread and butter, a *compote* of pears and two slices of walnut cake. 'She's just totally worn out. Quite grey with fatigue, she is.'

Cook nodded knowingly. 'Needs her strength building up, I don't doubt. I'll get a nice bit of lamb's liver for her lunch tomorrow. That'll do her the world of good.'

The household was less sympathetic towards Richard. Those who had joined the Leighs in London knew that it had been his propensity to get into undesirable company that had brought them to this dead-and-alive hole in the first place. They did not for one moment doubt that whatever had taken place had been for precisely the reason Eliza had put about—that India had been trying to get her brother out of some scrape or another—and it wouldn't have surprised them one little bit to have learned that Richard had got himself entangled with smugglers. Quite why the revenue men should have helped him home rather than carted him off to gaol was an interesting question but quite possibly Lord Bardolph's former friendship with Miss Leigh had something to do with it.

In any case, Richard's recovery was much swifter than his sister's. He had been in far worse case when he was brought home because he had been floundering in the water for some time before the dinghy reached him, whereas India had never been without some support, Lord Bardolph having provided it at the very moment that the horse began to be in difficulties. Richard had the resilience of youth and within twenty-four hours inactivity had become irksome and the walls of his bedroom a prison. Within forty-eight he was not only up and about but itching to be out and doing.

Since India was in no position to keep an eye on him, Eliza took it upon herself to exert an authority which she knew to be outside her normal power. Catching him on his way out of the house, she drew him to one side.

'Now I don't know where you're off to, Master Richard, and I dare say you'll tell me it's none of my business to enquire, but I'm enquiring all the same because your sister's far from well and, as far as I can see, it's largely your fault. She's in no condition to keep an eye on you so I'm doing it for her. I don't mind not knowing exactly where you're going or what you're going to be up to, but I want your word that it'll be nothing that would cause your sister one moment's anxiety.'

'I only want some fresh air,' Richard said. 'I probably shan't go outside the village. Will that satisfy you?'

'Then keep a watch on your tongue. There's a lot of gossip running around and it's my guess they'll pounce on you to try to get at the truth. I've told them your sister went off to drag you out of some scrape. They've had no details and they've not dared ask me any. Not,' she added in a burst of frankness, 'that I had any to give them, but that's not the point. Miss Leigh's reputation hereabouts is what you might call teetering on the brink, whether she was gallivanting about the countryside with free-traders or with revenue men. You stick to my story if you're asked, and if they want to know how come his lordship and the customs men were there be vague. You don't know. It was just one of those happy coincidences.'

Richard grinned. 'That's no lie—I *don't* know. Don't worry, Eliza. I'll be discreet. I'll be very vague—I can be when it suits me, you know. I'll make sure I say nothing to harm India. That's a promise. And I'll not do anything that would worry her if she knew about it. All right?'

'I'll take your word on it,' Eliza told him.

'Do you think I ought to go over to Old Fen Hall and thank Bardolph?' he asked.

'Not knowing all the circumstances, I can't say,' the maid replied truthfully. 'I think it might be safer to wait until your sister's fully recovered and ask her. Maybe she'll want the two of you to do it together.'

He nodded thoughtfully and then smiled engagingly. 'You can trust me, Eliza. Really you can.'

'I'm depending on it but, just in case you waver, remember that if you break your promise the side of your face might just collide with the flat of my hand — one of those nasty, unforeseen accidents, you understand, but none the less painful for that.'

Even when the overwhelming need to sleep had passed, India was disinclined to do anything more strenuous than lie back against her pillows and drift into a world which was half-thought, half-daydream. She reflected with wistful pleasure that this wasn't the first time Lord Bardolph had come to her rescue nor the first time she had felt his arms around her and known the comfort of their strength, even if on this occasion her consciousness of both facts had been short-lived.

At first, she thought he would call to see how she did or, at the very least, send a note wishing her well. When neither happened her disappointment was lessened by the thought that perhaps he had called when she was in the first depths of her exhaustion and unable to receive anyone. Perhaps, having learnt that, he was waiting until she was fully recovered. Eventually, unable to bear the uncertainty any longer, she tackled her maid about it.

'I don't suppose Lord Bardolph called in the first few days after he brought us home?' she said hopefully.

'No, Miss Leigh. Master Richard was wondering whether he ought to call on him and thank him, but I told him to wait until you were better. That you'd probably want anything of that sort to come from the both of you.'

'Yes, of course, but I'm not up to it just yet. Eliza, if his lordship should call, you won't refuse me, will you? Even if he has to kick his heels in the morning-room while you make me presentable.'

'No, madam, I'll not refuse you.'

The gentleman didn't come, however, and India's recovery was slow enough to alarm even the sufferer. The doctor, a sensible, down-to-earth country physician with no fancy city ideas about leeching bad humours out with the blood, told her all she needed was time, rest and good food and gave his opinion that the occasional brandy would lift her spirits and do her no harm.

'Give it time,' he said. 'You young things are always in such a rush. Good heavens above, it's not all that long since you lost your parents and then you had all the upheaval of leaving India and then you decided to abandon London in favour of the Fens. It's no wonder one small adventure, whatever its explanation, should leave you worn out.'

India listened to him, because he made sense, and reminded herself that he didn't know the half of it and the half he didn't know added still more weight to his advice.

But as the days passed and thought occupied more of her waking moments than unprofitable daydreams she became more and more depressed that there was still no word from the Viscount. No enquiry after her health, no request to be allowed to visit, not even a demand for explanations. Nothing. Then her common sense took over. The last thing he would want, as a landowner and more particularly as a magistrate, would be for India Leigh to lay information against him in connection with his smuggling activities. If he had thought she might not have known who had rescued her, that would be more explicable, but he must have realised the servants would have told her who brought her home. Therefore he was lying low in the hope that she would simply say nothing and, since whenever they met they ended up disagreeing with each other, he probably thought it wiser not to risk provoking her into a retaliation more severe than a mere tongue-lashing.

With that realisation she spent some almost pleasant hours devising plans whereby she would be able to convince him that, although she thoroughly disapproved of his activities, they were none the less his business, not hers, and he could depend on her discretion. If she suspected that she was only able to take this view, even in the privacy of her thoughts, because deep down she still had difficulty believing he was actively involved in smuggling, she refused to let that interfere with her mental plans.

Those plans were knocked sideways when Richard came into her room one afternoon.

'Am I disturbing you?' he whispered as he crept in, anxious not to wake her if she should be asleep.

'Not at all,' she said. 'I'm quite glad to see you. You seem to have recovered from the effects of that awful night more quickly than I.'

'Oh, goodness me, yes. I don't let a little thing like getting my feet wet keep me out of commission for long. I did promise Eliza to behave myself and not to do anything that would worry you if you knew about it,' he added anxiously.

'I'm sure you kept your word. To what do I owe the present honour?'

'I bumped into Bartram Chelworth this morning. Actually, he was on his way to find me.' Richard hesitated. 'I know it's not a friendship you're very happy about and I know you think he's been a bad influence — except that his brother thinks the influence has been the other way around. . .'

'With some cause on both sides, don't you think?'

'Well, yes, I suppose you could look at it like that.'

'I rather think we both do,' India said drily.

'Then you'll be glad to know you're not going to have to worry much more,' Richard told her. 'Guess what? Bardolph's given in!'

India sat up, her interest suddenly sharpened. 'What do you mean, he's given in?' she asked. Had the strain been too much for him? Had he gone to whoever magistrates went to when they wanted to confess to wrongdoing? Or did they just resign the Bench?

'To Bartram. He's decided to let Bart join the navy after all. He's bought Bart in and he was coming to say goodbye—he's off to London tomorrow and then Bardolph's taking him down to Portsmouth to join his ship.' Richard chuckled. 'I never thought he'd cave in as easily as that.'

'I doubt if he found it all that easy,' India said shrewdly. 'Or maybe he was buying his silence.'

Richard was genuinely puzzled. 'Why should he want to do that?'

'To stop Bartram telling anyone of his involvement with smuggling.'

'Oh, that.' Richard was scornful. 'The whole county knows about that. They don't love him any the more for it, of course, but they certainly respect him.'

India was silent. It was, she thought, a strange comment on a society more corrupt than she had thought. The subject was uncomfortable mainly because of Lord Bardolph's involvement so she hastened to shift the conversation sideways. 'I suppose this means you expect me to let you start farming straight away,' she suggested.

'Heavens above, no! I don't know a quarter of what I need to know. Besides, I'm not so dead set on it that I don't want to go to Cambridge first. Mind you,' he warned, in case she was getting quite the wrong idea, 'I still intend to farm. I just intend to do it intelligently.'

'No one can complain about that,' India told him.

'If anything else had been your goal, I'm afraid I'd have told you you were still too young.'

'I know that, silly. Bartram would like to say goodbye to you. I told him you were probably asleep. Do you want to see him?'

India hesitated. She ought to and the fact that she had never liked Bartram meant that she really should be punctilious in the observance of all the courtesies. Nevertheless, she didn't want to and at least she had a good excuse.

'I don't think so,' she said. 'You can tell him I was asleep if you like, or you can say I'm not receiving visitors yet but I wish him well.'

'It'll have to be that, then, or he'll wonder why I was so long. You'd better go back to sleep.'

Sleep was a long way off when India was alone once more. So Bartram was being quite literally shipped out of the way. It might well be true that 'the whole county' knew about Bardolph's illegal activities. It was much more likely that he wanted to eliminate the chance of positive information, as opposed to mere local rumour, reaching the ears of those with the power to do something about it. She wondered what he could do to keep her quiet. Richard posed less of a problem because of his age; it would be easy to convince someone that a fourteen-year-old boy's story was as much the product of his imagination as of his experience. India could not be so easily dismissed. Perhaps that was why he hadn't been near her: he hadn't let her drown — which would have solved the problem for good; perhaps he was regretting the rash decision to save her life and hoped by avoiding her to avoid the questions that she might reasonably be expected to ask and thereby lessen the chances of making some sort of representations to the relevant authorities. Lord Bardolph, after all, wasn't to know that she hadn't the slightest idea who were those relevant authorities, nor that, regardless of his more nefarious activities, she loved him.

For there lay the nub of it. It was no good pretending that she enjoyed his company, that she appreciated his sardonic humour, that she liked arguing with a man who argued back on equal terms and never, ever, wriggled out of a superior argument on her part by dismissing it as 'feminine logic'. All these were true but the real reason she would never inform on him, the real reason she was miserable, was quite simply that she loved him.

In India her choice had been between fortune-hunters whom she had had no hesitation in sending about their business and thoroughly worthy men, her rejection of whom no one else could understand. She had returned to England more or less resigned to remaining an old maid and had incomprehensibly fallen head over heels in love with a man whom she had designated — with some justification — arrogant, haughty and overbearing. Indeed, she had disliked him intensely. That dislike had gradually changed into a mixture of respect and gratitude. How long had she loved him? She found it impossible to pin down the precise moment. It might have been the moment when his tongue slipped and he used her given name; it might have been when he held her before him on his horse; when his finger casually flicked her cheek or tilted her chin. None of these was sufficient in itself to make a woman fall in love but in conjunction and over a period of time. . .

She knew now that when he had lifted her down from her horse and she had not wanted him to let go of her it hadn't been just his hands on her waist that she'd wanted. That was the closest he had ever come to holding her in his arms and she now realised that just now she would give a good part of her fortune for precisely that. She longed for the closeness of lovers and her heart responded even to the thought of what might have been with all the ardour of one encountering true love for the first time.

She knew — she supposed she had always known — that anything more than the little she had had was all she could expect. Smuggler or not, he was still a viscount with a well-developed sense of his own standing in the order of things. He had never made the slightest pretence of regarding her as anything other than what she was — the wealthy heiress to a fortune made in trade. She couldn't fairly complain of that, of course, because it was the case. What hurt was that her origins made her quite unacceptable to a man of his sort on any level other than that of purely social intercourse. If he had needed her money, he might have overcome his scruples, but India was honest enough to acknowledge that, had she suspected him to be in that position, she would have taken very good care not to let herself be led into the sort of feelings she was now experiencing.

Lord Bardolph might quite possibly believe that

she had an interest in his title. He must, after all, have come across as many women thus inspired as she had fortune-hunters. She knew she had no particular desire to be a viscountess and she hoped she'd never behaved in a manner that suggested otherwise. If he had ever done or said anything that thoughtful reflection suggested could justifiably be interpreted as serious interest, she might have tried assuring him of the truth. However, any softening of his attitude towards her had not been sufficiently pointed for her to be able to delude herself for long that it had any particular significance, and even if it had, she thought in a sudden burst of uncomfortable candour, her attempt would probably have been self-defeating.

No. She was, and would always be, trade. Pert and unbecomingly forward trade, at that. For whatever reason, Lord Bardolph had clearly decided to end the acquaintance and that was probably just as well. It confirmed her former idea that the best thing for her to do was to move well away from here. She would notify the London agent through whom she had found this house that she wished to discontinue her tenure and ask him to engage a house in London for a short time, while he found something equally quiet in a more congenial part of the country. Near Bath, perhaps. Richard wouldn't like Bath, of course, but there was no denying it was ideal for a spinster sister. He could still go to Cambridge if he wished — or perhaps he might change his mind and settle for Oxford.

Since India was not a woman to dilly-dally once

her mind had been made up, instructions to this effect went off next morning and the day after that she told the staff of her plans. Those that wished to come with her were welcome to do so; if not, their employment would cease at the end of the month.

'If a place is found before then, I'll of course make up your wages to the full month,' she told them.

Richard was more displeased than she had anticipated. 'How could you, India?' he protested. 'Just when I've got to know the place and the people and decided I want to farm round here, you decide to up sticks and go somewhere else. It's not fair.'

'That's what you said when I told you we were leaving London,' India pointed out. 'I don't think you've had many regrets. I'm sure you'll find any other rural area just as good for your purpose.'

'Yes, and just as soon as I find my feet you'll decide it no longer suits and we'll have to go somewhere else,' he retorted bitterly, and stomped out of the house, giving the front door a hearty and expressive slam as he went.

Lord Bardolph heard the news almost as soon as he returned from seeing his brother safely on the first rung of his naval career.

'I gather Mr Chelworth's young friend is leaving the neighbourhood,' Folksworth told his master as he laid out clothes suitable for an informal dinner at home.

'You don't waste much time catching up on the gossip,' Lord Bardolph replied, amused. 'Which friend is that?'

'Young Master Leigh. I gather he and his sister are relinquishing the house by the end of the month. Miss Leigh's been most generous, by all accounts. Those of her household who don't wish to go with them will still be paid to the end of the month even if she goes before.'

Lord Bardolph's face betrayed nothing though it seemed to his valet that he selected a diamond pin for his cravat with more than his usual care.

'I don't believe I've ever heard anyone complain that Miss Leigh was tight-fisted,' he said.

'No, my lord. By all accounts she strikes a nice balance between keeping a judicious eye on the household expenses and undue prodigality.'

Gidding, too, had wasted no time in catching up on local gossip.

'It looks as if the lady's saddle can be put aside for the foreseeable future, my lord,' he said next morning, apropos of nothing in particular.

'I wasn't aware that you had been anticipating its immediate re-use, anyway,' Lord Bardolph told him.

'No? Well, you never can tell, can you, my lord? Nice woman, that Miss Leigh, if you don't mind me saying so. Enjoyed riding and handles a horse well. Much liked in the village, too, by all accounts.'

'Indeed? I'm glad to hear it.'

'Far be it from me to speak out of turn, my lord, but it does seem a pity to let a woman like that go away without clearing the air, so to speak.'

The Viscount's lips twitched. 'Far be it, indeed,' he murmured.

'Not been at all well, by all accounts,' the groom

went on, undeterred by a comment he had no difficulty pretending he hadn't heard. 'The boy, now, he was up and about in a couple of days, but the sister's been confined to her room most of the time. Gone into quite a deep melancholy, so they say.'

'You seem to have access to a hitherto unsuspected store of private information about the Leighs,' his employer commented.

'As to that I couldn't say, I'm sure, my lord. It's just that my sister-in-law's cousin's boy, Will, helps out in the garden there and you know what youngsters are, my lord. Devil of a job to stop them gossiping.'

'Quite so.'

Gidding wisely judged that he had said enough for now, possibly even enough, full stop. Let his lordship mull that little lot over and hope he didn't mull for too long. He'd been like a bear with a sore head since that business at the river, not that Gidding had been there, but fortunately young Mr Chelworth was never a one to hold his tongue when he was in a sulk and he hadn't liked being dragged back home for the umpteenth time. Between the two of them, there wasn't much that Gidding and Folksworth hadn't deduced with reasonable accuracy even if they were content to let the lesser household mortals speculate without feeling any need to put them right.

India eased the cushion behind her back, put her book aside and reached for her tambour frame. She was deriving no particular pleasure from either activity but couldn't bear to be totally idle. If she were really honest, she thought, she'd amend that to not being able to bear to be *seen* to be totally idle, because idleness was all she felt good for. A letter lay on the little work-table beside her. It contained the news that Mr Risinghurst had found a house in the capital that was, in his estimation, ideal for her needs. It also urged her to authorise him to settle on her behalf without delay because he happened to know that the owner's statement that two other parties were interested in it was absolutely true and not just a ruse to obtain a tenant quickly.

She had no reason to doubt Mr Risinghurst's word, yet her heart had sunk when she had read his letter. The house he described was admirably situated and had all she required. There was absolutely no reason for not writing to him immediately with instructions to take it on her behalf. Yet she delayed. Not only that, but she found herself unwilling to re-read his letter, as if by ignoring it the letter would go away and the house remain unfound. She looked round the drawing-room. It was comfortable enough, but it wasn't the house of her dreams. She felt no ties to it. It was just a house.

She looked across to the window where the late afternoon sun could be seen already trailing clouds of red and gold. The sunsets were one of the glories of the Fens. In India the sun simply went down. Here it made a festival of it. She had at first assumed this was characteristic of England and it had been Lord Bardolph who had told her that the Fenland skies were nature's compensation for the flat landscape. She had looked at them with a new awareness after that and told herself she would be more loath to leave the skyscape than the house. It was not a calculation likely to raise her spirits or encourage her to write that letter to Mr Risinghurst.

Her melancholy reverie was interrupted by an apologetic Eliza. 'It's Lord Bardolph, Miss Leigh. He says he knows it's not the right time to come calling but hopes you'll forgive him.'

India started. 'Lord Bardolph? Are you sure?'

'Of course the woman's sure — do you take her for a fool?' Lord Bardolph appeared behind the maid. 'That will be all, Eliza. If you're needed, Miss Leigh will ring for you.'

The maid hesitated and looked at her mistress.

'Yes, Eliza, that will be all right,' India said and, as the door closed behind her, went on, 'That was remarkably high-handed of you, my lord.'

'Yes, wasn't it?' he agreed affably. 'It made it impossible for you to refuse me, however.'

India flushed. 'Did you think I would?'

'It crossed my mind as a distinct possibility. May I sit down?'

Flustered because he shouldn't have had to ask, India replied, 'Yes, of course,' and was even further taken aback when, instead of taking one of the chairs with which the room was amply provided, he sat on the sofa beside her, unceremoniously pushing her legs out of the way so that he had enough room. 'There are chairs, my lord,' she pointed out icily.

He glanced around. 'So there are, and very comfortable they look, too. I prefer to be here, however. Do you object to my being close enough for us to speak without shouting or would you prefer us to have to shout at each other across the room?'

'The room is quite small enough for neither of us to have to raise our voice.'

'Perhaps, but not small enough to enable us to talk sufficiently quietly to prevent those outside from hearing.'

'Are you suggesting that my servants listen at keyholes, sir?' India asked indignantly.

'If they don't, they must be unique.'

'If that's your experience at the Hall, I can only conclude you don't give them enough work to occupy their time,' India told them.

'I dare say you're right. I imagine they're sadly mismanaged. They lack the firm guiding hand of a mistress, you see.'

Suspecting that here lay a baited hook which she would do well to ignore, India shifted the focus of the conversation. 'In any case, I can't imagine that we have anything to say that we wouldn't want them to hear.'

'Can't you? Dear me, and I'd always thought your imagination was almost as vivid as your brother's.'

India blushed, uncertain how to respond, but he relieved her of the need to do so by picking up the letter that had slipped between her leg and the back of the sofa. He flicked open the folded sheet and saw the embossed address at the top. 'Ah, Risinghurst. I see you employ the best,' he said and began reading.

India snatched it from his hand. 'Do you always read private letters, my lord?' she said angrily.

'Very rarely, as a matter of fact,' he replied, unperturbed. 'So rumour doesn't lie?'

'What rumour would that be?'

'That you're leaving here. Or is it supposed to be a secret?'

'It can hardly be that; I've told the servants.'

He held up the letter. 'And will you take this house?'

'I haven't made up my mind.'

'It sounds ideal and, from what Risinghurst says, you'd be unwise to delay too long.'

'My lord, I've no desire to be offensive, but I am capable of reading and correctly interpreting a letter for myself,' India said stiffly.

'That's not entirely true,' he said and, as she opened her mouth to protest, held up a staying hand. 'You had every desire to be offensive. It seems to come over you whenever we meet, yet other people say it's a side of you they've never seen.'

'So you discuss me with all and sundry?'

He grinned. 'It was an educated guess but I'll wager it's true.'

Enough of this, India thought. When he had entered the room, it had been as if a dream had been answered. Now she was beginning to wonder how she could possibly have imagined herself in love with so provoking a man. The sooner she and Richard were gone the better.

'If you came here to find out whether the rumour

were true, my lord, you've succeeded. You don't
have to put yourself to the trouble of being sufficiently unpleasant to ensure that I don't change my
mind. There isn't the least chance of that. We're
going, so you may as well waste no more of your
valuable time but be on your way, too. And to put
your mind entirely at rest by answering the question
you probably dare not ask, I can assure you that you
need have no fear; your secret's safe with me. I shall
tell no one.'

If her intention had been to disconcert him, she
could only be gratified by her success. He stared at
her in blank astonishment.

'My secret? You'll tell no one?' he echoed. 'Tell
no one what? What secret?'

'Come, my lord—don't pretend to be obtuse
when we both know you're not. I shan't inform on
you.'

'I'm relieved to hear it but I'm still completely
mystified as to what I've done that might require me
to be informed upon.'

His bewilderment seemed so genuine that India
began to doubt even her own certainty. Hadn't she
led away the horses? Hadn't she seen him with her
own eyes? Hadn't he chased them to the river? The
only mystery was why he hadn't let them all drown.
All the same, the seeds of doubt had been sown.

'Do you deny that you've been involved in
smuggling?'

For the first time there was a gleam of comprehen-
sion in his eye but it was swiftly extinguished. 'No, I
don't deny that.'

'Do you deny you're a magistrate?'

'No, of course not.'

'Doesn't it strike you that the one activity is just a shade incompatible with the other?'

'No, not at all, given the particular circumstances.'

'I don't see how particular circumstances can alter it.'

'No? Perhaps that's because you're unaware of them.' He let the letter fall to the floor and caught both her hands and when he spoke there was a warmth and a tenderness she had longed to hear. 'My dearest India, I don't believe you have the smallest notion how much trouble you and the boys caused that night on the marshes. Yes, I was involved in smuggling—but in much the same way as the revenue men who were my companions. I was there in my capacity as a magistrate. You took away our horses, not—as Bartram seemed to believe— the smugglers'. The three of you came within yards of scuppering a plan which had taken months of careful observation and meticulous planning to set up. We wanted more than just the impoverished peasants using a pound of smuggled tea or a cask of geneva to provide the wherewithal to feed their families. We wanted the master of the *Amelia* and the man who co-ordinated the distribution from here.'

'Mr Huggate?'

'Who else?'

'Is he in gaol?'

'No. So far as we know, he's in London, but it's only a matter of time before he's caught and enough men have saved their own necks by offering to turn

King's Evidence to convict him. Had some of us not had to make off after the "smugglers" who stole our horses, we'd have had sufficient men to catch him there and then.'

'But we took your horses — not the smugglers,' India protested, baffled.

'As I soon discovered. At the time, however, we assumed that one of their look-outs had appropriated them. When I recognised Bartram — and then you — I knew we were wrong though I was completely mystified as to your real purpose. Bartram explained it all, of course.'

'I wish someone had explained it to me,' India said with some feeling.

'I know Bartram said something about it to Richard. I assumed your brother would have told you.'

India thought back. 'He did say something about everything being sorted out. There wasn't any detail. I suppose it didn't occur to him that I still didn't know.'

He raised her hands to his lips and kissed them one after the other. They were not the cursory kisses of social convention. 'What your brother needs is the constraining influence of a man, rather than that of a household of women.'

India's eyes flashed. 'So that he might turn out like Bartram, you mean?'

She saw the momentary anger in his eyes but it was swiftly replaced by rueful laughter. '*Touché*,' he said. 'Perhaps not. I wonder what other reason I can offer you?'

'Reason for what?'

'I'm trying to find an unanswerable reason for suggesting you should marry me.'

'Marry you?' India repeated.

'Is it so unappealing an idea?'

'Not unappealing, exactly,' India said with perfect truth, and was startled by his sudden laugh.

'I must thank you for so effusive a compliment,' he said sardonically.

She blushed with confusion. 'It's just that. . .well, my family is trade; I'm vulgar — you've often commented to that effect. Why on earth should you want to marry such a woman?'

'I've often asked myself the same question,' he said and then caught her to him. 'No, India, I don't mean it quite like that; it's just that you provoke me into saying the most outrageous things. Haven't you realised that I only say such things when I'm losing an argument?'

India cast her mind back and realised that it was indeed so. A slow smile lit up her face. 'Then we're going to have a sad marriage for, if I'm to believe you, I have either to let you win every argument or risk having my lack of breeding thrown in my face. Not a recipe for fairy-tale happiness.'

'True — if there is such a thing, which I take leave to doubt. On the other hand, it isn't a recipe for a boring marriage, either, and I know which I'd prefer.'

'But you can't think of a reason why I should marry you?'

'You don't need my fortune any more than I need

yours, and I don't think you care two hoots about
the title. We've already established that I'm not the
ideal person to exert a sort of paternal influence
over your brother. What other reason can I think
of?'

'You don't think that perhaps loving you might be
reason enough?'

His grey eyes looked down into her brown ones.
'It's the only really unarguable reason,' he said. 'I
just didn't think. . . I never imagined. . .'

'Then why on earth did you ask me?' India replied
softly.

'Good God, woman, hasn't it dawned on you?
Why do you think you make me so angry? It's
because I love you. I haven't been willing to admit
it, even to myself, but I think it's been so ever since
you answered me back when I brought Richard
home that time.'

India's heart clutched at his words though her
mind had difficulty grasping them. 'Is anger the way
you always express your love?' she asked, bemused.

'Yes. . .no. . . How should I know? I've thought
myself in love before but none of those ladies
provoked in me any of the feelings you do.'

India dropped her gaze demurely. 'Perhaps that
was because they were. . .ladies,' she suggested.

'Quite possibly that's the difference,' he agreed,
'and it's just as well you reminded me of it, or I
might have made the mistake of treating you like
one. As it is, I don't have to be so circumspect.'

So saying, his hitherto gentle hold became almost
savage as he crushed her to him and his mouth

descended on hers in a ruthless, demanding kiss to which her whole body responded as if this was what it had been yearning for since womanhood dawned. Nor was there any simpering, maidenly withdrawal when his embrace went far beyond the bounds of gentlemanly conduct. Her whole body told him that here, at last, he had found a woman whose passion equalled his own and for whom it would be the greatest pleasure in the world to open one by one the doors of pleasure through which their mutual desire would lead them. The fast-fading light created the fitting backdrop to the urgent, demanding consummation of passions so long held in check by misunderstandings and convention.

And when the thrusting surge that made them one had eased and India lay relaxed and secure within the strong circle of his arms, she sighed and snuggled closer to him. 'So much time wasted,' she murmured.

He lightly kissed the top of her head. 'We've plenty of time before us. Let's waste none on regrets.'

India's glance fell on the letter that had slipped unnoticed to the floor. She bent over and picked it up, holding it out between two fingers. 'Do you think I should write to Mr Risinghurst?' she asked.

'Immediately—and preferably to tell him you've changed your mind.'

India turned in his arms and looked up at him. 'You sound as if you think I might be having second thoughts about marrying you,' she said.

'You wouldn't be the first,' he reminded her.

She kissed him. 'You won't be so easily rid of me, my lord.'

'"My lord"?'

'Edward.'

He chuckled. 'I knew you'd see it my way in the end,' he said, and neither of them noticed when the last glimmerings of light drifted from the sky.